Ed McBain is one of the most illustrious names in crime fiction. In 1998, he was the first non-British author to be awarded the Crime Writers' Assocation/Cartier Diamond Dagger Award and he is also holder of the Mystery Writers of America's coveted Grand Master Award. His latest novel in Orion paperback is *Fat Ollie's Book*, and his latest hardback novel, *The Frumious Bandersnatch*, is also available from Orion. Visit his website at www.edmcbain.com.

By Ed McBain

FAT OLLIE'S BOOK

An 87th Precinct novel

Ed McBain

ORION

An Orion paperback

First published in Great Britain in 2002
by Orion
This paperback edition published in 2003
by Orion Books Ltd,
Orion House, 5 Upper St Martin's Lane,
London WC2H 9EA

A CIP catalogue record for this book
is available from the British Library.

Typeset by SetSystems Ltd,
Saffron Walden, Essex

Printed and bound in Great Britain by
Clays Ltd, St Ives plc

I realize this is getting boring . . .
But this, too, and yet another time . . .
Is for my wife,
Dragica Dimitrijević-Hunter

FAT OLLIE'S
BOOK

1.

RESPONSE TIME — from the moment someone at the Martin Luther King Memorial Hall dialed 911 to the moment Car 81, in the Eight-Eight's Boy Sector rolled up — was exactly four minutes and twenty-six seconds. Whoever had fired the shots was long gone by then, but a witness outside the Hall had seen someone running from the alleyway on its eastern end and he was eager to tell the police and especially the arriving TV crew all about it.

The witness was very drunk.

In this neighborhood, when you heard shots, you ran. In this neighborhood, if you saw someone running, you knew he wasn't running to catch a bus. This guy wasn't running. Instead, he was struggling to keep his balance, wobbling from one foot to the other. Nine, ten in the morning, whatever the hell it was already, and he could hardly stand up and he stunk like a distillery. He finally sat on one of the garbage cans in the alley. Behind him, rain water from a gutter dripped into a leader and flowed into an open sewer grate.

Slurring his words, the drunk immediately told the responding officers from Car 81 that he was a Vietnam vet, mistakenly believing this would guarantee him a measure of respect. The blues saw only a scabby old black drunk wearing tattered fatigue trousers, an olive-drab tank top, and scuffed black penny loafers without socks.

He was having trouble not falling off the garbage can, too. Grabbing for the wall, he told them he'd been about to go into the alley here, yessir, when he saw this guy come bustin out of it . . .

'Turned left on St Sab's,' he said, 'went runnin off uptown.'

'Why were you going in the alley?' one of the blues asked.

'To look inna garbage cans there.'

'For what?'

'Bottles,' he said. 'Takes 'em back for deposit, yessir.'

'And you say you saw somebody running out of the alley here?' the other blue asked. He was wondering why they were wasting time with this old drunk. They'd responded in swift order, but if they wasted any more time with him, their sergeant would think they'd been laggard. Then again, the TV cameras were rolling.

'Came out the alley like a bat out of shit,' the drunk said, much to the dismay of the roving reporter from Channel Four, a pretty blonde wearing a short brown mini and a tan cotton turtleneck sweater. The camera was in tight on the man's face at that moment, and the word 'shit' meant they couldn't use the shot unless they bleeped it out. Her program manager didn't like to bleep out too many words because that smacked of censorship instead of fair and balanced reporting. On the other hand, the drunk was great comic relief. The Great Unwashed loved drunks. Put a drunk scene in a movie or a play, the audience still laughed themselves to death. If they only knew how many battered wives Honey had interviewed.

'What'd he look like?' the first blue asked, mindful of the TV cameras and trying to sound like an experienced investigator instead of a rookie who'd just begun patrol duty eight months ago.

'Young dude,' the witness said.

'White, black, Hispanic?' the first blue asked, rapping the words out in a manner that he was sure would go over big with TV audiences, unmindful of the fact that the camera was on the witness and not himself.

'White kid,' the witness said, 'yessir. Wearin jeans and a whut chu call it, a ski parka, an' white sneakers an' a black cap with a big peak. Man, he was movin fast. Almost knocked me down.'

'Did he have a gun?'

'I dinn see no gun.'

'Gun in his hand, anything like that?'

'No gun, nossir.'

'Okay, thanks,' the first blue said.

'This is Honey Blair,' the Channel Four reporter said, 'coming to you from outside King Memorial in Diamondback.' She slit her throat with the forefinger of her left hand, said, 'That's it, boys,' and turned to her crew chief. 'Get him to sign a release, will you?' she said. 'I'm heading inside.' She was walking toward the glass entrance doors when the Vietnam vet, if indeed that's what he was, asked, 'Is they a reward?'

Why didn't you say that on the air? Honey thought.

THIS WAS, and is, and always will be the big bad city.

That will never change, Ollie thought. Never.

And never was it badder than during the springtime. Flowers were blooming everywhere, even in the 88th Precinct, which by the way was no rose garden.

Detective/First Grade Oliver Wendell Weeks had good reason to be smiling on this bright April morning. He had just finished his book. Not finished *reading* it, mind you, but finished *writing* it. He was still rereading the last chapter, which was back at the apartment. He didn't

3

think it would need any more work, but the last chapter was often the most important one, he had learned, and he wanted to make sure it was just right. He was now transporting the positively perfect portion of the book to a copying shop not far from the Eight-Eight.

He wondered if the sun was shining and the flowers were blooming next door in the 87th Precinct. He wondered if it was springtime in the Rockies, or in London, or in Paris or Rome, or in Istanbul, wherever that was. He wondered if flowers bloomed all over the *world* when a person finished his first work of fiction. Now that he was a bona fide writer in his own mind, Ollie could ponder such deep imponderables.

His book, which was titled *Report to the Commissioner*, was securely nestled in a dispatch case that rested on the back seat of the car Ollie drove hither and yon around this fair city, one of the perks of being a minion of the law, ah yes. The windows of the Chevy sedan were open wide to the breezes that flowed from river to river. It was 10:30 on a lovely sunlit Monday morning. Ollie had signed in at 7:50 (five minutes late, but who was counting?), had taken care of some odds-and-ends bullshit on his desk, and was now on his way to the copying shop on Culver Avenue, not four blocks from the station house. So far, the day –

'10–40, 10–40 . . .'

The dash radio.

Rapid mobilization.

'King Memorial, St Sebastian and South Thirtieth, man with a gun. 10–40, 10–40, King Memorial . . .'

Ollie hit the hammer.

HE PARKED ILLEGALLY at the curb outside the Martin Luther King Memorial Hall, flipped down the visor on

4

the driver's side to show the card announcing Police Department authorization, locked the car, flashed the blue-and-gold tin at a uniformed grunt who was already approaching with a scowl and an attitude, said, 'Weeks, Eighty-eighth Squad,' and barged right past him and the roaming television teams that were already thrusting microphones at anyone within range. He kept using his detective's shield like a real warrior's shield, holding it up to any barbarian who rose in his path, striding through the glass doors at the front of the building, and then into the marble entrance lobby, and then into the auditorium itself, where a handful of brass were already on the scene, had to be something important went down here.

'Well, well, if it isn't The Large Man,' a voice said.

Once upon a time, Ollie's sister Isabelle had referred to him as 'large,' which he knew was a euphonium for 'obese.' He had not taken it kindly. In fact, he had not bought her a birthday present that year. Ollie knew that there were colleagues in this city who called him 'Fat Ollie,' but he took it as a measure of respect that they never called him this to his face. 'Large Man' came close, though. He was ready to take serious offense when he recognized Detectives Monoghan and Monroe of the Homicide Division, already on the scene, and looking like somewhat stout penguins themselves. So someone had been aced. Big deal. Here in the Eight-Eight, it sometimes felt like someone got murdered every ten seconds. Monoghan was the one who'd called him 'The Large Man.' Monroe was standing beside him, grinning as if in agreement. A pair of bookends in black – the color of death, the unofficial color of Homicide – the two jackasses were the Tweedledum and Tweedledee of law enforcement. Ollie wanted to punch them both in the mouth.

'Who got it?' he asked.

'Lester Henderson.'

'You kidding me?'

'Would we kid a master detective?' Monoghan said.

'A super sleuth?' Monroe said, still grinning.

'Stick it up your ass,' Ollie explained. 'Anybody else from the Eight-Eight here?'

'You're the first.'

'Then that puts me in charge,' Ollie said.

In this city, the appearance of Homicide detectives at the scene of any murder was mandatory if not necessary. Presumably, they were here in an 'advisory and supervisory capacity,' which meant they only got in the way of the precinct detectives who caught the squeal. Since Ollie was the so-called First Man Up, the case was his. All he had to do was file his reports in triplicate with Homicide, and then go his merry way. He did not think he needed to remind the M&Ms that this was a fact of police life in this fair metropolis, ah yes. They knew full well that except on television, the glory days of Homicide were long gone.

The dead man lay on his back in a disorganized heap alongside a podium draped with red, white, and blue bunting. A sign above the podium read LESTER MEANS LAW. Ollie didn't know what that meant. The dead man was wearing blue jeans, brown loafers without socks, and a pink crewneck cotton sweater. The front of the sweater was blotted with blood.

'So what happened?' Ollie asked.

'He got shot from the wings,' Monroe said. 'They were setting up for the big rally tonight . . .'

'*Who* was setting up?'

'His people.'

'All these people here?'

'All these people.'

6

'Too *many* people,' Ollie said.

'Is right.'

'*What* rally?'

'Big fund-raiser. Putting up lights, American flags, cameras, bunting, the whole shmear.'

'So?'

'So somebody fired half a dozen shots from the wings there.'

'Is that an accurate count, or are you guessing?'

'That's what his aide told us. Five, six shots, something like that.'

'His aide? Who's that?'

'Guy with all those reporters over there.'

'Who let *them* in?'

'They were already here when we responded,' Monroe said.

'Terrific security,' Ollie said. 'What's the aide's name?'

'Alan Pierce.'

The corpse lay in angular disarray, surrounded now by the Mobile Lab techs and the Medical Examiner, who was kneeling beside the dead man and delicately lifting his pink cotton sweater. Not fifteen feet from this concerned knot of professionals, a man wearing blue jeans similar to the dead man's, and a blue denim shirt, and black loafers with blue socks stood at the center of a moving mass of reporters wielding pencils and pads, microphones, and flash cameras. A tall, slender man, who looked as if he jogged and swam and lifted weights and watched his calories – all the things Ollie considered a waste of time – Pierce appeared pale and stunned but nonetheless in control of the situation. Like a bunch of third graders waving their hands for a bathroom pass, the reporters swarmed around him.

'Yes, Honey?' Pierce said, and a cute little blonde with

a short skirt showing plenty of leg and thigh thrust a microphone in Pierce's face. Ollie recognized her as Honey Blair, the roving reporter for the Eleven O'Clock News.

'Can you tell us if it's true that Mr Henderson had definitely decided to run for the Mayor's Office?' she asked.

'I did not have a chance to discuss that with him before . . . before this happened,' Pierce said. 'I can say that he met with Governor Carson's people this weekend, and that was the main reason we flew upstate.'

'We've heard rumors that you yourself have your eye on City Hall,' Honey said. 'Is that so?'

'This is the first I'm hearing of it,' Pierce said.

Me, too, Ollie thought. But that's very interesting, Mr Pierce.

Honey would not let it go.

'Well, *had* you planned on running for Deputy Mayor? Assuming Mr Henderson ran for Mayor?'

'He and I never discussed that. Yes, David?'

A man Ollie had seen a few times here and there around City Hall shoved a microphone at Pierce.

'Sir,' he said, 'can you tell us where you were when Mr Henderson . . .?'

'That's it, thank you very much,' Ollie said, and strolled into the crowd. Flashing his shield like a proud father exhibiting a photograph of his first born, he said, 'This is all under control here, let's go home, okay?' and then signaled to one of the blues to get this mob out of here. Grumbling, the reporters allowed themselves to be herded offstage. Ollie stepped into Honey's path just as she was turning to go, and said, 'Hey, what's your hurry? No hello?'

She looked at him, puzzled.

'Oliver Weeks,' he said. 'The Eighty-eighth Precinct.

8

Remember the zoo? The lady getting eaten by lions? Christmastime?'

'Oh yes,' Honey said without the slightest interest, and turned again to go.

'Stick around,' Ollie said. 'We'll have coffee later.'

'Thanks, I have a deadline,' she said, and followed her tits off-stage.

Ollie showed Pierce his shield. 'Detective Weeks,' he said, 'Eighty-eighth Squad. Sorry to interrupt the conference, sir, but I'd rather you told us what you saw and heard.'

'Yes, of course,' Pierce said.

'You were here when Mr Henderson got shot, is that it?'

'I was standing right alongside him.'

'Did you see the shooter?'

'No, I did not.'

'You told the other detectives the shots came from the wings.'

'That's what it seemed like, yes.'

'Oh? Have you changed your mind about that?'

'No, no. I still think they came from the wings.'

'But you didn't see the shooter.'

'No, I did not.'

'Guy fired five, six shots, you didn't see him.'

'No.'

'How come?'

'I ducked when I heard the first shot.'

'I woulda done the same thing,' Ollie said understandingly. 'How about the second shot?'

'Lester was falling. I tried to catch him. I wasn't looking into the wings.'

'And all the other shots?'

'I was kneeling over Lester. I heard someone running

9

off, but I didn't see anything. There was a lot of confusion, you know.'

'*Were* you planning to run for Deputy Mayor?'

'I wasn't asked to do so. I was only Lester's aide.'

'What does that mean, anyway?' Ollie asked. 'Being an aide?'

'Like his right-hand man,' Pierce said.

'Sort of like a secretary?'

'More like an assistant.'

'So you don't have any political aspirations, is that correct?'

'I didn't say that.'

'Then you do?'

'I wouldn't be in politics if I didn't have political aspirations.'

'Excuse me, Alan,' a voice said.

Ollie turned to see a slight and narrow, precise little man wearing a blue blazer, a red tie, a white shirt, gray slacks, gray socks, and black loafers. Ever since the terrorist bombing at Clarendon Hall, everybody in this city dressed like an American flag. Ollie figured half of them were faking it.

'We're having a conversation here,' he said.

'I'm sorry, sir, but I wanted to ask . . .'

'You know this man?' Ollie asked Pierce.

'Yes, he's our press rep. Josh Coogan.'

'Excuse me, Alan,' Coogan said, 'but I was wondering if I should get back to headquarters. I know there'll be hundreds of calls . . .'

'No, this is a crime scene,' Ollie said. 'Stick around.'

Coogan looked flustered for a moment. He was maybe twenty-four, twenty-five years old, but he suddenly looked like a high-school kid who hadn't done his assignment and had got called on while he was trying to catch a nap. Ollie didn't have much sympathy for politicians, but all at once this seemed very sad here, two guys who all at once didn't know what to do with themselves. He almost felt like taking them out for a beer. Instead, he said, 'Were you here in the hall when all this happened, Mr Coogan?'

'Yes, I was.'

'Where in the hall?'

'In the balcony.'

'What were you doing up there?'

'Listening to sound checks.'

'While you were listening to these sound checks, did you happen to hear the sound of a gun going off?'

'Yes.'

'In the balcony?'

'No.'

'Then where?'

'From somewhere down below.'

'Where down below?'

'The stage.'

'Which side of the stage?'

'I couldn't tell.'

'Right or left?'

'I really couldn't tell.'

'Was anyone with you up there in the balcony?'

'No, I was alone.'

'Incidentally, Mr Pierce,' Ollie said, turning to him, 'did I hear you tell those reporters you went upstate with Mr Henderson?'

'Yes, I did.'

'Where upstate?'

'The capital.'

'When?'

'We flew up together on Saturday morning. I'm his aide. I *was* his aide,' he said, correcting himself.

'Did you fly back together, too?'

'No. I left on Sunday morning. Caught a seven A.M. plane.'

'So he spent all day Sunday up there alone, is that it?'

'Yes,' Pierce said. 'Alone.'

'You the detective in charge here?' the ME asked.

'I am,' Ollie said.

'Your cause of death is gunshot wounds to the chest.'

Big revelation, Ollie thought.

'You can move him out whenever you like. We may find some surprises at the morgue, but I doubt it. Good luck.'

Monoghan was walking over with a man wearing a red bandana tied across his forehead, high-topped workman's shoes, and bib overalls showing naked muscular arms, the left one tattooed on the bicep with the words SEMPER FIDELIS.

'Weeks, this is Charles Mastroiani, man in charge of decorating the hall here, you might want to talk to him.'

'No relation to Marcello,' Mastroiani promptly told Ollie, which was a total waste since Ollie didn't know who the hell he was talking about. 'My company's called Festive, Inc,' he said, exuding a sense of professional pride and enthusiasm that was all too rare in today's workplace. 'We're listed in the city's yellow pages under "Decoration Contractors." What we do is we supply everything you need for a special occasion. I'm not talking about a wedding or a barmitzvah, those we leave to the caterers. Festive operates on a much larger scale. Dressing the stage here at King Memorial is a good example. We supplied

12

the bunting, the balloons, the banners, the audio equipment, the lighting, everything. We would've supplied a band, too, if it was called for, but this wasn't that kind of affair. As it was, we dressed the hall and wired it, made it user-friendly and user-ready. All the councilman had to do was step up to the podium and speak.'

All the councilman had to do, Ollie thought, was step up to the podium and get shot.

'Will you get paid, anyway?' he asked.

'What?' Mastroiani said.

'For the gig. Him getting killed and all.'

'Oh sure. Well, I suppose so.'

'Who contracted for the job?'

'The Committee.'

'What committee?'

'The Committee for Henderson.'

'It says that on the contract?'

'That's what it says.'

'Who signed the contract?'

'I have no idea. It came in the mail.'

'You still got it?'

'I can find it for you.'

'Good. I'd like to see who hired you.'

'Sure.'

'All these people who were onstage with you when he got killed,' Ollie said. 'Were they regulars?'

'What do you mean, regulars?'

'Have you worked with them before?'

'Oh sure. All the time.'

'All of them reliable?'

'Oh sure.'

'None of them strangers to you, is that right? What I'm driving at, would any of these guys have come in here with a concealed . . .'

13

'No, no.'

'. . . weapon and popped Henderson, is what I'm asking.'

'None of them. I can vouch for each and every one of them.'

'Cause what I'll have to do, anyway, I'm gonna have to send some of my colleagues from up the Eight-Eight around to talk to them individually, just in case one of them got a bug up his ass to shoot the councilman.'

'I don't think you need to worry about that.'

'Yeah, well, I worry about such things. Which is why I'll need a list of all your people here on the job.'

'Sure. But they're all bonded, so I'm sure you won't find anything out of the way.'

'Why are they bonded?'

'Well, we sometimes do these very big affairs where there's jewelry and such laying around . . .'

'Uh-huh.'

'Precious antiques, things like that, on these big estates, you know . . .'

'You're saying these men are honest individuals, is what you're saying.'

'That's right.'

'Wouldn't harm a fly, is what you're saying.'

'Is basically what I'm saying.'

'We'll have to talk to them anyway,' Ollie said. 'So what *I'm* saying, after you give me all their names, you might advise them not to leave the city for the next couple of days, till my people have a chance to talk to them.'

'I'll be happy to do that.'

'Good. So tell me, Mr Master-yonny . . .'

'It's Mastroiani.'

'Ain't that what I said?'

'No, you said . . . I don't know what you said, but it wasn't Mastroiani.'

'You know, have you ever thought of changing your name?'

'No.'

'To something simpler?'

'No. Like what?'

'Like Weeks, for example. Short and sweet and easy to say. And people would think you're related to an American police detective.'

'I don't think I'd like to do that.'

'Entirely up to you, my friend, ah yes,' Ollie said.

'And I *am* American,' Mastroiani said.

'Of course you are,' Ollie said. 'But tell me, Charles, may I call you Charles?'

'Most people call me Chuck.'

'Even though most Chucks are fags?'

'I'm not.'

'You're not Chuck?'

'I'm not a fag.'

'Then should I call you Charles?'

'Actually, I'd prefer being called Mr Mastroiani.'

'Sure, but that don't sound American, does it? Tell me, Chuck, where were you exactly when the councilman got shot?'

'I was standing near the podium there.'

'And?'

'I heard shots. And he was falling.'

'Heard shots from the wings there?'

'No. From the balcony.'

'Tell me what happened, Chuck. In your own words.'

'Who else's words would I use?' Mastroiani asked.

'That's very funny, Chuck,' Ollie said, and grinned like a dragon. 'Tell me.'

The way Mastroiani tells it, the councilman is this energetic little guy who gets to the Hall at about a quarter to nine, dressed for work in jeans and a crewneck cotton sweater, loafers, real casual, you know? He's all over the place, conferring with his aide and this kid he has with him looks like a college boy, giving directions to Mastroiani and his crew, arms waving all over the place like a windmill, running here, running there, going out front to check how the stage looks every time a new balloon goes up, sending the college kid up to the balcony to hear how the sound is, then going up there himself to listen while his aide talks into the mike, then coming down again and making sure the podium is draped right and the sign is just where he wants it, and checking the sound again, waving up to the kid in the balcony who gives him a thumbs up signal, and then starting to check the lights, wanting to know where the spot would pick him up after he was introduced . . .

'That's what he was doing when he got shot. He was crossing the stage to the podium, making sure the spot was following him.'

'Where were you?'

'At the podium, I told you. Looking up at the guy in the booth, waiting for the councilman to . . .'

'What guy in the booth?'

'The guy on the follow spot.'

'One of your people?'

'No.'

'Then who?'

'I have no idea. My guess is he works here at the Hall.'

'Who would know?'

'You got me.'

'I thought you supplied everything. The sound, the lighting . . .'

'The *onstage* lighting. Usually, when we do an auditorium like this one, they have their own lighting facilities and their own lighting technician or engineer, they're sometimes called, a lighting engineer.'

'Did you talk to this guy in the booth? This technician or engineer or whatever he was?'

'No, I did not.'

'Who talked to him?'

'Mr Pierce was yelling up to him – Henderson's aide – and so was the councilman himself. I think the college kid was giving him instructions, too. From up in the balcony.'

'Was the kid up there when the shooting started?'

'I think so.'

'Well, didn't you look up there? You told me that's where the shots came from, didn't you look up there to see who was shooting?'

'Yes, but I was blinded by the spot. The spot had followed the councilman to the podium, and that was when he got shot, just as he reached the podium.'

'So the guy working the spot was still up there, is that right?'

'He would've had to be up there, yes, sir.'

'So let's find out who he was,' Ollie said.

A uniformed inspector with braid all over him was walking over. Ollie deemed it necessary to perhaps introduce himself.

'Detective Weeks, sir,' he said. 'The Eight-Eight. First man up.'

'Like hell you are,' the inspector said, and walked off.

2.

WHEN OLLIE GOT BACK to his car, the rear window on the passenger side door was smashed and the door was standing wide open. The briefcase with *Report to the Commissioner* in it was gone. Ollie turned to the nearest uniform.

'You!' he said. 'Are you a cop or a doorman?'

'Sir?'

'Somebody broke in my car here and stole my book,' Ollie said. 'You see anything happen, or were you standin here pickin your nose?'

'Sir?' the uniform said.

'They hiring deaf policemen now?' Ollie said. 'Excuse me. Hearing-*impaired* policemen?'

'My orders were to keep anybody unauthorized out of the Hall,' the uniform said. 'A city councilman got killed in there, you know.'

'Gee, no kidding?' Ollie said. 'My *book* got *stolen* out *here!*'

'I'm sorry, sir,' the uniform said. 'But you can always go to the library and take out another one.'

'Give me your shield number and shut up,' Ollie said. 'You let somebody vandalize a police vehicle and steal valuable property from it.'

'I was just following orders, sir.'

'Follow this a while,' Ollie said, and briefly grabbed his own crotch, shaking his jewels.

*

DETECTIVE-LIEUTENANT ISADORE HIRSCH was in charge of the Eight-Eight Detective Squad, and he happened to be Jewish. Ollie did not particularly like Jews, but he expected fair play from him, nonetheless. Then again, Ollie did not like black people, either, whom he called 'Negroes' because he knew it got them hot under the collar. For that matter, he wasn't too keen on Irishmen or Italians, or Hispanics, or Latinos, or whatever the tango dancers were calling themselves these days. In fact, he hadn't liked Afghanis or Pakis or other Muslim types infiltrating the city, even *before* they started blowing things up, and he didn't much care for Chinks or Japs or other persons of Oriental persuasion. Ollie was in fact an equal opportunity bigot, but he did not consider himself prejudiced in any way. He merely thought of himself as discerning.

'Izzie,' he said – which sounded very Jewish to him, the name Izzie – 'this is the first big one come my way in the past ten years. So upstairs is gonna take it away from me? It ain't fair, Izzie, is it?'

'Who says life has to be fair?' Hirsch said, sounding like a rabbi, Ollie thought.

Hirsch in fact resembled a rabbi more than he did a cop with more citations for bravery than any man deserved, one of them for facing down an ex-con bearing a grudge and a sawed-off shotgun. Dark-eyed and dark-jowled, going a bit bald, long of jaw and sad of mien, he wore a perpetually mournful expression that made him seem like he should have been davening, or whatever they called it, at the Wailing Wall in Jerusalem, or Haifa, or wherever it was.

'I was first man up,' Ollie said. 'That used to mean something in this city. Don't it mean nothing anymore?'

'Times change,' Hirsch said like a rabbi.

'I want this case, Izzie.'

'It should be ours, you're right.'

'Damn right, it should be ours.'

'I'll make some calls. I'll see what I can do,' Hirsch said.

'You promise?'

'Trust me.'

Which usually meant 'Go hide the silver.' But Ollie knew from experience that the Loot's word was as good as gold.

Like a penitent to his priest, or a small boy to his father, he said, 'They also stole my book, Iz.'

HE TOLD THIS to his sister later that night.

'Isabelle,' he said. 'They stole my book.'

As opposed to her 'large' brother, as she thought of him, Isabelle Weeks was razor-thin. She had the same suspecting expression on her face, though, the same searching look in her piercing blue eyes. The other genetic trait they shared was an enormous appetite. But however much Isabelle ate – and right this minute she was doing a pretty good job of putting away the roast beef she'd prepared for their dinner – her weight remained constant. On the other hand, anything Ollie ingested turned immediately to . . . well, largeness. It wasn't fair.

'Who stole your book?' Isabelle said. 'What book?' she said.

'I told you I was writing a novel . . .'

'Oh yes.'

Dismissing it. Shoveling gravied mashed potatoes into her mouth. Boy, what a sister. Working on it since Christmas, she asks *What* book? Boy.

'Anyway, it was in the back seat of the car, and somebody spotted it, and smashed the window, and stole it.'

20

'Why would anyone want to steal your book?' she asked.

She made it sound as if she was saying 'Why would anyone want to steal your *accordion*?' or something else worthless.

Ollie really did not wish to discuss his novel with a jackass like his sister. He had been working on it too long and too hard, and besides you could jinx a work of art if you discussed it with anyone not familiar with the nuances of literature. He had first titled the book *Bad Money*, which was a very good title in that the book was about a band of counterfeiters who are printing these hundred-dollar bills that are so superb you cannot tell them from the real thing. But there is a double-cross in the gang, and one of them runs off with six million four hundred thousand dollars' worth of the queer bills and stashes them in a basement in Diamondback – which Ollie called Rubytown in his book – and the story is all about how this very good detective not unlike Ollie himself recovers the missing loot and is promoted and decorated and all.

Ollie abandoned the title *Bad Money* when he realized the word 'Bad' was asking for criticism from some smart-ass book reviewer. He tried the title *Good Money*, instead, which was what writers call litotes, a figure of speech that means you are using a word to mean the opposite of what you intend. But he figured not too many readers out there – and maybe not too many editors, either – would be familiar with writers' tricks, so he abandoned that one, too, but not the book itself.

At first, the book itself was giving him trouble. Not the same trouble he'd had learning the first three notes of 'Night and Day,' which he'd finally got through, thanks to Miss Hobson, his beloved piano teacher. The trouble

21

was he was trying to sound too much like all those pissant writers out there who were not cops but who were writing what they called 'police procedurals,' and by doing this, by imitating them, actually, he was losing track of his own distinctiveness, his very Oliver Wendell Weekness, no pun intended.

And then he hit upon his brilliant idea.

Suppose he wrote the book like a Detective Division report? In his own language, the way he'd type it on a DD form, though not in triplicate. (In retrospect, he wished he had written it in triplicate.) Suppose he made it sound like he was writing it for a superior officer, his Lieutenant, say, or the Chief of Detectives, or – why not? – even the Commissioner! Write it in his own language, his own words, warts and all, this is me, folks, Detective/First Grade Oliver Wendell Weeks. Call the book *A Detective's Report* or *Report from a Detective* or –

Wait a minute.

Hold it right there.

'*Report to the Commissioner*,' he said aloud.

He'd been eating when the inspiration came to him. He yanked a paper napkin out of the holder on the pizzeria table, took a pen from his pocket, outlined a rectangle on the napkin . . .

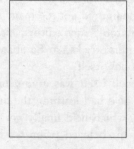

. . . and then began lettering inside it:

REPORT TO THE
COMMISSIONER

BY DETECTIVE/
FIRST GRADE

OLIVER WENDELL
WEEKS

And that was it.

He had found a title, he had found an approach, he was on his way.

'It was in the dispatch case you gave me,' Ollie said, 'he prob'ly thought it was something else. Up the Eight-Eight, the only thing anybody carries in a dispatch case is hundred-dollar bills or cocaine. He prob'ly thought he was making a big score.'

'Well, hey,' Isabelle said, 'your big *novel*!'

He would have to tell her sometime that skinny people shouldn't try sarcasm.

'Also they're tryin'a take away this big homicide I caught.'

'Maybe they'll show more respect once your big *novel* is published.'

'It's not that big,' Ollie said. 'If you mean long.'

'Anyway, what's the big deal? Print another copy.'

'Do what?'

'Print another copy. Go to your computer and . . .'

'What computer?'

'Well, what'd you do? Write it in longhand on a lined yellow pad . . .'

'No, I . . .'

'Write it in lipstick on toilet paper?' Isabelle asked, and laughed at her own witticism.

'No, I typed it on a *typewriter*,' Ollie said. 'You know, Isabelle, somebody should tell you that sarcasm doesn't work when a person weighs thirty-seven pounds in her bare feet.'

'Only large persons should try sarcasm, you're right,' Isabelle said. 'What's a typewriter?'

'You know damn well what a typewriter is.'

'Are you saying you don't have a *copy* of the book?'

'Only the last chapter. The last chapter is home.'

'What's it doing home?'

'I may need to polish it.'

'Polish it? What is it, the family silverware?'

'Nothing's finished till it's finished,' Ollie said.

'So as I understand this, everything but the last chapter of your book was stolen from your car this morning.'

'Five-sixths of my novel, yes.'

'What's it about?'

'About thirty-six pages.'

'Isn't that short for a novel?'

'Not if it's a good novel. Besides, less is more. That's an adage amongst us writers.'

'Didn't you writers ever hear of carbon paper?'

'That's why there are Kinko's,' Ollie said, 'so you don't have to get your hands dirty. Besides, I didn't have time for carbon paper. And I didn't know some junkie hophead was going to break into my car and steal my book. It so happens I'm occupied with a little crime on the side, you know,' he said, gathering steam. 'It so happens I'm a professional *law* enforcement officer . . .'

'Gee, and here I thought you were Nora Roberts . . .'

'Isabelle, sarcasm really . . .'

'Or Mary Higgins Clark . . .'

'I am Detective Oliver Wendell Weeks,' he said, rising from the table and hurling his napkin onto his plate. 'And don't you ever forget it!'

'Sit down, have some dessert,' she said.

DETECTIVE STEVE CARELLA first heard about Fat Ollie Weeks being assigned to the Henderson homicide on Tuesday morning, when Lieutenant Byrnes called him into his corner office and tossed a copy of the city's morning tabloid on his desk.

'Did you see this?' he asked.

The headline on the front page read:

88TH PCT CATCHES
HENDERSON HOMICIDE

The subhead read:

LOCAL FUZZ LAND BIG FISH

'Seems Fat Ollie caught the squeal,' Byrnes said.

'Good for him,' Carella said.

'Bad for us,' Byrnes said. 'Henderson lives in the Eight-Seven. Lived,' he corrected. 'Over in Smoke Rise.'

Smoke Rise was a walled and gated community of some seventy-five homes, all of them superbly located on sculpted terraces that overlooked the River Harb. The residents of Smoke Rise enjoyed the exclusive use of an indoor-outdoor swimming pool, a health club, and tennis courts lighted at night. There was a private school on the property as well, the Smoke Rise Academy, for grades one through eight, boasting its own soccer and baseball teams, their gray-and-black uniforms seeming to conjure the very image of rising smoke.

Long, long ago, in a galaxy far away, Carella had caught a kidnapping there, at the residence of a man named Douglas King, whose estate lay within the confines of the Eight-Seven, at the farthermost reaches of the precinct territory in that nothing but the River Harb lay beyond it and the next state. In this exclusive corner of the Eight-Seven, Smoke Rise provided the ultra-urban face of the city with an atmosphere at once countrified and other-worldly. Smoke Rise signified wealth and exclusivity.

It was here, on a tree-shaded street named Prospect Lane, that City Councilman Lester Henderson had lived with his wife and two children. And it was not seven miles away and a hundred miles distant – at the Martin Luther King Memorial Hall on St Sebastian Avenue in Diamondback, a black and Hispanic section of the city coiling like a rattlesnake on the fringes of civilization – that Henderson had been shot to death yesterday morning.

'Means we can expect Ollie any minute,' Byrnes said.

Both men looked at each other.

Carella actually sighed.

OLLIE DID NOT, in fact, show up at the precinct until twelve noon that Tuesday, just in time for lunch. Ollie's internal mechanism always told him when it was time to eat. Ollie sometimes believed it told him it was always time to eat.

'Anybody for lunch?' he asked.

He had opened the gate in the slatted rail divider that separated the squadroom from the long corridor outside, and was waddling – the proper word, Carella thought – across the room toward where Carella sat behind his desk.

On this bright April morning, Ollie was wearing a plaid sports jacket over a lime-green golfing shirt and blue Dacron trousers. He looked like a Roman galley under full sail. By contrast, Carella – who was expecting the imminent appearance of a burglary victim he'd scheduled for an interview – looked sartorially elegant in a wheat-colored linen shirt with the throat open and the sleeves rolled up over his forearms, and dark brown trousers that matched the color of his eyes. Ollie noticed for the first time that Carella's eyes slanted downward, giving his face a somewhat Oriental appearance. He wondered if there was a little Chink in the armor back there someplace, huh, kiddies?

'How's my eternally grateful friend?' he asked.

He was referring to the fact that around Christmas-time, he had saved Carella's life – twice, no less.

'Eternally grateful,' Carella said. In all honesty, he didn't enjoy the idea of being indebted to Ollie in any which way whatever. 'What brings you to this part of town?' he asked. As if he didn't know.

'Seems a resident here got himself aced yesterday morning, ah yes,' Ollie said.

'So I understand,' Carella said.

'Then why'd you ask, m'little chickadee?' Ollie said, once again doing his world-famous W. C. Fields imitation. The pity was – but he didn't realize this – nobody today knew who W. C. Fields was. Whenever Ollie did his impersonation, everyone thought he was doing Al Pacino in *Scent of a Woman*.

'Want to go get a bite to eat?'

'Gee, what else is new?' Carella said.

Sarcasm, Ollie thought. Everybody today is into sarcasm.

*

THE PLACE they chose was a diner on Culver and South Eleventh, which Ollie said was run by the Mob, which Carella doubted since he'd only been working in this precinct forever, and except for prostitution and numbers, the boys had pretty much ceded the hood to black gangs and Colombian posses. The black gangs used to devote their time to street rumbles until they realized there was money to be made dealing dope. The Colombian gangs knew this all along. Unfortunately, dope didn't stop anyone from killing anyone else. In fact, it seemed to encourage the activity.

'I need your help,' Ollie said. 'I'm gonna have my hands full checking out the Hall and how somebody could've got in and out of there with what Ballistics now tells me was a .32 aced Henderson. His views weren't particularly appreciated in the so-called Negro community, you know, so it ain't exactly unlikely that he was offed by some irate person of color, as they sometimes refer to themselves, ah yes.'

'What is it you'd like me to do?' Carella asked.

He was watching Fat Ollie eat, an undertaking of stupendous proportions to anyone not himself a glutton. Ollie had ordered three hamburgers to start, and was devouring them with both hands and a non-stop mouth, consuming simultaneously a huge platter of fries with ketchup, and drinking his second chocolate milk shake, a perpetual-motion, eating, drinking, slurping, slobbering, dripping, incessant ingestion machine.

'I want you to go up Smoke Rise,' Ollie said, signaling to the waitress, 'talk to the councilman's widow, see you can find out did he have any enemies besides the usual suspects . . . yes, darling, here's what I'd like if you could be so kind,' he said to the waitress. 'Bring me another shake, that's chocolate, and another hamburger, and that

28

apple pie – is it apple? – looks good, too, with some vanilla ice cream on it, please, make it two scoops, *is* it apple?'

'Actually, it's strawberry peach,' the waitress said, looking already weary at twelve-thirty in the afternoon, but Ollie appreciated women who appeared beaten and defeated.

'Yum, strawberry peach sounds good, too,' he said, 'two scoops of ice cream, okay?'

'Yes, sir.'

'And that uniform is very becoming,' Ollie said, 'ah yes, m'dear, have you ever considered modeling?'

The waitress smiled.

Ollie smiled back.

Carella bit into his grilled cheese sandwich.

'I'd like to take a look at the Hall,' he said. 'See what happened there before I go talking to any widow.'

'What's one thing got to do with the other?' Ollie asked.

'Well, a woman's husband gets shot, maybe she'd like to know some of the details.'

'I can tell you everything you need to know right now, you don't have to waste time. He was up there getting the lay of the land, helping his people set the stage for what was supposed to be a big rally last night. Somebody plugged him from the wings, or the balcony, or wherever – I'm still waiting for information on trajectory, flight curve, all the other garbage, from both the ME and Ballistics. I got three different acoustics reports from witnesses at the scene. One said . . .'

'Who were the witnesses?'

'Guy named Alan Pierce, who's Henderson's aide, and a guy from the company supplying the balloons, the bunting, all the other shit, both of them standing right next to the councilman when the bullets took him.'

'What'd they hear?'

'Pierce says the shots came from the wings. The other guy – his name is Chuck Mastroiani, one of your *paisans*,' Ollie said, and grinned as if he were telling a dirty joke, 'says the shots came from the balcony. Neither of them know Shinola from bow-waves, they were prob'ly talking about muzzle reports. Third guy, this young college twerp, was actually sitting in the balcony, which is maybe why he told me the shots came from downstairs. *Wherever* the shots came from . . .'

'How many?' Carella asked.

'Six. Ballistics says they were fired from a .32 Smith & Wesson, which means the shooter emptied the gun at him. Betokens rage, mayhap? Leading back to the possibility that a jig done it – oops, forgive me, I know you don't appreciate slang.'

'Some people might consider your "slang" racist,' Carella said.

'Pip, pip, my good fellow,' Ollie said, trying to imitate a British member of Parliament, but sounding instead like either W. C. Fields or Al Pacino. 'There's a vast difference between being politically incorrect and being racist.'

'Explain the difference to Artie Brown sometime.'

'Actually, Brown's a good cop,' Ollie said. 'For a Negro.'

'Explain "Negro" to him, too.'

'Steve, don't bust my chops,' Ollie said. 'I saved your goddamn life.'

'Twice, don't forget.'

'Don't forget is right.'

'I still want to take a look at that hall,' Carella said.

30

3.

YELLOW CRIME SCENE tapes defined a wide area leading from the sidewalk to the entrance doors of the hall. A row of uniformed cops stood outside the building, uneasily expecting the appearance of anyone with scrambled eggs on his cap. They all knew a city councilman had been shot to death inside here yesterday morning. They all knew the murder was all over the newspapers and television yesterday afternoon and early this morning. They also knew that last summer a series of gropings in Grover Park had attracted intense media scrutiny because some policemen appeared to have been inattentive to the needs of women whose panties were being yanked down. The cops here today did not wish to be considered derelict in their duty. So they stood outside the hall scratching their asses and wondering what the hell they were supposed to be doing here, while simultaneously trying to appear alert for future assassins. The appearance of two gold-and-blue shields on the scene made them uneasy.

'At ease, men,' Ollie said, though none of the uniforms had snapped to attention.

A sergeant who'd seen it all, and heard it all, and done it all merely looked at Ollie, who opened one of the glass doors and allowed Carella to precede him inside. The two made an odd-looking couple. Carella was some six feet tall in his stocking feet, weighing in at about a buck-eighty now that he was watching his weight, broad-shouldered and narrow-waisted, with the stride of a natural athlete – which he certainly wasn't. Ollie was somewhat shorter, with the pear-shaped body of a bell buoy floating off the harbor, but with a stride that actually surpassed Carella's, not for nothing was it rumored that fat men were light on their feet. Once, in fact, while vacationing in the Caribbean, Ollie had won a salsa contest – but that was another story. Marching side by side into the marbled entrance lobby, Carella actually had difficulty keeping up with him. Ollie flashed the tin at the gaggle of uniforms standing attentive guard in front of the inner doors, and again allowed Carella to walk ahead of him, this time into the vast auditorium itself.

The place had a ghostly silence to it, not unusual at the scene of a murder, but somehow more resolute because of the cavernous space. The stage was still partially hung with bunting and balloons, American flags and banners proclaiming the councilman's name. But the job hadn't been quite finished because someone had inconsiderately shot Henderson while he and his people were still setting things up. Like a woman who was dressed for a ball, but who hadn't yet put on her earrings or her lipstick, the stage sat only partially adorned, forlornly incomplete. The two men stood at the rear of the hall, looking toward the stage, outwardly appearing to be sharing the same thoughts and feelings, but actually experiencing quite different emotions. For Carella, there was only a sense of loss, the same pain he felt whenever he looked down at a torn and bleeding corpse on the sidewalk. Ollie looked at the stage and saw only a puzzle that needed to be solved. Perhaps that was the essential difference between the two men.

Silently, they walked down the center aisle. There were empty seats on either side of them, adding to the sense of an incomplete act, a performance postponed. Carella stopped midway toward the stage, turned, and looked up at the balcony. It seemed a hell of a long way for .32-caliber bullets to have traveled.

'Had to be the wings, don't you think?' Ollie asked, reading his mind.

'Maybe.'

'Thing is, nobody *saw* anything. Pierce and your *paisan*' – and again, the knowing leer – 'were standing right next to him. Workmen are all over the place. Bam, bam, somebody drops Henderson and disappears. Nobody seen nothing.'

'Workmen doing what?'

'Putting up the flags and stuff.'

They were standing on the stage now, the flags and stuff hanging above them. A podium behind which Henderson would never stand was under a huge banner that stated LESTER MEANS LAW. Neither of the detectives knew what that meant.

'How many workmen?' Carella asked.

'A dozen or so. I have the list.'

'None of them *saw* anything?'

'I got some of my people out talking to them now. But I doubt we'll get lucky.'

'But they were all there working when he got shot, is that it?'

'They were all on the stage here, putting up things, testing mikes, whatever they do.'

'Nobody in the wings?'

'Just the shooter.'

'Let me get this straight . . .'

'Sure.'

'Henderson is onstage with his people and a dozen workmen . . .'

'Is the way I got it.'

'. . . when six shots are fired.'

'Two of them taking him in the chest. Four went wild.'

'And by the time anyone reacts, the shooter is gone.'

'That's the long and the short of it,' Ollie said.

HE TOLD THE uniformed guard in the gate house booth that he was here to see Mrs Henderson, and the guard checked his clipboard list, and then picked up the phone when he didn't see Carella's name on it.

Apparently Pamela Henderson gave the okay; the guard told him it was the first house on the right on Prospect Lane, and then waved him on through.

It was a lovely spring day.

Carella drove on winding roads past men and women in white playing tennis under clear blue skies, boys and girls on the fields behind stolid Smoke Rise Academy, playing soccer and baseball in their gray-and-black uniforms, their vibrant voices oddly recalling a youth he thought he'd long forgotten. The Henderson house was a vast stone structure set on a good two acres of wooded land. He parked the car in the gravel driveway, walked to the front door, and pressed the bell under a brass escutcheon that read simply '26 Prospect.' A uniformed housekeeper answered the door and told him she would fetch Mrs Henderson.

Pamela Henderson was a woman in her mid-forties, Carella guessed, tall and slender and exuding the sort of casual confidence women of wealth and influence often did. But she was not an attractive woman, he realized, her eyes somehow too small for her face, her nose a trifle too large. Newspaper reports would undoubtedly describe her as 'handsome,' the death knell for any woman who aspired to beauty.

Poised and polite, already wearing black – albeit jeans and a cotton turtleneck – she greeted Carella at the door, and led him into the living room of her home perched on the river, afternoon sunlight streaming through French doors, a glimpse of the Hamilton Bridge in the near distance, the cliffs of the adjoining state bursting with the greenery of spring. Her eyes were as green as the faraway hills. She wore no makeup. A simple oversized gold cross hung on the front of the black cotton turtleneck.

'I understood from the newspapers that a . . . different detective was investigating the case,' she said, hesitating slightly before the word 'different,' as if disapproving of either the false information in the papers or the unexpected turn the investigation had taken.

There was a certain formality here, a strict observance of the rules of sudden death and subsequent grief. Here were the stunned widow and the sympathetic but detached investigator, together again for the first time, with nothing to talk about but what had brought them to this juncture on this bright spring afternoon. A man had been robbed of his life. To Carella, Lester Henderson was a vague political figure in a city teeming with strivers and achievers. To Pamela Henderson, he had been husband, father, perhaps friend.

'Would you care for some coffee?' she asked.

'Thank you, no,' he said.

She poured coffee from a silver urn resting on a table before sheer saffron colored drapes. She added cream and two lumps of sugar.

'What are the chances?' she asked. 'Realistically.'

'Of?'

'Of catching whoever killed him.'

'We're hopeful,' he said.

What do you say to a widow? We lose as many as we catch? Sometimes we get lucky? What do you say when you can see that all her outward calm is vibrating with an almost palpable inner tenseness? Her hand on the saucer was shaking, he noticed. Tell her the truth, he thought. The truth is always best. Then you never have to remember what you lied about.

'There were a dozen or so people onstage with him when he was shot,' he said. 'Detective Weeks and his colleagues at the Eight-Eight are questioning them more fully now. They're also doing a canvass of the area around the Hall, trying to locate any . . .'

'What do you mean by questioning them more fully?'

'They already had a first pass at them.'

'And?'

'No one saw anything. The shots were described as coming from different sections of the hall. This is common. Eye witnesses are notoriously . . .'

'Is it possible there were two shooters?'

He noticed the word 'shooters.' Everyone watches television these days, he thought.

'We're still waiting for reports from the ME and Ballistics.'

'When will you have those?'

'It varies.'

Tell her the truth. Always the truth. In this city, with the number of homicides committed here every day of the week, any kind of report could sometimes take a week or ten days to get back to you. 'We're hoping, given the

36

magnitude of the case, it'll be sooner rather than later,' he said.

'The magnitude of the case,' she said, and nodded.

'Yes, ma'am.'

'Meaning my husband was important.'

'The case is attracting attention, yes, ma'am.'

'What do I tell the children?' she asked, and was suddenly weeping. She put down the coffee cup. She groped for a tissue in the box on the table, found the tag end of one, yanked it free, and brought it to her eyes. 'I kept them home from school today, I don't know what to tell them. My son was supposed to have baseball practice. My daughter's on her soccer team. What do I tell them? Your father's dead? They think he's still upstate. What do I tell them?'

Carella listened silently. He never knew what to say. He never knew what the hell to say. She kept sobbing into the tissue, crumpled it, took another from the box. He waited.

'I'm sorry,' she said.

He nodded.

'Why are you here?' she asked.

'There are some questions we need to ask. If you'd rather I came back some other . . .'

'No, please. Ask me.'

He hesitated, took his notebook from the inner pocket of his jacket, opened it, and looked at the list of questions he and Ollie had prepared. They seemed suddenly stark. Her husband had been killed. He cleared his throat.

'Can you tell me what time he left here yesterday morning?'

'Why is that important?' she asked.

'We're trying to work up a timetable, ma'am. If we can ascertain when . . .'

37

'I wish you'd stop calling me "ma'am,"' she said. 'I'd guess we're about the same age, wouldn't you? How old are you, anyway?'

'I'm forty, ma'am.'

She looked at him.

'Mrs Henderson,' he corrected.

'I'm forty-two,' she said.

He nodded.

She returned the nod.

The ice had been broken.

THERE WERE REPORTERS waiting outside the station house when he got back there at a quarter to four that afternoon. A pair of blues were standing on the wide front steps, barring the way like soldiers outside the gates of ancient Rome. Carella moved past the teeming crowd on the sidewalk, approaching the steps with an authority that told them at once he was connected.

'Excuse me,' one of them said, 'are you . . .?'

'No,' he said and went past them, and through the entrance doors with their glass-paneled upper sections adorned with the numerals '87' on each. Behind the muster desk, Sergeant Murchison was busy fielding phone calls. He looked up as Carella went past him, rolled his eyes, said into the phone, 'You'll have to contact Public Relations about that,' and hung up. Carella climbed the iron-runged steps to the second floor, stopped in the men's room to pee, washed his hands, and then went down the corridor and into the squadroom. Everything seemed more or less normal here. He almost breathed a sigh of relief.

Meyer Meyer, bald and burly and blue-eyed, was at his desk talking to a woman who looked like a hooker but who was probably a housewife who'd got all dressed up in her shortest skirt to come report something-or-other terrible to the police. The woman appeared extremely agitated although scantily dressed. Meyer merely looked patient. Or perhaps bored.

At his own desk, Bert Kling, blond and hazel-eyed and sporting a beard that was coming in blond and patchy, but which he felt was essential to an undercover he was working, was on the phone with someone he kept calling Charlie, who was probably on a cell phone because Kling kept saying, 'Charlie? Charlie? I'm losing you.'

Artie Brown, looking huge and menacing and dark and scowling, stood at the bulletin board, pondering the multitude of posters, notes, and announcements hanging there, glancing as well at the latest posted e-mail jokes from other police stations all over the country. Carella thought he detected a smile from him. He turned as Carella went by, waved vaguely in his direction, and then went back to his desk, where the phone began ringing furiously.

Another day, another dollar, Carella thought, and knocked on the lieutenant's door.

DETECTIVE-LIEUTENANT PETER BYRNES did not like high-profile cases. Given his druthers, he would have preferred that Lester Henderson had not lived in Smoke Rise, had instead lived across the river in the next state, or anyplace else but the Eight-Seven. He would have preferred that Ollie Weeks had not come calling with his courtesy request, although asking payback for saving someone's life – twice, don't forget – possibly qualified as something more substantial than a mere exchange of good manners. It was not unusual for cops in this city to ask favors of other precincts. Usually, but not always, they offered to share credit for any ensuing bust. Ollie had not deemed such an offer necessary. But, hey, he had saved Carella's life. *Twice!*

The first time was when a lion was about to eat him.

Yes.

A lion was sitting on Carella's chest, don't ask.

Ollie shot the beast between the eyes, end of lion, end of story. Carella could still smell the animal's foul breath.

The second time was a week or so later, when a blonde carrying an AK-47 was not about to *eat* Carella, more's the pity, but was instead ready to shoot him in the eye or someplace when who should arrive upon the scene but the large man from the Eight-Eight – wham, bam, thank you, ma'am, though he did not kill her as dead as he had the lion. Carella could still smell *her* breath, too. A whiff of Tic Tacs, as he recalled, spiked with that selfsame stink of imminent extinction.

Ollie had a right, Byrnes guessed. But he sure as hell wished nobody but the usual suspects had got killed yesterday morning.

'So what'd she have to say?' he asked Carella.

'Her husband wasn't home Sunday night.'

'What do you mean?'

'I asked her when he left the house yesterday morning, she told me she didn't know, he wasn't home.'

'So where was he?'

'Upstate. Meeting with the Governor's people.'

'That's very nice, the Governor's people,' Byrnes said.

'His wife told me they were trying to convince him to run for mayor.'

'Oh, Jesus, don't tell me this is going to get political,' Byrnes said.

'It could. He's a politician, Pete. Was.'

'Too much bad blood between Democrats and Republicans these days,' Byrnes said, shaking his head.

'You think a Democrat killed him?'

He was smiling. The idea of a Democrat killing a Republican was somewhat amusing. For that matter, so was the idea of a Republican killing a Democrat.

'I don't know who killed him,' Byrnes said. He was not smiling. 'You know something else? I don't even *care* who killed him. This case belongs to His Lord Fatness, I don't know how the hell we got involved in it.'

'Payback time, Pete.'

'You should try not to get yourself killed so often. And you should try to avoid obese saviors.'

'I'll try.'

'Where'd Henderson stay upstate? Did she say?'

'I'll ask her.'

'Call whichever hotel it was, find out what time he checked out, did he drive, did he take the train, did he fly, whatever. Give Ollie an ETA at the hall, and then tell him goodbye.'

'Yes, sir, is that an order, sir?'

'I don't want this case,' Byrnes said.

AT SEVEN O'CLOCK that Tuesday night, while Carella was at the dinner table with his wife and two children, Ollie Weeks called to say he was sorry he'd missed him at the office earlier today, but was it convenient for him to talk now?

'I'm in the middle of dinner,' Carella said.

'That's okay,' Ollie said, 'so am I.'

Carella had the feeling that somehow Ollie was *always* in the middle of dinner. Or lunch. Or breakfast. Or something.

'Can I call you back later?' he asked.

'Well, sure,' Ollie said, sounding offended, and hung up.

Carella called him back at a little past eight, after the twins were in bed. Ollie picked up the phone, said, 'Weeks,' and then belched.

'Ollie, it's Steve.'

'Yes, Steve.'

Still sounding offended.

'I wanted to report on what I learned from Mrs Henderson . . .'

'Yes, Steve.'

His tone was saying I only saved your life, you know.

'I had a long telephone conversation with her this afternoon. She . . .'

'I thought you were going to see her personally,' Ollie said.

'I did. This was *after* I saw her.'

'Uh-huh.'

'She said her husband flew up to the state capital on Saturday . . .'

'Uh-huh.'

'. . . stayed the weekend at the Raleigh Hotel there . . .'

'Okay.'

'Probably flew back early Monday morning . . .'

'What do you mean *probably*?'

'He didn't come home. She thinks he must have gone directly from the airport to King Memorial.'

'What do you mean she *thinks*?'

'Ollie,' Carella said, '*non mi rompere*, okay?'

'What?'

'I'm trying to tell you what I've got here. The lady doesn't know for *sure* where he was when. The last time she spoke to him was from the Raleigh. The next thing she knows he's shot dead at King Memorial. So she's assuming he flew back and went directly . . .'

42

'Okay, I get it, I get it,' Ollie said. 'Did you call the airport?'

'There are two non-stop flights leaving here early in the morning, both on US Airways. Takes about an hour to get to the capital. Any connecting flight doesn't pay, you can just as easily drive up these days, the long lines.'

'How about coming back?'

'Same thing. Two early morning flights. I called the hotel. Henderson checked out at six Monday morning. He could've caught either one of them, been here in the city by eight, eight-thirty. A cab from the airport would've put him at the Hall by eight-thirty, nine. Which is about right, more or less.'

'Where's his suitcase?'

'What?'

'He had to have a bag, no? So if he went straight to the Hall, where's the bag?'

'Good question.'

'We'll find out tomorrow. Meet me up the precinct at eight o'clock.'

'Uh . . . Ollie . . . my boss wants me off this.'

'Oh? Why?'

'He thinks it's too uptown for us.'

'We been uptown together before, my friend, ah yes.'

'The Loot isn't sure he wants to go there again.'

'Even if we share the bust?'

'I just don't think he wants any part of it.'

'You negotiating with me, or what?'

'Would I even dream?'

'We crack this one, we're made men.'

'I thought only the Mob had made men.'

'The Police Department is a mob, too, believe it or not. Tell your loot we share the bust, we'll all be glory boys.'

'How do you figure that, Ollie?'

'Guy about to run for mayor, he gets snuffed? Hey, this is bigtime stuff, Steve-a-rino.'

'How do you know he was going to run for mayor?'

'His aide told me. Alan Pierce, Mr Wasp from Waspville. Steve, I know it don't mean nothing I saved your life . . .'

'Enough already, Ollie.'

'Talk to your loot. Tell him we'll all get rich and famous.'

'He's already rich and famous.'

'Sure. Like my Aunt Tillie. Tell him we'll be on television and everything.'

'You know what we caught this morning, Ollie?'

'Tell me what you caught this morning, Steve.'

'A hundred-and-four-year-old lady drowned in her bathtub.'

'Not unusual. These old broads, they sometimes . . .'

'She was stabbed in the eye first, Ollie.'

'Extraordinary,' Ollie said. 'But it ain't gonna get your picture in the papers. You want the Eight-Seven to remain a shitty little precinct the rest of your life, or you want to step up to the plate and knock one out of the ball park?'

'I want to go say goodnight to my kids.'

'Call your loot instead, what's his name? Bernstein?'

'Byrnes.'

'I thought he was a Yid, like my boss. Tell him does he want another juicy one like that money money case we caught around Christmastime . . .'

'Money money *money*,' Carella said.

'Or does he just want another old lady moldering in a bathtub?'

'I think he might prefer the old lady.'

'Then he's an old lady himself, your boss. Tell him you got to grab this city by the balls before it grabs you first. Tell him opportunity knocks but once, tell him it's not every cop in the world gets invited to talk on *Larry King*. Tell him Oliver Wendell Weeks has spoken.'

'I'm sure he'll be impressed.'

'Tell him.'

'I'll tell him.'

'Don't forget the old lady metaphor,' Ollie said, and hung up.

4.

DETECTIVE/SECOND GRADE EILEEN BURKE did not know how she felt about being transferred to the Eight-Seven.

Lieutenant Byrnes voiced it for her.

'Eileen, you're a good cop,' he said, 'and I'm glad to have you with us. But there's this thing with Bert.'

The lieutenant was referring to the fact that in the not too distant past, Eileen had enjoyed an arduous but brief (well, brief in the annals of the Eight-Seven) relationship with one of his detectives. The look on Byrnes's face indicated he did not want problems related to ancient love affairs. Eileen read the look, and registered his words, and didn't know quite what to say. She had not seen Bert Kling in a very long time, and she knew he was now involved with someone else.

Standing before her new boss's desk, wearing brown slacks and brown low-heeled pumps, an olive-green crew-neck sweater with a matching cardigan over it, sunshine streaming through the Loot's corner windows and setting her red hair ablaze, she wondered what gave him the right to intrude on her personal life, wondered if he would give the male half of this prior romance the same warning, and was tempted to tell him to go to hell. He must have read the look in her green eyes, must have seen County Cork flaring; he was Irish himself, after all.

'Not that it's any of my business,' he amended.

'I'm sure there won't be any problem, sir,' Eileen said.

Byrnes noted the 'sir.' They had worked together before, when Eileen had been loaned to him as an undercover decoy, and back then it had been 'Pete.' Now it was 'sir,' which meant he'd got off on the wrong foot with her, something he didn't particularly wish. In apology, he said, 'You're the first woman I've had on my squad, Eileen.'

'I know that, sir.'

'Make it Pete, can you?'

'Pete,' she said, and nodded.

'You may find it quiet around here,' he said. 'After Hostage Negotiating.'

'In this city, nothing's quiet,' she said.

As a matter of fact, hostage-taking had cooled down a bit in recent years. Oh sure, you had the occasional nut who shot his wife and two of his kids and was holding the third kid at gun point in a ratty apartment someplace in Majesta while the cops promised him an airplane to Peru and three dozen Hershey bars, but for the most part the bad guys had bigger things on their minds. You didn't – in fact, couldn't – send a negotiator to talk to some fanatic who had taken over an airliner. Maybe the Eight-Seven *would* seem a little tame after standing face to face with a hostage-taker holding an AK-47 on his grandma, but maybe Eileen needed a rest in the country. Besides, from the inter-departmental jive she'd heard, the boys up here had recently been involved in a very big case involving the Treasury Department, the CIA, and God knew what else.

Byrnes was thinking he should tell her he'd try his best not to partner her with Kling – but that sounded apologetic. He was thinking he'd tell her that very often the working relationship between two detectives made the difference between life or death – but that sounded corny.

'Eileen,' he said simply, 'we're a tight-knit family here. Welcome to it.'

'Thank you. sir,' she said. 'Pete.'

Which was when a knock sounded on the lieutenant's door.

'Come,' Byrnes said.

The door opened – and speak of the devil.

AT TWENTY MINUTES to nine that Wednesday morning – some fifteen minutes after he'd stepped into the lieutenant's office to encounter a redheaded ghost – Bert Kling was at the wheel of an unmarked police sedan driving himself and Carella uptown to the Eight-Eight.

'I have to tell you the truth,' he said, 'my heart stopped.'

Carella said nothing. He had called the lieutenant the night before, and told him about Ollie Weeks's offer of a fifty-fifty bust, if ever there was one. He had told the lieutenant that you had to grab this city by the balls before it grabbed you first. He had told him that opportunity knocks but once, and it wasn't every cop in the world who got invited to talk on *Larry King*.

'Oliver Wendell Weeks has spoken,' he'd said.

Byrnes had responded, 'Let's go for it.'

So here he was on the way uptown again, listening to Kling tell him all about how he'd felt upon seeing, after all this time, the woman who had once been the love of his life.

It had begun raining.

The Eight-Seven had investigated a case one March where it had rained almost constantly. They would later refer to it as 'The Rain Case,' even though it had involved finding a severed hand in an airline bag. In this city, rain could actually be pleasant sometimes. Not this morning.

The rain was driving and incessant, falling from the sky in buckets – to coin a phrase – cascading onto the windshield where the wipers worked in vain to maintain some semblance of visibility.

'I felt like telling her I used to love her a lot,' Kling said. 'But the Loot was sitting right there, and besides I didn't want to give her the idea there might be anything there anymore.'

'So what *did* you say?' Carella asked.

'Well, Pete told me she'd be working with us from now on, so I said, "Glad to have you aboard," or something stupid like that, and we shook hands. It felt strange shaking hands. I mean . . . we were together a long time, you know, we were a *couple*. And now we were just shaking hands. Like strangers. That's when I felt like telling her I used to love her a lot. While we were shaking hands.'

'We can park behind the station,' Carella said, 'go in the back way.'

Kling leaned over the wheel, squinting through the windshield to locate the driveway, and then swung the car into the lot. He parked in a space as close to the building as he could find, but they both almost drowned before they'd stepped a foot out of the car to begin a mad dash to the rear door of the station house.

All of these old precincts had the same layout. They could just as easily have been entering the Eight-Seven as the Eight-Eight. They came into a long corridor illuminated by a naked light bulb. No one inside the door, it occurred to Carella that some lunatic with a bomb could just march in. He made a mental note to mention this to Byrnes when they got back home. Down the corridor, past an old defunct coal-burning furnace, up a flight of wooden steps to a door that opened onto the first-floor muster room. Same muster desk as the Eight-Seven's, different sergeant behind it. He either recognized Carella and Kling, or else didn't give a damn that they might be desperate terrorists.

Mobile radio rack to the left of them, rack with vests to the right. Up the iron-runged stairs to the second floor, past a men's room, and a ladies' room, and then through a gate in a slatted wooden railing identical to the one back home, and there you were, face to face with His Royal Girth.

'You're late,' Ollie said, grinning.

It was 9:01 A.M.

Here, too, were the familiar sounds and smells. The ringing telephones, the aroma of coffee brewing on a hot plate, the stale odor – especially on a rainy day – of a room that had seen too many days and nights of use and abuse, and there, yes, the faintest trace of a scent only cops could identify as coming from the black ink on the fingerprint table across the room. One of the windows across the room was open just a crack. There was even an unaccustomed whiff of fresh air. All so very familiar. Especially if you watched television.

'We found the bag,' Ollie said.

Kling wondered what bag.

For a moment, Carella wondered the same thing.

'Oh, the bag,' he said, remembering.

Ollie rose from his swivel chair like a whale off the coast of Mexico. He waddled across the room to where one of those small black airline bags on wheels rested near the water cooler. Yanking out the handle, he wheeled the bag over to his desk, hoisted it onto its top and – like a magician about to pull a rabbit from a top hat – unzipped the bag, and threw back the flap.

'This is what a city councilman packs for an overnight

trip,' he said, and opened his hands wide. 'Found it sitting on the stage, near the rear wall.'

The clothing in the bag was stuffed into it like laundry – which is what it undoubtedly was. These were the clothes Henderson had worn during his two-night stay in the state's capital. Packed in the bag were a pair of men's undershorts, two pairs of dark blue socks, a blue, long-sleeved, button-down shirt, a similar white shirt, a blue tropical weight suit, a blue-and-green-striped silk tie, a pair of black shoes, a toilet kit, and an electric razor.

'He was wearing jeans, loafers, and a faggoty pink sweater when he got killed,' Ollie said. 'Probably wore them home on the plane.'

'Tells us nothing,' Kling said.

Ollie looked at him.

Carella braced himself for whatever was coming. With Ollie, you never knew. But nothing came. Ollie merely sighed heavily. The sigh could have meant 'How come I always get stuck with stupid rookies?' (which Kling certainly wasn't) or alternatively, 'How come it's raining on a day when we have so much to do?'

'How much time can you guys give me today?' he asked.

'The Loot says we're at your disposal.'

'Really? Who's gonna take care of the old lady in the bathtub?' Ollie asked, as if he gave a damn who'd stabbed her in the eye. Carella recognized the question as rhetorical. Kling didn't know what they were talking about. 'Here's what I'd like to do today,' Ollie said, and began ticking the points off on his left hand, starting with the pinky. 'One, *I'll* go chase down this guy who was on the follow spot when Henderson caught it Monday morning, nail down what he saw, what he heard, and so on. Nobody leaves alive. Next,' ticking it off on his ring finger, 'I want *you* guys to talk to the Reverend Gabriel Foster about a little fracas him and Henderson got into just a week or so ago.'

'Why us?' Carella asked.

'Let's say the rev and me don't get along too well, ah yes.'

'Gee, I wonder why.'

'What kind of fracas?' Kling asked.

'Name calling, fists flying, like that.'

'Where was this?'

'A Town Hall debate. Hizzoner was there, too, *that* shmuck.'

'You don't really think Foster had anything to do with Henderson's murder, do you?' Carella said.

'I think where there's a nigger in the woodpile, you smoke him out,' Ollie said.

Kling looked at him.

'Something?' Ollie said.

'I don't like that expression.'

'Well, gee, shove it up your ass,' Ollie said.

Carella stepped in at once. 'Where do we see you later?'

'You mean when shall we three meet again?' Ollie said. 'Ah yes. How about right here, back at the ranch, let's say three o'clock.' He looked Kling in the eye and said, 'I hope you know Henderson was for stiffening drug laws.'

'So?'

'So some people in the so-called black community might've thought he was trying to send their so-called brothers to jail.'

'So?'

'Targeting persons of color, they might have thought,' Ollie said. 'What some people up here call profiling. You ought to keep that in mind when you're talking to him.'

'Thanks, we'll keep it in mind,' Kling said.

'What I'm suggesting is Foster's a well-known Negro agitator and rabble rouser. Maybe he got himself all agitated and aroused Monday morning.'

'Or maybe not,' Carella said.

'Or maybe not,' Ollie agreed. 'It's a free country, and nobody's hassling the man.'

'Except us,' Kling said.

'Asking pertinent questions ain't hassling. Unless you're a Negro, of course, and then everybody in the whole fucking world is hassling you. Foster's been around the block once or twice, so watch your ass, he's slippery as a wet condom. Then again, they all are. This is where the big bad city begins, Sonny Boy, right here in the Eight-Eight, the home of the jig and the land of the spic.'

'One more time, Ollie,' Kling said.

'What the fuck's with you?' Ollie said, genuinely puzzled.

'See you at three,' Carella said, and took Kling's elbow and steered him out of the squadroom.

Behind them, Ollie called, 'You new in the job, or what?'

IT OCCURRED TO CARELLA that it had been raining the last time he'd visited the Reverend Gabriel Foster here at the First Baptist Church. This time he took an umbrella from the car. In this city, you never saw a uniformed cop carrying an umbrella and you hardly ever saw a detective carrying one, either. That was because law enforcement officers could walk between the drops. Walking between the drops now, Carella hunched with Kling under the large black umbrella, and they splashed their way together to the front doors of the church.

The First Bap was housed in a white clapboard structure wedged between a pair of six-story tenements whose red-brick façades had been recently sandblasted. There were sections of Diamondback that long ago had been sucked into the quagmire of hopeless poverty, where any thoughts of gentrification were mere pipe dreams. But St Sebastian Avenue, here in the Double-Eight between Seventeenth and Twenty-first, was the hub of a thriving mini-community not unlike a self-contained small town. Along this stretch of avenue, you could find good restaurants, markets brimming with prime cuts of meat and fresh produce, clothing stores selling designer labels, repair shops for shoes, bicycles, or umbrellas, a new movie complex with six screens, even a fitness center.

Carella rang the doorbell.

The middle of the three doors opened.

A slight black man wearing a dark suit and glasses peered out at them.

'Come in out of the rain,' he said.

Inside, rain battered the roof of the church, and only the palest light trickled through stained-glass windows. The pews echoed themselves row upon row, silent and empty. Carella closed the umbrella.

'You're policemen, aren't you?' the man said.

'Detective Carella,' he said.

'You've been here before.'

'Yes.'

'I remember. Did you want to see the Reverend?'

'If he's here.'

'I'm sure he'll want to talk to you. I'm Deacon Ainsworth,' he said, and offered his hand.

Both detectives shook hands with him.

'Come with me,' he said, and led them down a side aisle to a door to the right of the altar. The door opened onto a narrow passageway lined with windows on the street side. They walked past the windows to another door at the far end. Ainsworth knocked. A voice within said, 'Yes, come in.' Ainsworth opened the door.

According to police records, the Reverend Gabriel Foster's birth name was Gabriel Foster Jones. He'd changed it to Rhino Jones when he enjoyed a brief career as a heavyweight boxer, and then settled on Gabriel Foster when he began preaching. Foster considered himself a civil rights activist. The police considered him a rabble rouser, an opportunistic self-promoter, and a race racketeer. His church, in fact, was listed in the files as a 'sensitive location,' departmental code for anyplace where the uninvited presence of the police might cause a race riot.

Six feet, two inches tall, with the wide shoulders and broad chest of the heavyweight fighter he once had been, his eyebrows still ridged with scar tissue, Foster at the age of forty-nine and fast approaching fifty still looked as if he could knock your average contender on his ass in thirty seconds flat. He extended his right hand the moment the detectives entered the rectory. Grinning, he said, 'Detective Carella! Nice to see you again.'

The men shook hands. Carella was mindful of the fact that the last time he was here, Foster hadn't been at all happy to see him.

'This is Detective Kling,' he said.

'Nice to meet you,' Kling said.

'I know why you're here,' Foster said. 'You're shaking the tree, am I right?'

'We're here because the last time you and Henderson debated, it ended in a fist fight,' Carella said.

'Well, that's not quite true,' Foster said.

'It's our understanding of what happened.'

'Oh, we came to blows, all right, that part of it is most certainly true,' Foster said, grinning. 'It's the "debate" part I would challenge. I wouldn't exactly call his diatribe a debate.'

Kling was trying to decide whether he liked the man or not. He had become overly sensitive in his dealings with black people ever since he'd begun living with a black woman. What he tried to do was see all black people through Sharyn's eyes. In that way, all the color bullshit disappeared. The first thing he'd learned from her was that she despised the label 'African-American.' The second thing he'd learned was that she liked to kiss with her eyes open. Sharyn Cooke was a medical doctor and a Deputy Chief in the Police Department, but Kling never saluted her.

He guessed he liked the mischievous gleam in Foster's eyes. He knew the man was a troublemaker, but sometimes troublemakers were good if they raked up the right kind of trouble. He was wondering how Lester Henderson had managed to survive a fist fight with the man who'd once been Rhino Jones. Henderson's pictures in this morning's paper showed him as a slight man with narrow shoulders and the sort of haircut every politician on television sported, a non-partisan trim that Kling personally called 'The Trent Lott Cut.' Weren't the Reverend Foster's hamlike fists registered as deadly weapons? Or had he pulled his punches? And when, exactly, had that boxing match taken place, anyway?

Reading his mind, Carella said, 'Tell us about that fight, Reverend Foster.'

'Most people call me Gabe,' Foster said. 'It was hardly what I'd call a fight, either. A fight is where two people exchange punches with the idea of knocking somebody unconscious. That is what a fight is all about. Or even

56

killing the other person – which I understand might be a sensitive subject at the moment, considering what happened to that S.O.B.' Foster grinned again. 'A week ago Sunday, Lester threw a punch at me, which I sidestepped, and I shoved out at him, which caused him to fall on his ass, and that was the end of that. Photo op for all the cameras in town, but no decision.'

'Why'd he punch you, Gabe?' Kling asked.

'He did not *punch* me, per se, he *tried* to punch me. I saw it coming all the way from North Dakota, and was out of the way before it was even a thought.'

'Why'd he *try* to punch you?' Kling asked.

'Are you the brother dating Sharyn Cooke?' Foster said.

'Brother' was not a word Kling might have used. Neither was 'dating.'

'What's that got to do with the price of fish?' he asked.

'Just wondered. I used to know Sharyn's mother. Cleaning lady up here in Diamondback. She helped around the church every now and then. When I was just starting out.'

'Why'd Henderson try to punch you?' Kling asked. Third time around. Maybe he'd get lucky.

'Gee, I really don't know,' Foster said. 'You think it's cause I called him a racist pig?'

'Now why'd you go say something like that?' Carella asked. His eyes, his faint smile betrayed the knowledge that Lester Henderson had been called this before, in many variations on the theme, the most recent one from a state senator, who'd called him 'Hitler without a mustache.'

'It's a known fact that he was targeting Diamondback for extinction,' Foster said. 'If I'm not mistaken, Detective Carella, you yourself investigated a case just recently where the drug problem up here played an important role. Well, Henderson was all for toughening the state's already Draconian drug laws, laws that are methodically clearing young black people off the streets . . .'

Here comes a speech, Kling thought.

'. . . and throwing them into already overcrowded prisons that are costing taxpayers a fortune to maintain. Instead of helping these youths to become productive members of a thriving community, we are instead turning them into criminals. I pointed this out to Lester, and I casually mentioned that only a racist pig would pursue a course as politically motivated as the one he was promoting. That was when he tried to pop me.'

'Small wonder,' Carella said. 'So where were you around ten-thirty Monday morning, Gabe?'

'Oh dear,' Foster said.

'Oh dear indeed.'

'I fear I was asleep in my own little beddie-bye, all by my little self.'

'Which would have been where?'

'1112 Roosevelt Av Apartment 6B.'

'And what time did you get *out* of your little beddie-bye?'

'I came to the office here at eleven. I had a scheduled eleven-thirty interview with a reporter.'

'What time did you leave the apartment?' Kling asked.

'Around ten-thirty. Whenever the weather is good, I walk to work.'

'So you weren't anywhere near King Memorial at ten-thirty Monday morning, is that right?'

'Nowhere near it at all.'

'Be nice if someone had been in bed with you,' Carella said.

'Yes, it's always nice to have someone in bed with you,' Foster said.

'But no one was.'

'No one at all.'

'*What'd* you say your address was again?' Kling asked.

'1112 Roosevelt.'

'That's between Twenty-eighth and Twenty-ninth, isn't it?'

'No, it's further uptown.'

'Near King Memorial?'

'A few blocks away, yes.'

'Where exactly?' Carella asked.

'Between Thirty-first and -second.'

'The Hall's on St Sab's, corner of Thirtieth,' Kling said.

'So it is,' Foster said.

'If you'd walked one block over, you could've passed it on your way to work.'

'*If* I'd walked one block over,' Foster said. 'But I came straight down Roosevelt. Same way I always do.'

'You walk the ten blocks down to Twenty-first here . . .'

'Yes, and then I walk the block crosstown to St Sab's.'

'Nice walk.'

'If the weather's nice, yes.'

'It certainly was nice Monday,' Kling said.

'It certainly was,' Carella said.

'Fellas, let's cut the idle bullshit, okay?' Foster said. 'You know I didn't kill that prick, so it doesn't matter *where* I was Monday morning. I could've been home in bed with the entire Mormon Tabernacle Choir, or I could've been right outside King Memorial tying my shoelaces. I may have done some foolish things in my lifetime, but killing a man a week after we had a brawl is definitely not one of them.'

'I tend to agree,' Carella said.

'Me, too,' Kling said.

'But we have to ask,' Carella said.

'You know how it is,' Kling said.

'Thanks for your time, Gabe. If you happen to hear anything . . .'

'What would I hear?'

'Well, you *do* have your finger on the community pulse. Maybe somebody saw something, heard something, feels it's his duty to report it to a community leader . . .'

'That's yet *more* bullshit,' Foster said. 'I'm still a suspect, right?'

'Teach you to sleep alone,' Carella said.

5.

TO TELL THE God's honest truth, Ollie was more interested in finding whoever had stolen his book than he was
in finding whoever had murdered Lester Henderson.
Toward that end, he had already coerced the Mobile
Crime Unit into coming all the way uptown to dust his
car for prints, the operative theory being that the perp
hadn't been wearing gloves on a nice spring day, and had
therefore left telltale evidence all over the place.

Sure.

That was for fiction.

The MCU boys hadn't come up with anything at all –
which didn't surprise Ollie, those jackasses – but which
still left *somebody* out there who had smashed Ollie's car
window (in plain view of the deaf, dumb, and blind blues
standing outside King Memorial, don't forget) and
reached in to unlock the door and run off with Ollie's
precious manuscript. He didn't think anyone up here
knew how to read, so he didn't suppose they could discern
he or she was looking at something written by a police
officer, which if it wasn't returned pronto, could put his
or her ass in a sling.

The dispatch case bearing the manuscript had been a
gift from Isabelle two Christmases ago. Like everything
else his dumb sister ever gave him, he'd had no use for it
until he placed his book inside it to carry to Kinko's. He
figured the only use the thief had for the case was to hock

61

it, so he'd already sent out a flier to all the hock shops in the Eight-Eight and neighboring precincts. Junkies – if indeed a junkie had stolen it – were territorial by nature and basic by instinct.

In the three months it had taken him to write the book, he had learned a lot about so-called mystery fiction. After he'd thrown away his first feeble attempts at *Bad Money*, he'd started all over again by reading most of the crap on the bestseller list, much of it written by ladies who were not now, nor had ever in their entire lives been cops or private eyes or medical examiners or game wardens or bounty hunters, or any of the other things they professed to be. He then began reading all the book reviews posted on Amazon Dot Com.

Before he himself got on the Web, he used to think Amazon Dot Com was a very large broad named Dorothy Kahm. Now he knew better. To him, the reviews on this bookselling site seemed like the book reports he had to write when he was in the sixth grade. In fact, the reviews on Amazon seemed to be written by soccer moms who'd never been to school at *all*, it looked like, who were also not cops or private eyes or anything else, and who weren't very good writers in the bargain. He wondered why Amazon, presumably in the business of selling books, would post bad reviews about books they were trying to sell, but hey, that was *their* business. Besides, these so-called book reviews were very informative to Ollie.

What he learned from them was that any book with more than half a dozen characters in it, or more than a single plot line, was too confusing to be understood by some hick down there in Green Beans, Georgia, or out there in Saddle Sores, Texas. The answer was simplicity. Keep it simple. If simpletons were out there reading mystery fiction or detective fiction or crime fiction or thrillers or whatever anyone chose to call these so-called stories, then anybody actually writing the stuff had better learn how to keep it simple. Simplicity for the simpletons.

Simple.

So what he'd done was to scrap the literary approach he'd formerly been striving for in *Bad Money*. For example, in the original version of his book, there had been high-flown language like:

The sound of music came from somewhere inside the apartment. Its noisome beat filled the hallway tremblingly.

In the next version, Ollie changed this to:

Loud music hammered the halls.

Period.

Simple.

He thought he had found his voice.

There was no sense trying to explain 'voice' to anyone who wasn't a writer. He had once tried to define it for his jackass sister Isabelle, and she had immediately said, 'Oh, are you gonna be a singer now?' To a writer, voice had nothing to do with singing. Voice was as intangible as mist on an Irish bog. Voice was something that came from the very heart and soul. Voice was the essential essence of any novel, its perfume, so to speak. Try explaining that to a jackass like Isabelle.

And then, all at once, he had a truly brilliant idea.

In the first version of the book, he had called his lead character Detective/First Grade Oswald Wesley Watts. He had, in fact, described him like this:

Tall and handsome, broad of shoulder and wide of chest, slender of waist and fleet of foot, Detective 'Big Ozzie' Watts, pistol in hand (a nine-millimeter semi-automatic Glock, by the way) climbed the steps to the fourth floor of the reeking tenement and knocked on the door to apartment 4C.

But after realizing that most of the mysteries on the

bestseller list were written by *ladies*, Ollie took an entirely different approach. The revised version of his book started like this:

I am locked in a basement with $2,700,000 in so-called conflict diamonds, and I just got a run in my pantyhose.

He had found a voice at last.

IT DID NOT TAKE Emilio Herrera long to realize that he had stumbled upon something very large indeed. He was not talking about the dispatch case itself. He had already sold that for five dollars. He was talking about what was inside the case. What he had just finished reading was a private report to the Police Commissioner from one of his female detectives:

REPORT TO THE
COMMISSIONER

BY DETECTIVE/
FIRST GRADE

OLIVIA WESLEY
WATTS

What he was just about to start reading again, more carefully this time, was an intensely personal account of a massive diamond deal that had gone awry. What he was hoping to discover – if he was smart enough to crack the code – was the location of millions of dollars in so-called conflict diamonds.

Emilio was a fast reader. One of his best subjects in school, before he dropped out to become a dope addict, was English Literature. It took only a matter of minutes for him to realize that the detective writing the report was using a sort of code known only to herself and the Police Commissioner. For example, when the detective used the word 'Rubytown,' Emilio knew right off she was talking about Diamondback, right here where he lived. And no matter *what* she called the city in her report, Emilio knew that Detective Olivia Wesley Watts was talking about this city right here, this big bad city where Emilio was born and raised and corrupted.

Emilio knew he had been corrupted. That is to say, he knew he was a drug addict. Lots of junkies told you they were not addicted, they could walk away from it anytime they chose, they could take it or leave it alone. But Emilio preferred not lying to himself; he knew he was hooked clear through the bag and back again. He did not start out life planning to become a drug addict. He had not told his mother, 'Hey, *jefita*, you know what I wish to become when I grow up? A drug addict!'

As a matter of fact, what he wished to become was a baseball player. A second baseman. Instead, he had become a drug addict. That was one of the things you had to watch out for in this city. You could start out wanting to be President of the United States but there were people who had other ideas for you, and all of a sudden you were sniffing your life up your nose. Just like that. One day you were playing ball on the diamond under the bridge near the drive, and the next day you were breaking a car window because you saw a brown leather dispatch case on the back seat and you figured maybe there was dope inside it.

But, you know . . .

It all worked out in the long run, didn't it?

Here in Emilio's hands was the key to millions of dollars. In a way, this was better than winning the lottery. All he had to do was read Detective Watts's report again and again, backwards and forwards, decipher which code names in the book stood for which real place names in the city, and he would know where the gang in the book had stashed what amounted to $2,700,000 in diamonds before they locked poor Olivia in the basement with a run in her pantyhose, which to tell the truth excited Emilio to read about a girl's underwear so honestly.

THE ELECTRICAL GUY'S name was Peter Handel.

The rain had stopped and he was playing chess in the park outside Ramsey U downtown when Ollie found him. Both Handel and his chess partner were people who, in Ollie's estimation, could have stood losing a few pounds. Like giant pandas, the two men hunched over the stone-topped table, pondering their next moves. Not wishing to break their hugely intense concentration, Ollie waited a moment before flashing the tin and introducing himself.

'I'd like to talk to you privately, Mr Handel,' he said. 'If your friend here doesn't mind.'

'I'm three moves away from checkmate,' his friend said.

Ollie wondered how chess players knew such things.

'Take a walk around the block,' he suggested. 'It's turning into a nice day.'

'He'll figure out my game plan,' the man complained, and waddled off grudgingly.

Ollie took his place at the chess table. He and Handel sat in dappled sunshine. Women strolled by pushing baby carriages. Across the street, young dealers were selling dope to college students. Ollie wondered where the hell all the cops were in this city.

'I understand you were in the booth up there when Henderson got shot,' Ollie said.

'Yeah,' Handel said.

Over a plaid sports shirt, Handel was wearing a brown woolen cardigan with darker brown buttons, what Ollie's sister called a 'candy-store sweater.' Combined with wide-waled brown corduroy trousers, the ill-fitting sweater made him look exceptionally stout. Ollie wondered why such people didn't go on diets.

'Tell me what you saw,' he said.

'I was following him from stage left, the spot on him all the way. Somebody shot him just as he reached the podium.'

'Where'd the shots come from, do you know?'

'Stage right.'

'What does that mean, stage right, stage left?'

'The person's right or left. The person standing on stage. *His* right or left. Looking out at the audience.'

'So, if he was approaching the podium from the left . . .'

'*His* left, yes.'

'You're saying somebody fired at him as he approached.'

'Somebody fired from stage *right*, yes.'

'How many shots did you hear?'

'Quite a few.'

'Five, six?'

'At least.'

'Did you see anyone sitting in the balcony?'

'I wasn't looking at the balcony. I was looking at the stage. My job was to keep that spot on him.'

'Are you sure those shots didn't come from the balcony?'

'I'm positive. I saw the muzzle flashes.'

'But not the shooter?'

'Not the shooter. Just the muzzle flashes. And then he was falling. I kept the spot on him as he fell. Those were my instructions. Keep the spot on him. I kept the spot on him till somebody yelled for me to turn it off.'

'Who was that, would you know?'

'No, sir, I would not. I guess it was somebody running the show. So I turned it off. And then somebody turned on the house lights.'

'When the house lights came on, did you see anybody in the wings?'

'Nobody. I guess whoever'd done the shooting was gone by then.'

'Stage right, you say.'

'Was where I saw the muzzle flashes.' Handel hesitated. Then he said, 'It can be confusing. Would you like me to draw a diagram?'

CARELLA AND KLING were waiting for Ollie when he got back to the Eight-Eight's squadroom at five minutes to three that Wednesday afternoon. Ollie was carrying two white pizza cartons. He opened one of them, shoved it across his desk, said, 'This is for you guys, my treat,' and then opened the second carton and began eating even before they sat down. Kling, who had never seen Ollie eating before, watched in amazement.

'Something, Sonny Boy?' Ollie asked.

'Nothing,' Kling said, but he continued shaking his head in wonder.

It was like a juggling act. With only two hands, Ollie seemed to keep three slices of pizza in constant motion from the box to his mouth. But now, adding to the splendor and mystery of the act, he added a fourth element. As if suddenly growing another hand, he reached into the breast pocket of his jacket, and took from it a folded sheet of paper, which he tossed onto the desk top, never missing a pizza-beat, pizza to mouth, paper to desk, more pizza to mouth, incredible.

'Take a look at this,' he said, and nodded at the sheet of paper while biting into what appeared to be two slices of pizza at the same time.

'What is it?' Carella asked.

'Diagram from the electrical guy.'

Carella put down his slice of pizza, unfolded the sheet of paper, and flattened it on the desk top.

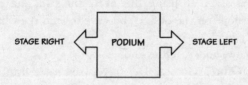

'The podium's in the center there,' Ollie said. 'Henderson came on stage left, walked across to it, got shot just as he reached it. The shooter was in the wings stage right. The electrical guy saw repeated muzzle flashes, are you guys going to finish that pizza or what?'

'Go ahead, have a slice,' Kling said.

He was eager to see if Ollie could juggle four slices simultaneously.

'Kept the follow spot on him all the way to the floor, dedicated, huh?' Ollie said, hands reaching, mouth working, teeth biting, sauce and toppings and cheese dripping all over his hands and his shirt and the desk top. Astonishing, Kling thought.

'Is there a Detective Weeks here?' someone said.

They all turned toward the slatted wooden railing that divided the squadroom from the corridor outside. A female police officer was standing there. She was holding a minilla envelope in her right hand. The word EVIDENCE was printed across the face of the envelope.

'I'm Detective Weeks,' Ollie said.

'Officer Gomez,' she said, and opened the gate in the railing and walked over to the desk. She was trying to learn attitude. Fresh out of the Academy, her uniform trimly tailored, the buttons all shiny and bright, even her shield looking glistening new, she walked with a sort of sidelong gait that tried to negate her obvious femininity while emphasizing the authority of the Glock on her hip.

'I was asked to bring this over,' she said, and placed the envelope on the desk. 'You have to sign the Chain of Custody tag.'

'I know, honey,' Ollie said.

'It's Officer Gomez, Detective,' she said, firmly but politely correcting him.

'Oh my, so it is,' Ollie said, glancing at the name tag pinned above her perky left breast, which read P. GOMEZ in white on black. He signed for the envelope, hefted it on the palm of his hand, and said, 'Would you happen to know what's inside here, Officer Gomez?'

'Yes, sir,' Gomez said. 'I was there when it was recovered at the scene.'

'And where would that have been, this scene, Officer Gomez?'

'In the alley outside the auditorium at King Memorial. Down the sewer there, sir.'

'I see, ah yes,' Ollie said, and opened the envelope.

Someone diligent seemed to have retrieved what looked like a .32-caliber Smith & Wesson revolver.

OLLIE WAS JUST LEAVING the squadroom at a quarter to six that evening when the call from Ballistics came. The detective calling had a thick Hispanic accent. Ollie could hardly understand him. He wondered why these people didn't learn to speak English. He also wondered why every time you called a movie theater to find out what was playing or what time the show went on, the person on the recorded message was somebody who'd learned English in Bulgaria. You had to call the number two, three times to get the message played all over again because you couldn't figure out if it was Meg Ryan in the damn picture or Tom Cruise. He figured this was some kind of dumb-ass equal-opportunity program. If you had to record a telephone message essential to your business, what you did was choose the person in your company who couldn't speak English at all. The thing was, Ollie hadn't realized till now that this practice had spread to the Police Department.

From what he could gather, the .32 Smith & Wesson recovered from a sewer in the alley off the western end of the King Memorial auditorium either was or was not the pistol that had fired the fatal shots into Lester Henderson. From what he could gather further, a pistol bearing the serial numbers of the recovered weapon either was or was not registered to someone in this city.

'Listen,' Ollie said, 'is there somebody there speaks English?'

The dope got insulted and hung up.

Ollie dialed back at once.

Another guy who couldn't speak English answered the phone.

'What is this?' Ollie asked. 'Did Castro invade the United States?'

'*Quien es?*' the guy asked.

'Detective/First Grade Oliver Wendell Weeks,' Ollie said. 'Give me somebody speaks English down there.'

He heard the phone rattling onto a counter top down

there. Probably dangerous weapons all over the place down there, nobody could speak English.

'Detective Hogan,' somebody said.

'Hooray,' Ollie said.

'Who's this?'

'Weeks, the Eight-Eight. You got an evidence piece we sent down for Comp and ID, I'm tryin'a get a report on it.'

'Didn't somebody call you?'

'Somebody called me.'

'So?'

'So now *I'm* callin *you*. Did you test-fire the piece, and if so did you get a match?'

'Test bullets were positive for the evidence weapon, yes,' Hogan said. 'Anything else?'

Ollie figured he was pissed off cause his spic buddies couldn't speak English too good. 'If it's not too much trouble,' he said sweetly, 'can you perhaps tell me if you ran a computer check on the evidence weapon?'

'Serial numbers were obliterated,' Hogan said. 'Anything else?'

'Yes. What's your first name, Hogan?'

'Why?'

'Cause I don't like your attitude is why. I'm investigating a homicide here, of a *councilman* no less, and you happen to have in your possession the *murder* weapon. So if you don't mind, Mr Hogan, and if it ain't too much trouble, what I'd like you to do is *restore* those numbers for me and then run the piece to see who might *own* the thing. Do you think you might know how to do that, Mr Hogan? First you clean the site of the numbers . . .'

'I know how to do it,' Hogan said. 'So do my partners.'

'Well, good, maybe the numbers are written in Spanish. After you bring 'em up, let me know what you find in the system, okay? I'll be waiting. So will the Mayor's Office, cause Lester Henderson wasn't just some punk on the street, you know?' He paused for emphasis. 'I wouldn't be bothering you with all this, Mr Hogan, cause I know how valuable your time is, but it so happens the only prints on the weapon were smeared, and we got nothing to go on. Which is why your expertise in the matter is so urgently demanded, ah yes,' Ollie said.

'The numbers were filed deep,' Hogan said. 'Gonna be tough to bring 'em up.'

'Well now, gee, that's your job, ain't it?' Ollie said, and hung up.

6.

ANDY PARKER didn't particularly like being partnered
with women, especially any woman who'd been hurt on
the job. The way he understood it, Eileen Burke had been
slashed while serving as an undercover decoy in a case
she'd been working with the Rape Squad. Blue wisdom
maintained she'd also been violated at the time, so to
speak, but nobody talked about that because Burke had
friends with short tempers, among them Bert Kling who
Parker knew for a fact had been going steady with her
when all this occurred. What went on between them – or
even between her legs, for that matter – was none of his
business. What happened on the job when you were
partnered with someone who'd been cut or shot was
another matter. They were never the same again, he knew
that for a fact, too.

The man they were talking to this Wednesday night
was a person Parker had been working with ever since
February. His name was Francisco Palacios, and he owned
and operated a cozy little shop that sold medicinal herbs,
dream books, religious statues, numbers books, tarot
cards, and other related items.

His silent partners, however, were named Gaucho
Palacios and Cowboy Palacios, and they ran a shop *behind*
the other shop, and *this* one offered for sale various
unrelated and medically approved 'marital aids' like
dildoes, French ticklers, open-crotch panties, plastic

vibrators, leather executioners' masks, chastity belts, whips with leather thongs, penis extenders, aphrodisiacs, inflatable life-sized female dolls, condoms in every color of the rainbow including vermilion, books on how to hypnotize and otherwise overcome reluctant women, ben wa balls in both plastic and gold plate, and a highly popular mechanical device guaranteed to bring satisfaction and imaginatively called Suc-u-lator.

Francisco, The Gaucho, and The Cowboy were in fact one and the same person, and they were collectively a police informer, a stoolie, a snitch, or in some quarters even a rat. At the back of El Castillo de Palacios, as The Gaucho called his bifurcated shop, he sat with the two detectives and tried to fill them in on what was about to come down next Tuesday night. He found it somewhat difficult to concentrate on business, however, because his eyes kept wandering to the redheaded detective's crossed legs, and he kept wondering what it would be like to put her in a pair of *bragas sin entrepierna* and leather anklets studded with chrome.

The Gaucho wondered if she found him good-looking.

He himself thought he was one cool *hombre*. As tall and as lean as a matinee idol, with dark brown eyes and a mustache he hadn't sported a year or so ago, he still wore his long black hair in a high pompadour, the way kids used to wear it in the fifties. He did not admit to having four wives because that was against the law – *having* them, not *admitting* to having them. But none of them was redheaded. In fact, he had never been to bed with a redheaded woman in his life. He wondered if it was true that they were even more passionate than blondes. None of his wives was blond, either. Not really blond, anyway. He wondered if Eileen Burke here, with her splendidly crossed *gambas* and the faintest trace of a scar on her left cheek was, in fact, a *real* redhead. Does the carpet match the drapes, he wondered, or is she merely Miss Clairol's cousin?

'What is going to happen next Tuesday at midnight,' he said, 'is a very large quantity . . .'

'When you say *Tuesday* at midnight,' Parker interrupted, 'do you mean *Tuesday* night when the . . .'

'Yes,' Palacios said.

'. . . clock strikes twelve . . .'

'Yes.'

'Or *Monday* night when the clock strikes twelve?' Parker asked, cleaving the air with the edge of his hand.

Palacios looked at him.

'What I'm asking is . . . Let's say it's eleven fifty-nine P.M., and then it's midnight, and then the minute hand moves to twelve-oh-one . . . is this *Tuesday* night we're talking about, or *Monday* night?'

'I am talking about *Tuesday* at midnight,' Palacios said. 'It is eleven fifty-nine on Tuesday night, and then it is midnight, and then it is twelve-oh-one on Wednesday morning. The shit will go down on Tuesday night at midnight.'

'Wouldn't it be easier to look at a calendar?' Eileen suggested.

Men, she thought.

There was, in fact, a calendar on the wall of The Gaucho's shop, and it showed a picture of a dark-haired, spread-legged woman wearing nothing but an open Japanese fan. Palacios put his finger on the square for Wednesday, April 24. 'This is today,' he said. He moved his finger down to the next row of dates. 'And this is Tuesday, April thirtieth, the last day of the month. That is when the shit will go down. Tuesday night at midnight.'

'Is that clear, Eileen?' Parker asked.

She looked at him.

Palacios caught the glance.

Very nice, he thought, and wondered if she would care to be spanked by him some day.

Parker was thinking, Well, pardon me all to hell, lady, but these are not kindergarten kids we're playing with here, and I would not like to show up a day late and a dollar short, and lose the whole damn bust, if you don't mind. What he was afraid of, in fact, was that they'd break down the door next week and go down the basement steps, and Burke here would see a gun or even a box cutter and pick up her skirts and run right into everybody else in her haste to get out of there.

'These people are not amateurs,' he said aloud.

'They are very definitely not amateurs,' Palacios said, smiling at her to let her know he realized her partner here was being condescending merely because she was a ravishingly beautiful redhead he would love to take to bed sometime. 'The ones selling the candy, anyway. They've been working on this deal for a long time now,' he said. 'They are not going to like you going down their basement and messing with them.'

You can hardly see where she was cut, Parker thought. On the face, he understood. Psychologically bad, especially for a woman. Still, they did wonders with cosmetic surgery these days. And yet . . .

'Where is this basement of theirs?' Eileen asked.

'That's one of the problems,' Palacios said.

'I didn't know there were any problems,' Eileen said, and looked at Parker again.

'The problem is it keeps changing,' Palacios said.

'What keeps changing?'

'The basement where the dope is.'

'They keep moving the dope, is that what you mean?'

'So far, yes, it's been in three different locations.'

'Why is that, do you suppose?'

'They're being cautious,' Parker said.

'Careful,' Palacios agreed, nodding.

'They're not amateurs,' Parker reminded her again.

'*Or*,' Eileen said.

Both men looked at her.

'They're onto us,' she said.

HOGAN GOT BACK to Ollie at ten that night.

Ollie was enjoying a snack before going to bed. He hated any of his meals being interrupted, and was almost sorry he'd given Hogan his home number.

'What I did,' Hogan explained, 'was first I cleaned the site, filed it down smooth, and polished it with Carborundum till I had it looking like a mirror. Then I kept swabbing it with hydrochloric acid till the numbers came up. Took me three hours altogether.'

Don't tell me your fuckin troubles while I'm eating, Ollie thought.

'So what'd the computer have to say?' he asked.

'The gun was registered to a guy named Charles McGrath. He used it in a bank holdup five years ago, shot the guard and a lady making a deposit. He still had the piece in his possession when he got busted two months later.'

'Where is he now?'

'Castleview. Doing a max of twenty on a B-felony conviction. He should be coming up for parole in a year or so.'

'Meanwhile he's behind bars, is that what you're saying?'

'That's what the computer says.'

'What happened to the gun?'

78

'What do you mean?'

'After they sent Mr McGrath to the country.'

'I told you. It was recovered in his possession.'

'Yeah, but how'd it get on the street again?'

'Well now, gee, that's *your* job, ain't it?' Hogan said, and hung up.

SHARYN EVERARD COOKE was the Police Department's Deputy Chief Surgeon, the first black woman ever to be appointed to the job – though 'black' was a misnomer in that her skin was the color of burnt almond. She wore her black hair in a modified Afro, which – together with high cheekbones, a generous mouth, and eyes the color of loam – gave her the look of a proud Masai woman. Five feet, nine inches tall, she considered herself a trifle overweight at a hundred and thirty pounds. Bert Kling thought she looked just right. Bert Kling thought she was the most beautiful woman he'd ever met. Bert Kling loved her to death.

The only problem was where to sleep.

Sharyn's apartment was at the very end of the Calm's Point subway line, some forty minutes from Kling's studio apartment across the river and into the trees. From his apartment, it took him twenty minutes to get to work in the morning. From her apartment, it took him an hour and fifteen minutes. Sharyn still had her own private practice, but as a uniformed one-star chief, she still worked fifteen to eighteen hours a week at the Chief Surgeon's Office, which was located in Rankin Plaza in that part of the city known as Majesta. Majesta happened to be forty-five minutes by subway from Kling's apartment. So it all got down to where they should sleep on any given night. All couples should have such a problem.

They had planned to spend that Wednesday night in

Sharyn's apartment, but because a cop had got shot downtown, and Sharyn was here in The City, anyway –

No matter where you lived in this city, Isola was still called The City. If you lived in Riverhead or Majesta or Calm's Point or even Bethtown, and you were taking the subway or a bus downtown, you were going into The City. That was it. Sharyn lived in Calm's Point, but Kling lived in The City, and since she was *in* The City anyway that day, they decided to sleep at his place, talk about lengthy exposition.

His place was a studio apartment.

His place wasn't too very comfortable.

But she loved him, so what could you do?

'Did your mother really work for Gabe Foster?' he asked.

She was in the bathroom brushing her teeth. She was still wearing a half slip and a bra and the sandals she'd worn to work that morning, strappy and buckled, with a medium-sized heel. She had rinsed out her pantyhose, and they were hanging over the shower rod. He liked her things hanging all over the place. He liked anything that reminded him of her.

'My mother worked for everyone in the world,' she said. 'How do you think I got through college and med school?'

'Foster said she used to help around the church every now and then. When he was just starting out.'

'That's possible,' Sharyn said. 'I'll have to ask her.'

She was cold-creaming makeup off her face now. It took her a half-hour every night to get ready for bed. She always came to bed smelling sweet and clean and fresh and beautiful. He loved the way she smelled. He loved everything about her.

'You ever meet him?' Kling asked.

'Foster? Once. There was a liquor store holdup in

Diamondback, and one of the cops who responded was a brother. He got shot twice in the chest. Foster showed up at the hospital to do his thing.'

'What's his thing?'

'False compassion for anyone who's black, indignation for any imagined slight to the black man – or woman, he claims, though I understand he favors honkie trim. He's a rabble rouser who wants to be mayor of this city one day. How'd you happen to talk to him?'

'Ollie Weeks thinks . . .'

'Bigot.'

'I know. Maybe that's why he thinks Foster might have had something to do with the councilman's murder.'

'Are you on that case?'

'Sort of.'

'What does that mean, sort of?'

'We're sharing the bust with Ollie. If we make one.'

'Is Foster a suspect?'

'Not really. Not yet, anyway. But he had a fist fight with Henderson . . .'

'Uh-oh.'

'Well, maybe. Be sort of dumb to shoot a guy you just brawled with, though.'

'Not something I would do, that's for sure.'

'Especially if you're in the public eye, the way Foster is.'

'So ask him where he was when the shooting took place.'

'We did. He could have been in the neighborhood.'

'Then he *is* a suspect.'

'Maybe. In police work . . .'

'Yes, dear, tell me all about police work.'

'In *police* work, wise guy, everyone's a suspect until he's no longer a suspect.'

'Gee,' Sharyn said, and rolled her eyes in mock amazement.

She was standing in the bathroom door now, the light behind her, looking tall and magnificent and lovely and wonderful. She put her hands on her hips. She looked across the room to where he was lying on the bed in his undershorts. The window was open. There was the sound of traffic below, moving toward the Calm's Point Bridge.

'Are we going to make love tonight?' she asked.

'I don't know. Do you feel like it?'

'Do you?'

'I think I could be persuaded.'

'What I'm asking . . .'

'I know.'

'Should I put the diaphragm in?' Her voice lowered. 'Is what I'm asking.'

'Well, if you're going to look so sexy and beautiful and all in that transparent slip with the light behind you, I think you ought to put in your diaphragm and take the pill and do everything possible to protect yourself because I'm but a mere mortal who can't possibly resist you, is what I think.'

'Sweet talker,' she said, and smiled, and went back into the bathroom, and closed the door.

In a little while, she came to him.

THE THING ABOUT being with him was the shared intimacy. Before him, she had never been intimate with another man. She didn't mean sexually intimate, she'd had sex with a dozen men, at least, before she met Kling. Having sex with a man wasn't the kind of intimacy she meant. You could be sexually intimate with any man, she supposed, white or black, although Kling was the first white man she'd ever been to bed with. She never expected to go to bed with any other white man in her life. Any other black man, either. Being sexually intimate

82

with some man wasn't the point of it all. She had finally discovered the point of it all with Bert Kling, the least likely candidate for the job.

To begin with, she outranked him in spades, no pun intended, and political correctness be damned. That was one of the things she meant about being intimate with him. She could happen to say, 'Besides, I outrank you in spades,' and he could put on a big Sammy Davis, Jr watermelon accent and answer, 'You can say *that* again, honey chile,' and she could laugh at the racial allusion and not get angry, the way a black woman in America – especially a black woman who wanted to become a doctor – could sometimes get very damned angry in America. And besides, she *did* outrank him in spades, which meant that she was a Deputy Chief who earned sixty-eight grand a year, and he was but a Detective/Third Grade who earned a whole hell of a lot less than that, a fact she had to remind him of every time he insisted on picking up a restaurant check, God, how she loved this man.

That had been one of the early problems, their relative positions in this small paramilitary force known as the Police Department, wherein fraternization between a chief and the lowest grade of detective was – if not forbidden by fiat – at least discreetly frowned upon. Not to mention this other small matter of their disparate coloration, or *lack* of coloration as the case actually was, black and white being an absence of hue rather than a plain statement like red or green for stop or go. That was what they'd had to decide rather early on. Stop or go.

Oddly, her rank was what had troubled him most.

She could remember him calling for the first time from one of those open plastic phone shells, standing in the rain and asking her if she'd care to have dinner with him. He thought it might make a difference that he was just a detective/third and she was a one-star chief. No mention of his blond hair or her black skin.

'Does it?' he'd asked.

'Does what?'

'*Does* it make a difference? Your rank?'

'No,' she'd said.

But what about the other? she'd wondered. What about whites and blacks killing each other in public places? What about that, Detective Kling?

'Rainy day like today,' he'd said, 'I thought it'd be nice to have dinner and go to a movie.'

With a white man, she'd thought.

Tell my mother I'm going on a date with a white man. My mother who scrubbed white men's offices on her knees. You hear this, Mom? A white man wants to take me out to dinner and a movie.

Bring the subject up, she'd thought. Face it head on. Ask him if he realizes I'm black. Tell him I've never done anything like this before. Tell him my mother'll jump off the roof. Tell him I don't need this kind of complication in my life, tell him . . .

'Well . . . uh . . . do you think you might *like* to?' he'd asked. 'Go to a movie and have dinner?'

'Why do you want to do this?' she'd asked.

'Well,' he'd said, 'I think we might enjoy each other's company.'

She supposed the intimacy between them had started right that minute.

It was an intimacy that had nothing to do with protecting or defending their right to be together in these racially divided United States of America, nothing to do with this white man and black woman having unimaginably found each other long before the slogan 'United We Stand' came into vogue again. Nor did their intimacy have anything to do with his whiteness or her blackness although each found this disparity enormously attractive. They both realized that terrorism wouldn't last forever, all wars ended sooner or later, and there would still be an America where blacks and whites could never be intimate unless they first forgot they were black or white.

Sharyn Everard Cooke and Bertram Alexander Kling had forgotten that a long time ago. In the dark there were only two people making love. But this was sexual intimacy, and they had both enjoyed that before, albeit never with anyone who wasn't color-coordinated. Now that they were equal opportunity employers, so to speak, they had to admit that sex with someone of a different tint was actually something of a kick.

'How about all this stuff I hear about black men?' Kling once asked.

'Why?' she said. 'Are you feeling underprivileged?'

'I'm just curious.'

'You know the joke, don't you?'

'Which one is that?'

'Man loses his penis in an automobile accident, he goes to see a surgeon who says he can give him a penis implant.'

'Yeah?'

'Guy says, "That's great, but how will I know what I'm getting?" The surgeon says, "I'll show you some samples." He goes in the back room, comes back with a penis six inches long, shows it to the guy. The guy says, "Well, since I'll be getting a new one, I was hoping . . ." The surgeon holds up his hands, says, "I understand completely," goes in the back room, comes back with a penis *eight* inches long. The guy says, "Well, to be perfectly frank, I was hoping for something with a bit more authority." The surgeon goes off again, comes back

85

with a penis *twelve* inches long. The guy says, "Now you're talking! Does it come in white?"'

Kling burst out laughing.

'Do that answer yo question, honey chile?' Sharyn asked.

The intimacy went beyond white and black.

The intimacy was based on the knowledge that living together with *anyone* was something that required constant care and attention. Intimacy demanded utter honesty and complete trust. Intimacy meant never being afraid of revealing yourself to another person, exposing yourself to this person, warts and all, without fear of condemnation or derision.

Kling, who was not Jewish, described intimacy as a 'shlep,' a Yiddish word that actually meant 'to carry, or pull, or drag, or lag behind,' but which he took to mean 'a long haul,' as in the expression 'Man, that was a shlep and a half!' common to everyone in this city regardless of stripe or persuasion, United We Stand, and God Bless America! They were both in this for the long haul. And though they knew true intimacy wasn't easy, they realized that once you got the knack of it, everything else seemed so very simple.

Sharyn found a yarn shop near Rankin Plaza that would needlepoint a small pillow to her specifications. Actually, she had two of the pillows made, one for his apartment, the other for hers, one in white letters on black, the other in black letters on white. Each pillow read:

Share
Help
Love
Encourage
Protect

86

Kling was bone-weary when he got to her apartment that night. He had taken the subway out to Calm's Point, and didn't get there till almost nine-thirty. He'd grabbed a hamburger at the squadroom, but he was grateful nonetheless for the soup and sandwich she had waiting for him. He didn't see the pillow until after he'd eaten. In fact, he was lying on the sofa in her living room, watching the Eleven O'Clock News, his head resting right *on* the pillow, when Sharyn suggested that he might be more comfortable with a softer pillow, and he said, 'No, I'm fine, hon,' and she said, 'Here, let me help you,' and she took the pillow from under his head and replaced it with a down pillow from the bedroom, and then she put the smaller pillow on his chest, and he *still* didn't look at it, what was *wrong* with this man? Patience, she told herself, you did get through med school, you know.

So she waited until the news went off, and they were both ready for bed, and then she came into the bedroom stark naked, holding the pillow with both hands at the joining of her legs, covering the wild tangle of her pubic patch, and he squinted at her, and said, 'A definite improvement,' and she burst out laughing and threw the pillow at him.

He read the needlepoint:

> Share
> Help
> Love
> Encourage
> Protect

'That says it all,' he told her, and took her into his arms.

Now, with her in his arms again, spent and somewhat

damp from their exertion, the lights of the bridge twinkling in the distance, he told her that Eileen Burke had been transferred to the Eight-Seven and would be working there from now on, and Sharyn asked, 'Does that bother you?' and he said, 'I don't know.'

And that was honest.

And that was what the two of them were all about.

7.

IT WAS WHILE OLLIE was investigating what in his mind would always be known as 'The $$$ Case,' that he'd received a letter from a knowledgeable editor at the publishing firm of Wadsworth and Dodds, which later turned out to be a front for a big drug-running operation and God knew what else – but that was another story. Anyway, a woman up there named Karen Andersen had given him a form letter from an editor up there named Henry Daggert, and it was from this letter that Ollie had learned everything he knew about writing bestselling thriller fiction. The letter read:

Dear Aspiring Writer:
   I often receive inquiries from writers who wonder about the most effective way to get a suspense novel on the bestseller list. After years of experience, I have discovered that there are some hard and fast rules to be followed in the writing of successful suspense fiction. I would like to share these rules with you now, if I may.

IF YOU WANT TO CRACK THE BESTSELLER LIST

   1) **You must create a plot that puts an ordinary person in an extraordinary situation.** Your

protagonist must be an 'Everyman.' However, you must have at least one complex female character as well. Don't forget, you want to capture both male and female readers.

2) **You must create a plot that plays out a universal fantasy.** You must put the reader in a situation that tests him in ways he's always wanted to be tested, vicariously.

3) **You must come up with a plot that passes the 'cool' test.** You must find an idea that makes readers want to read the book simply on the basis of the idea *alone*!

4) **Your plot must involve high stakes.** You must make clear that the fate of the world hangs in the balance – or, at least, the fate of a character we desperately care about.

5) **You must introduce a ticking clock.** You must give your protagonist only a limited amount of time to solve his problem, and the reader should be regularly reminded of the urgency via 'COUNT-DOWN CUES.'

Ollie deciphered all this to mean that a bestselling suspense novel had to tell a simple story about an ordinary person who found himself in an extraordinary situation that tested him in ways he'd always wanted to be tested, vicariously. Moreover, the plot had to include at least one complex male or female character in it, and the fate of the world had to be hanging in clock-ticking suspense.

But there was yet more to learn.

6) **Be sure to avoid ambiguity!** You must avoid situations where points in favor of both sides diminish the reader's ability to root intensely for one side

over another. For example: Novels about the IRA. Novels about murky Central American conflicts. Novels about Pro Choice versus Right-to-Life disputes.

7) **Avoid writing about what's in the news!** Editors (and especially *this* editor) will be seeing a slew of books on *whatever* it is, believe me! Be especially wary of plots about Computer Hackers, Genetic Engineering, Air Disasters, Terrorist Attacks, etc.

Good luck!

>Sincerely,
>*Henry Daggert*
>Henry Daggert

Before Ollie went to bed that night, he reread the last chapter of his novel yet another time. It seemed to him that it was perfect. He had completely mastered all the rules of bestselling suspense fiction, which was why he'd been able to bend them a little. Hence the multiple twists, turns, and edge-of-the-seat suspense in *Report to the Commissioner*.

Small wonder some cheap thief had stolen the book.

I am locked in a basement with $2,700,000 in so-called conflict diamonds and I just got a run in my pantyhose.

I am writing this in the hope that it will somehow reach you before they kill me.

You will recall having met me once, Mr Commissioner, when I received a Police Department bravery citation for having foiled, as they say, an imminent robbery at the Stillwater Trust on King Street in Rubytown, as that section of the city is called. They were giving away free toasters when the Attempted Rob occurred. I spilled a glass of red wine, do you remember? Not during the holdup attempt. I mean at the reception following the award. On your white linen suit.

I am a female police detective, twenty-nine years old, five feet, eight inches tall, and weighing one hundred and twenty-three pounds, which is slender. My hair is a sort of reddish brown, what my mother used to call auburn. I wear it cut to just above the shoulders, what my mother used to call a shag cut. My eyes are green. I look very Irish, although Watts is a British name, I think, although Olivia is Latin, which I'm not. My friends call me Livvie. I am a single woman, Mr Commissioner; I notice from the newspapers that you are recently divorced, by the way; my condolences. My weapon is a Glock nine I carry in a tote bag, but this was taken from me along with all my identification when I was locked in here. A black woman brings me my meals. She is armed with an Uzi.

I have not been killed yet because they are waiting for orders from someone higher up. I can't imagine why anyone would want me dead. Then again, nothing is ever simple in police work, is it, Mr Commissioner? I guess you know that better than me. Or perhaps even better than I. I don't even know where I am. Otherwise I would give you the address and make things really simple. But I was driven here blindfolded from the underwear factory. Which makes it somewhat complicated. So I guess I'd better take it from the top, and tell you everything that

happened, and get this report out of here somehow. Then maybe for the love of God you can
piece it all together and get to me in time.

Let's start with Margie Gannon and me, or
perhaps Margie and I, having an after-hours
beer last Monday night in a bar called
O'Malley's a few blocks from the station house.
Margie is sometimes partnered with me,
although I'm known in the squadroom as 'Livvie
the Lone Wolverine,' which of course is the
female tense of 'The Lone Wolf.' Margie has
blond hair she also wears short, and blue eyes,
and we make a good team together, partnered
or otherwise. We were sipping beer when these
two detectives from the Oh-One waltzed over to
join us, nice guys we worked with once on a joint
narcotics bust sometime back. (I was surprised,
to tell the truth, that the little police action back
then hadn't netted at least somebody a citation,
but I know you have a lot of other things on
your mind.)

Anyway, Frankie Randuzzi, who is with the
Oh-One, and was on that Colombian bust I was
telling you about, is getting married in June,
and he was showing us this rather modest diamond engagement ring, I must say, but you
know how much detectives are paid in this city,
don't you, even First Grades like Frankie and
me. The guy with him, Jerry Aiello, another
paisan, couldn't help remarking that he'd seen
bigger chips than that left by cows in a pasture,
to which Frankie replied it was a legit diamond
and not one of these diamonds had cost some
kid in Africa the loss of an arm or a leg. I didn't

know what the hell he was talking about, excuse the French, Commish.

Margie, it so happens, knows quite a bit about diamonds. She has been married and divorced twice and has therefore sported engagement rings of various sizes on the third finger of her left hand, more's the pity I have not. In fact, she is fond of telling the boys around the squad-room that she gets divorced every six years and shot every three, which happens to be true. I was with her once when she took one in the left shoulder. She never wears off-the-shoulder gowns to police functions anymore, but she is very well constructed otherwise, witness the way Jerry Aiello was trying to peer down the front of her blouse.

Margie explained that there'd been a war going on forever in the Sierra Leone and in Angola, over there in Africa someplace, wher-ever, I always thought Angola was a max secur-ity prison in Louisiana. She said that so-called conflict diamonds were what funded the rebel groups fighting over there.

'They call themselves the RUF, which stands for the Revolutionary United Front. They're eleven-year-old kids armed with AK-47s and machetes,' she said. 'They chop off people's arms and legs, that's how they maintain con-trol. But you're wrong if you think these rocks are cheaper than a legit diamond, Frank. In fact, once this rough ice is traded and polished, it's impossible to know where it came from. That may be one of them you're showing us right this minute.'

I never knew Margie was so smart.

Before then, I thought she was just a good-looking babe who got shot and divorced all the time.

It just goes to show.

I did not make the acquaintance of Mercer Grant till the next day. That is not his real name. He told me right off it wasn't his real name. He said it would be too dangerous for him to give me his real name. Grant (or Lee or Jackson or Jones or Smith or whatever his real name might have been) was a tall, light-skinned Jamaican with a neat little mustache under his nose. He came up to the squadroom around ten o'clock on that Tuesday morning in question, and he asked to talk to a police detective, of which there were only eight or nine in the squadroom that minute, it's a wonder he didn't trip over one of us. I signaled him over to my desk, and offered him a chair, and asked him his name.

'My name is Mercer Grant,' he said. 'But that is not my real name.'

'Then what is your real name, Mr Grant?'

'I can't tell you my real name,' he said. 'It would be too dangerous to tell you my real name.'

All of this in that sort of Jamaican lilt they have, you know? Like Harry Belafonte doing 'Hey, Mr Taliban.'

'Because, you see,' I said, 'we're required to fill in the name and address spaces on these complaint forms. Plus a lot of other information.'

'I am not making a complaint,' Mercer said.

'Then why are you here?' I asked.

'I am here because my wife is missing,' he said.

'Well, that's a complaint,' I said.

'Not in the case of my wife,' he said, and grinned, because he was making a joke, you see. He was saying nobody was complaining that his wife was missing. He had a gold tooth in the center of his mouth. The tooth had a little diamond chip in one corner. His mouth lit up like a Christmas tree when he grinned. He thought his little joke was pretty funny. He kept grinning.

'Well,' I said, 'what is your wife's name then?'

'I can't tell you her name,' he said. 'It would be too dangerous.'

'Then how am I supposed to find her if you won't give me her name?' I asked reasonably.

'You're the detective, not me,' he said reasonably. 'Although I must tell you I've never dealt with a female detective before, and I'm not sure how happy I am about it,' the sexist pig.

'What kind of detectives have you dealt with before, Mr Grant?'

'I have never been in trouble with the law,' he said. 'I'm reporting my wife missing because it's my duty as a citizen. My cousin Ambrose said I should report her missing.'

'Ambrose what?' I asked at once.

'Ambrose Fields. But that's not his real name, either.'

'Does anyone in your family have a real name?'

'Yes, but these names would be too dangerous to reveal.'

'Can you tell me where you live?'

'No.'

'Can you give me your phone number?'

'No.'

'Well, Mr Grant, let's suppose by some weird stroke of luck – me being a female detective and all – I _do_ find your wife. How am I supposed to let you know I've got her?'

'I will stay in touch.'

'I have to tell you, you don't sound too _eager_ to find her, now do you?'

He thought this over for a moment. Then he said, 'The truth is I don't think you _will_ find her.'

'Why do you say that?'

'I think she may already be dead.'

'I see.'

'Yes.'

'So you're here to report a murder, is that it?'

'No, I am here to tell you my wife is missing. As is my duty.'

'But you think she may be dead.'

'Yes.'

'Do you also think you know who killed her?'

'No.'

'It wouldn't be _you_ who killed her, would it, Mr Grant? This wouldn't be a confession here, would it?'

Grant, or whatever his name was, leaned closer to me.

'Have you ever heard of the RUF?' he asked.

'Yes,' I said. 'Once. Last night, in fact. Why? Do you think the RUF had something to do with your wife's death?'

'No.'

'If, in fact, she is dead.'

'Oh, she's dead, all right, oh yes.'

'How do you know that?'

'She wrote me a note.'

'Saying she was dead?'

'No. Saying if I didn't hear from her by Tuesday, she might be dead.'

'Today is Tuesday,' I said.

'Yes. So she must be dead, am I correct?'

'Well, she only said she might be dead.'

'She must have had an inkling,' Grant said.

'What else did she say in this note?'

'Here, read it for yourself,' Grant said, and took a folded sheet of paper from his pocket, and unfolded it, and smoothed it neatly on my desk top. The note read:

Dear Mercer . . .

'That's not my real name,' he said at once.

'Then why did she address you as such?'

'I told you. She must have had an inkling.'

Dear Mercer,
By the time you read this, I will be gone. Do not try to find me, it is too dangerous. If I am not back by Tuesday, I guess I will be dead.
Your loving wife,
Marie

'That's not her real name, either,' Grant said.

'I know. She must have had an inkling.'

'Exactly.'

'So you think the RUF had something to do with her disappearance, is that it?'

'No,' Grant said.

'Then why did you bring them up?'

'I thought you might have heard of them.'

'Is that diamond in your mouth a so-called conflict diamond?' I asked.

'What is a conflict diamond?' Grant asked.

'Is your wife – or was she, as the case may be – involved in any way with the sale or transport of illicit diamonds in Sierra Leone or Angola?'

'My wife and I never discussed her private affairs. You will have to ask her personally. When you find her. If you find her. But you won't find her because it's Tuesday and she said she'd be dead.'

'Well, you've filed a complaint . . .'

'I'm not complaining,' he said, and grinned again.

'. . . so I guess I'll have to investigate. Can you tell me what your wife looks like, please?'

'If she's still alive, she is a dark-skinned woman of about your height and weight, with black hair and brown eyes.'

'How old is she?'

'About your age.'

'Twenty-nine?'

'I should have thought twenty-five,' he said, and grinned his charming gold-and-diamond grin.

'Any visible scars or tattoos?'

'None that I ever noticed.'

'How long have you been married?' I asked.

'Too long,' he said, and then suddenly ducked his head, perhaps to hide a falling tear. 'She was a good woman,' he murmured.

The challenge now seemed clear: Find a good woman in this city. Which was not as simple as it first appeared. With all due respect, Commish, nothing is ever simple in police work, nothing is ever uncomplicated.

To begin with, if this woman . . .

Now hold it right there, Emilio thought.

Before things get *too* complicated here, let's just take a peek at the phone book and see if there really *is* a person or persons named Mercer Grant or Marie Grant or, for that matter, anybody named Olivia Wesley Watts, though he didn't think a detective would be so stupid as to list herself in the phone book. Emilio had only two directories in the apartment, one for Isola, the other for Riverhead, and neither one of them listed either a Mercer or a Marie Grant, which wasn't surprising since the guy in Livvie's report (Emilio was already fondly thinking of her as Livvie) had himself told her it wasn't his real name. There was no Margie Gannon in either of the books, either, nor anybody named Frank Randuzzi or Jerry Aiello, or Ambrose Fields, so he had to figure Livvie had made up these names for her own protection. There was no O'Malley's Bar, either, hey, big surprise!

But Livvie had written:

Let's start with Margie Gannon and me, or perhaps Margie and I, having an after-hours beer last Monday night in a bar called O'Malley's a few blocks from the station house.

So okay.

Somewhere in this city, a few blocks from a police station, there was a bar. Find that bar, whatever its real name was, and Emilio would be well on the way to finding a redheaded detective named Olivia Wesley Watts.

Let the games begin, he thought.

The clock is ticking!

8.

FIRST THING OLLIE DID that Thursday morning was hit the pawnshops again. This time, he had a double incentive. Not only had someone possibly hocked the dispatch case his dumb sister Isabelle had given him two Christmases ago, but someone *else* (presumably not the same asshole junkie) had also possibly hocked a gun that had been used in a bank heist five years ago. He did not expect to win the daily double, and was in fact surprised when even one of his horses came in.

Of course, nobody knew anything at all about the gun.

It would have been a miracle if anyone had.

Not that a great many .32-caliber Smith & Wessons hadn't been pawned in this fair city over the past five years, plenty of which could be traced through their serial numbers. But whereas a reluctant Detective Hogan had been persuaded, ah yes, to bring up the numbers on the piece that had caused the untimely demise, ah yes, of Councilman Henderson, those serial numbers had presumably been filed off *before* the bank robbery, lo, those many years ago. So, assuming the gun had been requisitioned, so to speak, from the Property Clerk's Office by some enterprising police officer who knew that a weapon without a serial number was the equivalent of a naked man in a busy whore house, and *further* assuming that the weapon had been sold on the street by said opportunistic cop and had eventually found its way into a pawnshop, it would *still* be unidentifiable without any numbers on it, and therefore untraceable, a clean gun that had remained clean five years after it had done its dirty deed.

So he knew the answer to the first gun question even before he asked it.

'Anybody buy a .32 Smith & Wesson from you recently?'

'Sure. Vot's the serial numbers?'

Fat Jew pawnbrokers wearing yarmulkes who only three weeks ago had celebrated Passover, when they were closed for religious reasons, and not even a poor alcoholic writer on a so-called lost weekend could hock his typewriter to buy a bottle of booze. True high artists sure had it tough all over these days. He could just imagine how difficult it was for poor Jonathan Franzen, whom Ollie admired a great deal because he'd dissed a Negress like Oprah Winfrey.

Even when Ollie gave them the serial numbers Hogan had brought up, he knew they wouldn't ring a bell because if the gun *had* by some amazing phenomenon been hocked, with the serial numbers filed off it was like trying to identify a bare-assed newborn baby who hadn't yet been given a name.

He asked the gun questions only because he had to.

The dispatch case was another matter.

'A Gucci dispatch case,' he told them, 'tan pigskin, single brass clasp, monogrammed with the letters OWW.'

First ten pawnshops he hit hadn't seen hide nor hair of a pigskin dispatch case from Gucci.

'Hide nor hair, you get it?' one of the pawnbrokers asked him, chuckling, making witty reference to the pigskin, Ollie guessed, which in *any* case Jews weren't allowed to eat, pig, nor Muslims, either, same as Catholics weren't allowed to eat meat of any kind on Good Friday, man, these religions. Ollie sometimes felt if everybody in the world was allowed to eat whatever the hell he wanted, there wouldn't be wars anymore. It all got down to eating. Which reminded him that it was almost twelve noon and he was getting hungry again.

He struck paydirt of sorts in the eleventh pawnshop he visited that morning.

A bell over the door tinkled as Ollie entered, causing him to look up in an attempt to identify the source, encountering at first glance a ceiling hung with musical instruments of every persuasion. Well, no pianos. But here in front of the counter was a gleaming brassy array of trumpets, tubas, trombones, and other alliterative instruments Ollie could not identify. And behind the counter was a hanging woodwind section of saxophones, clarinets, oboes, and bassoons, not to mention more guitars than could be found in a strolling mariachi band. A young woman with a sweet ass was standing at the counter, expectantly watching the shop owner, Ollie presumed, who had a jeweler's loupe to his eye and what looked like a diamond ring in his hand.

He put down the loupe. He handed the ring back across the counter. 'It's glass,' he said. 'I can't give you a nickel.'

Ollie felt like telling the woman there was a massage parlor up the street where she could get work if she was really hard up.

'Guy gave it to me last night,' she told both the pawnbroker and Ollie. 'Which means I got stiffed.'

Which meant she was already a working girl.

Ollie wondered if he should arrest her.

Years ago, he used to arrest hookers just to scare them into freebie blowjobs. Nowadays, they all had civil rights

104

lawyers who took their cases all the way up to the Supreme Court. Well, what could you do?

'Girl can't be too careful these days,' he suggested.

'Tell me about it,' she said, and swiveled her splendid ass out of the shop.

Ollie flashed the tin.

The pawnbroker nodded.

'Pigskin dispatch case,' Ollie said. 'Gucci label. OWW monogram. Seen it?'

'Came in Monday afternoon,' the pawnbroker said. 'Sold it in a minute.'

Ollie looked at the framed license on the wall behind the counter. The name on it was Irving Stein.

'Tell me, Irv,' he said, 'was there anything in that case when you received it?'

'Nothing.'

'Did you know the case was stolen?'

'No, I did not.'

'Didn't you receive a flier I sent out Tuesday?'

'I didn't see anything on any flier about any dispatch case worth a big five dollars.'

'Oh, is that what you thought a stolen Gucci dispatch case was worth, Irv?'

'That's all it was worth to me. And I didn't know it was stolen.'

''Cause you didn't see my flier, right?'

'I get fliers from all over the city. Every fecockteh precinct gets a Timex wrist watch stolen, they send me a flier. If I read every flier I got, I'd have no time for anything else,' Irving said. 'What's so important here, anyway? Whose dispatch case was this? Bin Laden's?'

'No, it was *mine*. And my book was in it.'

'Must be some book, all this commotion.'

'It's a book I *wrote*,' Ollie said.

'I thought you were a cop.'

'I am a cop.'

'But you also write books, huh?'

'Is that so strange? There are many cops and former cops and district attorneys and lawyers who write mystery novels. In every corner of this great nation, there are former . . .'

'A mystery book writer, how about that?' Irving said. 'Next you'll be telling me you play trombone.'

'No, I play piano.'

'Piano, I shoulda guessed.'

'I play "Night and Day" on the piano.'

'You play night and day, when do you find time to write and be a cop?'

'Did you get my flier, or didn't you?'

'I told you no, I don't remember getting it. I don't remember seeing anything at all about a pigskin dispatch case.'

'Cause pork is against your religion, right?'

'No, cause I don't remember seeing it.'

'Cause if you *did* get the flier, and you *did* know the case was stolen, and you knowingly received stolen goods, you'd be looking at a goodly amount of time in the slammer. Want to think about *that* one a while, Irv?'

'Give me a break, willya?' Irving said. 'A piece of dreck worth five dollars? Who's kidding who here?'

'You won't think I'm kidding if I go after your license.'

'So go after it. For what? For making a bona fide purchase for value?'

'Ah, the man suddenly understands legal distinctions,' Ollie said to the ceiling full of hanging musical instruments.

'I didn't know the case was stolen,' Irving said. 'Period.'

'Because if you knew it was stolen, you knew you'd be looking at a D-felony, am I right?'

'Yes, Detective, you are perfectly right. *If* I knew the case was stolen. Which I didn't.'

'Who brought the case in here, can you tell me that?'

'A girl named Emmy.'

'Emmy what?'

'I didn't get her last name.'

'You buy and sell goods without taking last names, is that it?' Ollie said.

'So I didn't ask her last name, so sue me,' Irving said. 'She gave me the case, I gave her five bucks, end of transaction.'

'What'd she look like?' Ollie asked.

'Like any other hooker comes in here.'

'Oh, she was a hooker, huh?'

'Yes.'

'She marched in and said, "Hi, I'm a hooker, I have this Gucci dispatch case, I want to . . ."'

'Please, I don't know a hooker when I see one? They come in here day and night, night and day. Black, white, Puerto Rican, Chinese, they all look the same.'

'What was this one?'

'Puerto Rican. Short skirt, high heels, net stockings, purple blouse, a hooker.'

'Describe her.'

'I just did.'

'What color eyes, hair . . .?'

'Brown eyes, blond hair.'

'A blond Puerto Rican, huh?'

'*Bleached* blond. Frizzy. Long earrings, thick lipstick, tits out to here.'

'When did this bona fide purchase for value take place?' Ollie asked.

'I told you. Monday afternoon.'

'And you sold the case when?'

'Tuesday.'

'Who bought it?'

'I don't know her name.'

Ollie looked up at the ceiling again. 'Man runs a hock shop, he doesn't take last names, he doesn't take *any* names,' he said to the hanging instruments, and shook his head in disbelief.

'You know what my profit was on this transaction?' Irving asked. 'After overhead and incidentals?'

'What incidentals?'

'Incidentals, incidentals. Items stolen from this shop every day of the week, night and day, day and night.'

Ollie looked at him.

'Are you making fun of me playing the piano?' he asked.

'Why would I make fun of a cop who plays piano?'

'You think I'm kidding, don't you?' Ollie said. 'If you had a piano in here, I'd play it for you.'

'Too bad you don't play trombone,' Irving said. 'I got lots of trombones.'

'What happened?' Ollie asked, looking up at the ceiling. 'Did the Philharmonic go bust?'

'The point is,' Irving said, 'I make a lousy two-dollar profit on a shitty dispatch case, you come hokking my tchynik. A diamond bracelet gets stolen from one of my display cases, it takes you guys three months to get here cause you're too busy writing a mystery book or playing the piano. Do me a favor. *Go* after my license. Please. It would be a mitzvah.'

'What'd she look like, this woman who bought the case?' Ollie asked. 'Would you remember?'

'She was *fat*,' Irving said – putting undue emphasis on the word, Ollie felt.

'What else? Was *she* a hooker, too?'

'No, she didn't look like a hooker.'

'What *did* she look like?'

'An opera singer.'

'What color opera singer?'

'White.'

'Hair, eyes?'

'Brown hair, brown eyes.'

'Ever in here before?'

'No.'

'Ever see her around the neighborhood?'

'No.'

'Here's my card. If she comes in again, call me.'

'Sure. I got nothing else to do.'

Ollie looked at him.

'Irving,' he said, 'I'm very serious here. Call me if she comes in again.'

'A lousy dispatch case,' Irving said, shaking his head.

'A dispatch case that maybe has that blond hooker's fingerprints on it.'

'And mine, too, don't forget,' Irving said.

'Ah yes,' Ollie said. 'But *you* didn't steal my book.'

'Thanks God,' Irving said.

OLLIE TOLD HIMSELF he did not wish to become engaged in any long boring conversations with any of the know-it-all sergeants or other pompous assholes who'd super-vised the search for the murder weapon. He much preferred discussing the whys and the wherefores with a simple and straightforward individual like Officer P. Gomez who, by her own admission, had been present

109

when the weapon was 'recovered at the scene,' as she'd put it, and whose breasts besides looked very perky and alert in her fresh-out-of-the-Academy blues.

He checked the Thursday duty roster for uniformed cops, and learned that an Officer Patricia Gomez had signed in at 7:45 that morning, for foot patrol in the Eight-Eight's Adam Sector. Since Adam Sector was where King Memorial was located, and since there was a very good diner on St Sab's and Thirty-second, not two blocks away from the hall, Ollie drove over there on the off-chance that Officer Gomez might be enjoying her noon repast along about this time. As fate would have it, she was not. Or at least, she was not taking her lunch break here in the Okeh Diner.

Ollie cased the joint, and sighed when he realized she wasn't there – but what would the odds on that have been, anyway? Then, so it shouldn't be a total loss, he took a booth near one of the windows and ordered four hamburgers, two sides of fries, two glasses of milk, and a blueberry pie with a double scoop of vanilla ice cream. On his way out, he bought a Milky Way from the display on the counter near the cash register. He knew many cops who would not have paid for the Milky Way. But whereas there once was a time, ah yes, when Ollie might have considered himself a so-called coffee-and-cruller cop, those days were gone forever. It was not that he was now more honest than he used to be. It was merely that cops all over the USA had been under such close scrutiny in recent years that the booty wasn't worth the risk. Although he had to admit that cops were being looked at in a more favorable light ever since all the World Trade Center heroics. So perhaps a return to the good old days was in sight, who knew? Meanwhile, he paid for the candy bar. Munching on it contentedly, he walked back to the car and began cruising the sector in search of Officer Patricia Gomez.

He found her strutting up the avenue with that peculiar sidelong gait of hers, the Glock in its holster thrusting her right hip forward a bit sooner than the left one. A lot of Hispanic males, so-called, affected a similar walk, which they thought made them look deadly. On Officer Patricia Gomez, it merely looked sexy as hell. The males, they thought it was *muy macho* to make kissing sounds on the air and yell 'Hey, mama, *mira, mira*!' whenever a good-looking babe walked by. Ollie was willing to bet two cents and a collar button that Officer Patricia Gomez would break the head of any young spic who kissed the air and yelled '*mira, mira*' at her.

Just for the hell of it, he rolled down the window on the street side, and yelled, '*Mira, mira!*' but he didn't kiss the air. Officer Patricia Gomez stopped dead in her tracks, the left hip catching up with the right one, her right hand going to the Glock in the holster on her right hip – damn if she wasn't about to shoot him!

'It's me!' he yelled. 'Ollie Weeks! I'm just practicing my Spanish.'

He pulled the car over to the curb, and she walked over to it with that same sidelong gait, gun hip leading, visored cap tilted kind of saucily, he noticed, sooty black ringlets showing below it, brown eyes sweeping the sidewalk as she came toward the car, checking the perimeter, she'd be a good cop one day, maybe already was one. The uniform *had* to be hand-tailored, the way it fitted her so snugly here and there.

'Get in,' he said. 'I need some help.'

She looked puzzled for a moment, but then she yanked open the door on the curb side, climbed in, and pulled the door shut behind her.

'What's up?' she asked.

'You were there when they found the murder weapon, right?'

'Is it?' she asked. 'The murder weapon?'

'Turns out, yes,' he said. 'It is.'

'Well, good,' she said, and seemed very pleased. Actually nodded. One for our side.

'Can you take me to where that was?' he said.

'Sure. The alley, you mean? Sure. But I have to clear it with my sergeant first.'

She was already reaching for the walkie-talkie on her belt.

'No need for that,' Ollie said. 'I'll square it later.'

'You sure? I don't want to get in trouble.'

'Well, if you're concerned, buzz him now and I'll talk to him. Who is he?'

'Jackson. Yes, I'd rather we cleared it first, if that's okay with you.'

'Jackson, sure,' Ollie said. He was thinking, Colored sergeant, expect bullshit. Black Means Flak, was what he was thinking. Patricia was already punching in the call numbers.

'Sergeant Jackson,' a voice said.

'Sarge, I've got Detective Weeks here,' Patricia said. 'He'd like a word with you.'

Ollie took the radio.

'Hey, Jackson,' he said, 'how are you?'

'Fine,' Jackson said warily. 'What's on your mind?'

'I need Officer Gomez for a while, show me around the alley where the evidence weapon was retrieved, that okay with you?'

'Which evidence weapon might that be?' Jackson asked.

'The gun used in the Henderson murder.'

'You mean you want to take her off post?'

'Is what I mean,' Ollie said. 'If that's okay with you.'

'I don't know how my captain might feel about that.'

'Well, all I know is how the Chief of Detectives feels about one of our councilmen getting killed, is all I know,' Ollie said. 'So maybe you can spare Gomez for an hour or so.'

'Let me talk to her,' Jackson said.

'Sure,' Ollie said, and handed Patricia the radio.

'Yes, Sarge?' she said. She listened and then said, 'Ainsley and Thirty-fifth.' She listened again. 'Thanks, Sarge.'

'Tell him I appreciate it,' Ollie said.

'Detective Weeks says he appreciates it,' she said, and listened, and then nodded, and thumbed the OFF button. 'He's sending somebody to cover for me,' she said. 'Wants me back on post by two-thirty. That enough time for you?'

'Yes, indeed,' Ollie said, 'ah yes. What'd he say?'

'About what?'

'When you told him I appreciated it.'

'Oh. Nothing, actually.'

'No, I'm curious, what'd he say?'

'Well . . .'

'Come on, tell me.'

'Well, what he said, actually, was "Tell Detective Weeks to shove it up his ass." Was what he said.'

'No kidding?'

'Well . . . yeah.'

'Thank you for your honesty, Patricia, may I call you Patricia?'

'Well . . . sure.'

113

'Thank you. And you may call me Ollie. Now let's go look at that alley, okay? And fuck Sergeant Jackson.'

'**ARE YOU SURE** this is where you found the gun?' Ollie asked.

'Well, I didn't find it myself, personally,' Patricia said. 'But, yes, I was with the search team when the weapon was recovered, yes.'

'Here in this alley right here.'

'Yes, right here. In the sewer against the wall there.'

'Here on *this* side of the auditorium.'

'Yes. Here,' Patricia said.

'Mmm,' Ollie said.

He hoped he was impressing her with the exactitude and precision of his detective work. In truth, he was merely confusing her. This was where they'd found the gun, yes, right here in this alley, in the goddamn sewer, yes, so why did he keep asking her over and over again if this was where they'd found it? Was he a little hard of hearing?

'Because you see,' he said, 'the shooter nailed him from stage right.'

Patricia didn't know what he was talking about.

'Let me show you something,' he said. 'I know this can get confusing,' he added, hoping that the impression he was giving was that of Patient, Experienced, Worldly Sleuth Mentoring Novice Investigator. Patiently, he reached into the inside breast pocket of his jacket and took out the folded diagram the electrical guy had made for him. Patiently, he unfolded it, and handed it to Patricia.

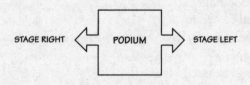

'You see where it says "Stage Right" there?' he asked.

'Yes?'

'That's where the shooter was standing when Henderson got aced.'

'Why is it called stage right when it's on the left?' Patricia asked.

'I don't know why that is,' Ollie said. 'It's one of life's little mysteries. The point is, let's say the shooter ran out into the alley afterward, and dumped the gun down that sewer . . .'

'Which is actually what did happen,' Patricia said.

'Well, that's the problem,' Ollie said. 'Tell me where we are,' he said.

'What do you mean?'

'Where are we now?'

'In the alley outside the auditorium,' she said and blinked in further confusion. He knew where they were. They were in the alley. She had told him a hundred times where they were. What was the matter with this man?

'Which alley? There are two alleys, one outside stage right, the other outside stage left. Where is this alley we're standing in now?' he asked. 'Which side of the auditorium?'

'Well . . . I don't know.'

She looked at the metal doors at the far end of the alley, and she looked at the brick walls enclosing the alley, and then she looked at the garbage cans lining one wall. Nothing gave her a clue as to which side of the auditorium this was. Well, it was easy to get disoriented because Ollie had parked the car on St Sebastian Avenue and they had entered King Memorial through the big glass doors at the front there. And then they'd walked across the lobby to where the auditorium was, and had gone into the auditorium itself and walked down the acenter aisle to the stage . . .

'Take a look at the drawing again,' Ollie said.

Patricia looked at it.

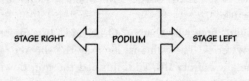

'Well,' she said, 'if the shooter was standing here at stage right . . .'

'Yes, that's where he had to be standing. Henderson was crossing from left to right, and he got shot in the chest, so the shooter had to be standing in the wings stage right. And if whoever shot him ran into the alley stage right and dumped the gun in the sewer on *that* side of the building, we'd right now be standing in that very same alley, am I right? Cause this is where you found the gun, am I right? In the sewer right here.'

'Yes, this is where we found the gun.'

'This very same alley.'

'Yes. In the sewer there.'

'Only problem is,' Ollie said, and here he smiled understandingly and comfortingly, 'this is the alley outside stage *left*.'

Patricia looked at him.

'So how'd the shooter end up on the opposite side of the building?' Ollie asked. 'You want a cup of coffee or something?'

PATRICIA WAS NERVOUS about the time. She kept looking at her watch. Ollie told her not to worry about Sergeant Jackson, he'd take care of Sergeant Jackson if the man gave her any static. They were sitting in a Starbucks – Ollie knew the location of every eatery in the precinct – not far from where Ollie had picked her up earlier, and where she was expected to relieve on post again at two-thirty. It was now ten minutes past two. Ollie had ordered cappuccinos for both of them, and had also brought back to the table a pair of what he called 'everything' cookies, which were oatmeal cookies with raisins and chocolate chips and M&Ms in them.

'Do you like to eat?' he asked her, chewing on one of the cookies, washing it down with his coffee.

'Yes, but I have to watch my weight,' Patricia said.

'Oh, me, too,' Ollie agreed. 'I try not to have more than five meals a day. The Rule of Five. Otherwise it can get out of hand. This is very good cappuccino, don't you think?' he asked, and before she could answer, he said, 'Making cappuccinos is like everything else in life. You either know what you're doing or you don't. If you have to tell a person to put a lot of foam on it, then she doesn't know how to make a cappuccino in the first place. Cappuccino is like a religion, you know. The same way Muslims have to fall on their knees, five times a day, I think it is, some people have to go for cappuccino at ten or eleven in the morning and again at two or three in the afternoon. There are different denominations of the Cappuccino faith, and different houses of worship all over the city, Starbucks is only one of them, you know. They're like mosques and churches and temples in other religions, except people go there to sit and drink Ca-poo-*chee*-no,' he said, throwing his arms up, and grinning. 'But there has to be lots of foam on it, or it ain't kosher, are you going to finish that cookie, or what?'

'Help yourself,' she said, and moved the paper napkin with the cookie on it closer to him on the table.

'Cause, you know, it's a sin to let food go to waste,' he said, and reached for the cookie.

Patricia watched him eating.

'Why are you studying Spanish?' she asked.

'What?' he said.

'You said you were practicing your . . .'

'Oh, yeah. Right, right, *mira, mira*. Well, in this polyglot city, I like to be able to communicate with all types of individuals,' he said, chewing, drinking. 'For example, I'm trying to learn how to say "What can you do?" in five different languages. I got one language to go.'

'Why five?' she asked.

'The Rule of Five,' he said. 'All good things come in five. For example, I'll bet you're five feet, five inches tall, am I correct?'

'No, I'm five-seven,' she said.

'That's even better,' he said.

'I'm too short, right?' she said, and pulled a face.

'No, five-seven is perfect for a woman, ah yes,' he said.

'Is that W. C. Fields?' she asked.

'Why, yes, it is,' he said.

'I thought so.'

'Ah yes, m'little chickadee,' he said, and flicked ashes from an imaginary cigar.

Patricia laughed.

'The Rule of Five, huh?' she said.

'The Rule of Five, yes. I'm learning how to play five songs on the piano, too. Do you know "Night and Day"?'

'Oh sure.'

'I'll play it for you sometime. Is there some song you'd like me to learn for you? Maybe some Spanish song? Let me know, and I'll ask my piano teacher. Right now, she's teaching me "Satisfaction."'

'I like that song.'

118

'Yes, it's a nice tune,' Ollie said.

'Why'd you pick that particular phrase? "What can you do?"'

'Well, it's like saying "Go fight City Hall," ain't it? Except it's easier to translate. "What can you do?"' he said, and shrugged.

'*Que puede hacer?*' Patricia said, and shrugged in imitation.

'That's it in Spanish, you're absolutely right,' he said. 'Do you know how to say it in Italian?'

'No, tell me.'

'*Che si puoi fare?*' he said, and hunched his shoulders and opened his hands to show the palms.

'*Che si puoi fare?*' she said, imitating him again.

'Perfect,' Ollie said. 'Here it is in French. *Qu'est-ce qu'on peut faire?* How's that? I know my accent ain't so hot . . .'

'No, that sounded very French.'

'Did it?'

'Absolutely. You should grow a mustache to go with it.'

'You think so? You're kidding me, right?'

'I'm kidding you. But it is a very good French accent. What other language do you know it in?'

'Chinese.'

'Get out of here!'

'I mean it. Well, not Cantonese. I only know it in Mandarin.'

'Let me hear it.'

Ollie squinted his eyes. Cleaving the air with the edge of his palm, he shouted '*May-oh BAN fa!*' and burst out laughing. Patricia laughed with him.

'That's remarkable,' she said.

'Yeah, I know,' Ollie said. 'I want to learn it in Arabic, too. So when I arrest some terrorist hump and he complains about his civil rights, I'll tell him to go fight City Hall in his native tongue.'

Patricia's walkie-talkie went off.

She pulled it from her belt, flipped it on, said, 'Gomez,' and listened. 'I was just on my way, Sarge,' she said. 'Right away. Yes, Sarge. This very minute.' She turned off the radio, pulled a face, and said, 'I have to go. I'm sorry.'

'Maybe we can have coffee again sometime,' Ollie said.

'Maybe we could,' Patricia said.

'Think up a Spanish song for me,' he said. 'I'll ask my teacher to get the sheet music for me.'

'You read music and everything?'

'Oh sure, everything,' he said. 'I even wrote a book.'

'Get out of here!'

'I did. Some hump stole it from my car. I'm searching for him now, I'll bust his ass when I find him.'

'Wow,' she said.

'Yeah,' Ollie said modestly.

'I'll try to think of a song,' she said, and rose, and said, 'Thanks for the coffee. Let me know when you figure out how that gun got over to the wrong side of the hall.'

'I will. You think about it, too. Maybe we can come up with something together.'

'Maybe so,' she said, and looked at him for a moment, and then said, 'Well, I have to go,' and smiled, and raised her hand in farewell, and then turned and walked away from the table, one hip heavy with the weight of the Glock, swiveling toward the front door. He kept watching her till she was out of the shop. Then he went to the counter and bought another cookie.

9.

The challenge now seemed clear: Find a good woman in this city. Which was not as simple as it first appeared. With all due respect, Commish, nothing is ever simple in police work, nothing is ever uncomplicated.

To begin with, if this woman was, or even were still alive, she could be anywhere in the city, which I don't have to tell you is a very big city. But more than that, if she was or were still alive, did she even exist? By Mercer Grant's own admission, Marie Grant was a phony name, what we call a misnomer. But then again, so were Mercer Grant and his alleged cousin Ambrose Field. I have been a cop for a long time now, so the first thing I did was check the phone books for all five sections of the city . . .

Wow, that's just what *I* did, Emilio thought. Well, just Isola and Riverhead. But still.

. . . and discovered in a flash that there were a voluminous multitude of Grants here, which seemed to be a very popular name, but there were no Mercer Grants or Marie Grants and no Ambrose Fields, either, though there seemed to be plenty of other Fields in this fair city. Which meant that Mr Grant, or whatever his name was, had been telling the truth, in which case why had he been lying? That is to say, why had he lied about his name and his wife's name and his cousin's name? What was Mercer Grant hiding? In addition to all those names, of course. And if he was or were hiding something, why had he gone to the police in the first place?

Well, Emilio thought, for that matter, why are you yourself lying, Livvie? Because there is no Olivia Wesley Watts in the phone book, either. Which Emilio thought was somewhat understandable, though, her being a cop and a woman both. If he himself were or was either a cop or a woman, he wouldn't have put his name in the phone book, either. In fact, he prided himself on having thought exactly the way Livvie had, on both levels, as a cop *and* as a woman.

On this Thursday afternoon at a little past three o'clock, Emilio sat with Livvie's report in his lap, his Japanese silk kimono open, his La Perla silk stockings and lace-fringed garter belt exposed where the robe fell loose over his legs and thighs. A frizzy blond wig was sitting on top of the dresser across the room. He would put on the wig and his spike-heeled strappy Prada pumps when he dressed for the stroll tonight. When times were good and heroin was cheap, Emilio earned enough as a hooker to afford nice things like the shoes and the lingerie and all his leather minis and long-sleeved silk blouses that hid the track marks on his arms. Times were not so very good these days. The shortage of heroin from Afghanistan had caused the price of the drug to sky rocket. He hoped the situation was only temporary. Not the war, he knew *that* would go on forever. But if he could find the diamonds Livvie was talking about in her report . . .

Okay, so stop day-dreaming, man. Get back to it.

What was Mercer Grant hiding? In addition to all those names, of course. And if he was or were hiding something, why had he come to the police in the first place?

In police work – as well you know, Commish – we detectives frequently make use of informers, what we call in the trade snitches. These are people upon who or even whom we usually have something we can hold over their heads. As for example, The Needle is a Jamaican informer who used to be a drug dealer before we busted a posse that had originally operated out of London. In London, young Jamaican males involved in violence and/or drugs are called Yardies – a little known fact, but true. The point is, The Needle ratted out half a dozen of these so-called Yardies when we busted the posse, this in exchange for dropping all charges against him. Temporarily, that is. We still have enough on him to put him away for a goodly number of years, were we so disposed. The Needle knows this. He also knows that if we let it be bruited about that he was the one who sold out the posse, oh dear, he might find himself down a sewer one night with his throat slit. So he is very inclined toward helping us whenever we come calling.

I went calling on him that Tuesday afternoon, shortly after Mr Grant left the office. What Mr Grant did not know was that when I asked him to please wait for me in the corridor outside while I checked with the Loot to see if he, the Loot, had any questions he might care to ask, what I was doing in actuality was talking to Barry Lock, a detective who works with me. What I was asking Barry to do was follow Mr Grant home so that we could perhaps get a true name and address for the gentleman. So when I came back out and told Mr Grant the Loot had nothing to add to what we'd already discussed, Barry had already gone downstairs and would be waiting for Mr Grant when he came out of the station house. Mr Grant didn't know anything about this, of course. That is why it is called detective work.

Nor did he know that I myself was on my way to meet with The Needle.

The Needle was not so-named because he is tall and thin, which he is. Nor is that his name because he has only one eye, which he has. No, he is The Needle because when he was but a mere youth, he used to run a dope parlor where you could come up and flop while he injected heroin in your arm or sometimes into the inside of your thigh if you were a girl and didn't want track marks to show for all to see. Also, if he used a thigh, it being so proximate and all, chances were good he might get a little something besides money in exchange for his product, one of the perks of being a dope dealer with female clients. It is not only the Taliban who took advantage of women, you know. I hate to say this, Mr Commissioner, but I have been in precincts where rookie female cops, no names mentioned, have had their lockers broken into and their shoes pissed into, pardon my French. It is not an easy life we women lead, cops or not.

Anyway, The Needle is this very tall, very thin, one-eyed but not unhandsome Jamaican individual, if you like Jamaicans, who was in the drug trade long before we busted the Yardie posse, and who – for all I know – is still dealing drugs this very minute. I really don't know, and I don't care. We have enough on him to send him away for a long time as it is, without adding anything else to it, so 'Don't Ask, Don't Tell' is my policy. Except that when I ask, The Needle better tell, or I pull the chain on him.

'What do you know about a Jamaican fellow named Mercer Grant?' I asked.

We were sitting in the kitchen of The Needle's apartment, which is not too far from the station house and also O'Malley's, the bar where all of this started. Because if it hadn't been for Margie Gannon mentioning all that stuff about conflict diamonds, and if it hadn't been for Mr Grant bringing up the matter of the Revolutionary United Front, I wouldn't be sitting here in a basement waiting for somebody to kill me. The Needle's true and proper name, by the way, is Mortimer Loop. I am told there are a lot of Loops in Kingston. He is a very personable fellow with one annoying habit – well, two if you count his drug addiction. The other annoying habit is that he fancies himself to be a rap artist. That is to say, he constantly talks rap.

'Mercer Grant, Mercer Grant, do dee mon be

Jamaican? How you laks yo' eggs, wid some sausages or bacon?'

'Yes, he's Jamaican,' I said.

He was standing at the stove, cracking eggs for omelets. This was already two in the afternoon, but The Needle had just woken up. He was, in fact, still wearing pajamas. To those not familiar with police work, this may seem unusual, a man in pajamas cooking eggs for a woman wearing beige slacks and tan French-heeled shoes, and a green long-sleeved blouse and a brown jacket, and carrying a nine-millimeter Glock automatic in a tan leather tote bag that matched the shoes when they were not even sharing any kind of personal relationship, the man and the woman. But in many respects, a law enforcement officer is similar to a physician. And so a cheap thief will often feel perfectly comfortable while dressed casually, let us say, in the presence of a female detective dressed for business. Besides, The Needle and I had worked together before, and the pajamas were very nicely patterned with a sort of peony design on black silk.

'And I'll have sausages,' I said. 'If you've got them.'

'Sausages,' The Needle said, and then went into another rap riff that carried him over to the refrigerator. 'Dee lady want sausages, Dee Needle want bacon. She lookin for a mon she say be Jamaican.' Carrying the meats, he trotted back to the stove again on the heels of yet another rap. 'What he do, this mon, do he break

126

dee law? Otherwise, why dee cop, what she comin here for?'

I told The Needle that so far as I knew, Mercer Grant hadn't committed any crime, but that he had come up to the squadroom with a whole bundle of phony names and a diamond chip in his front tooth . . .

'Oh, dee man got a di'mon, should be easy to fine. Is he tall, is he short, is he five feet, nine?'

I told The Needle that Grant was more like six-one, six-two, a tall angular man with a light complexion and a trim little mustache under his nose. I told him that Grant wasn't even his real name, nor was Marie his wife's real name, who by Tuesday would be dead, anyway, by her own estimate, which was today.

'So the wife be dead, but her name ain' Marie. And the husband ain' Grant, so what you want from me?'

'What do you know about conflict diamonds?' I asked him.

'Is he link to the war in Sierra Leone? Or he movin dee ice by hisself all alone?'

'I have no idea. He told me his wife was gone, and then he asked me if I'd ever heard of the RUF, which stands for Revolutionary United Front . . .'

'You think she got whacked by the RUF?'

'Well, that crossed my mind. But . . .'

'Cause they mean mothah-fuckers, and I rather be deaf.'

The Needle forked strips of bacon out of the frying pan, and placed them on paper towels.

Then he dropped four links of sausage into the sizzling bacon fat, and went back to stirring half a dozen eggs in a bowl. On the range, several squares of butter were melting in a second frying pan. The Needle dropped two slices of bread into a toaster on the counter top. I was beginning to work up an appetite.

'I was thinking of writing a cook book,' I told him. 'Livvie Watts's Recipes, how does that sound?'

'Shitty,' The Needle said, and didn't go for a rhyme.

'Kay Scarpetta wrote a cook book,' I told him.

'Who dee fuck be she, what she mean to me? Would you lak some coffee, shall I brew some tea?'

We had breakfast, or lunch, or brunch, or whatever it was at a small table near a window that overlooked the street below. I could hear the sounds of little girls skipping rope downstairs. I could see pigeons flying from the rooftop across the way. It was springtime in the city, and the sausages and eggs were delicious. Even as The Needle promised me he would look for the elusive Grant and his missing, or perhaps already dead wife . . .

'Have no fear, I go on the ear. A mon with a di'mon, his wife ain' Marie. I hear what I hear, I see what I see.'

'. . . I had not even a glimmer that I would soon be placed in a situation that would test me in ways I'd never dreamt I'd be tested. Little did I know that the clock had already started ticking and that the fate of the world was hanging in the balance, not to mention my own fate.

But I'm getting ahead of myself.

You're not going too fast for me, honey, Emilio thought. You're giving me clue after clue. If I don't find you by Sunday, I'll eat my rhinestone-studded thong panties. You have just told me that your informant is a tall, thin, one-eyed Jamaican who is known as The Needle, big surprise, but whose real name is Mortimer Loop, which is probably not his real name, either, they are so fuckin cagey, these people. But let's take a look in the phone book, anyway, just to verify, as they say.

Not to Emilio's great surprise, there were no Mortimer Loops listed in either of the two directories he owned, but there was a Henrietta Loop who sounded interesting, and also a Loretta Loop, who sounded like Henrietta's twin sister though their addresses were different. He wondered why Livvie would be using a fake name for her informant, but perhaps that was to protect herself in case her report got into the wrong hands before it was delivered to the commissioner. Emilio had no intention of delivering the report to anyone engaged in law enforcement. All he wanted to do was find that basement where all the diamonds were, give Livvie a big kiss of gratitude, and then leave for Rio de Janeiro.

Toward that end, he called a friend of his who used to be a bartender.

IN OLLIE'S NOVEL, his stool pigeon was a razor-thin, one-eyed Jamaican named Mortimer Loop, alias The Needle. In real life, this was a white man named William 'Fats' Donner. Ollie had changed Donner's name and description for fictitious purposes and also because he did not wish to get sued later on by a fat junkie snitch.

In fact, Donner was not merely fat, he was Fats. And 'Fats' was 'fat' in the plural. Fats Donner was obese. He was immense. He was mountainous. He also had a penchant for young girls and Turkish baths. In his novel, Ollie had changed these character traits to a fondness for cooking and rapping. He figured this was literary license.

On Thursday afternoon at three twenty-seven, Ollie found Donner at a place called The Samuel Baths, on Lincoln and South Twenty-ninth. The Baths had been named for a black faggot named Albert Samuel, who had made his money running a numbers game, and who needed a place where his fruity friends could gather to jerk each other off. Ollie didn't think Donner was gay. He figured he came here only because, unlike Stockholm, there was a paucity of steam baths in this town. He was sitting now with a towel draped across his crotch, sucking in steam, thick layers of flesh quivering all over his sickly white body. He was altogether a somewhat disgusting person who did perverse things with twelve-year-old girls, but this was the big bad city and Donner was a very good informer. Sometimes you had to make allowances.

Ollie came in with his own towel and took a seat beside Donner on the wooden bench. Together, they looked like a pair of giant white Buddhas. Steam swirled around them.

'I'm looking for a hooker named Emmy,' Ollie said. 'Blond hair, big tits. Ring a bell?'

'Most hookers these days got blond hair and big tits,' Donner said.

'Not the Puerto Rican ones,' Ollie said.

'Ah, we're closing in,' Donner said.

'You know her?'

'Only what you just told me, dad. Blond, big tits, a spic. What part of town is she working?'

'She hocked a Gucci dispatch case in a pawnshop on Ainsley and Fifth. Broker's a guy named Irving Stein.'

'No last name, this chick?'

'Stein didn't ask for one. It was a two-bit transaction,' Ollie explained. 'I'm looking for the case, too, if you get anything on it. A fat lady bought it from Stein.'

'Does she have a name, this fat lady?'

'No.'

'How fat is she?'

Not as fat as you, Ollie was tempted to say, but didn't.

'She looked like an opera singer,' he said. 'White. Brown hair, brown eyes.'

'Let's get back to the hooker, dad. Not many of them work that stretch of turf. Is it possible Emmy *lives* near the pawnshop?'

'I don't know where she lives. And besides, Stein told me he gets *lots* of hookers in there.'

'I'm only saying that ain't a stretch they normally stroll, man. You talking Hookerland, try Mason Avenue.'

'Are you telling me lots of hookers *live* near Ainsley and Fifth?'

'Lots of hookers live everywhere in this city. Most of 'em don't eat where they shit, though, is all I'm saying.'

'Then why'd Stein tell me he gets lots of hookers in his shop?'

'Maybe he does.'

'Who live in the neighborhood?'

'It's possible. Lots of them big old buildings used to have Jewish families in them, the ones south of Ainsley.'

'Yeah?'

'Could be hookers in them buildings now.'

'The queen could be king, too, if she had balls,' Ollie said.

'I'm only tryin'a zero in, dad,' Donner said. 'If I can get a bead on her territory, maybe I can find her for you. Where'd she get this dispatch case?'

'She stole it from a parked car outside King Memorial.'

'Ah-ha!' Donner said. 'Now you're talkin, man. That's hooker turf, the King area. Lots of events there, lots of white men on the town uptown, lookin for bars, lookin for black pussy, spic pussy, now you're talkin. Let me go on the earie.'

'I'm eager to find this broad,' Ollie said.

'How much are we talkin here?' Donner asked. 'You tell me the Gucci was a two-bit transaction . . .'

'I'm thinking a C-note if you find her for me.'

'You're thinking small, dad. This is the twenty-first century.'

'And Castleview is still a penitentiary,' Ollie said.

'Oh dear, don't threaten me, dad.'

'It's all I know how to do,' Ollie said, and grinned like a barracuda.

'Make it a deuce,' Donner said.

'Let's see what you come up with.'

'Emmy,' Donner said. 'Let's see.'

AT A QUARTER to four that Thursday afternoon, just as the night shift was gathering before the muster desk downstairs, preparing to relieve on post at four P.M., and just as detectives were beginning to wend their separate ways up the iron-runged stairway that led to the second-floor squadroom, Pamela Henderson stopped at the desk and asked Sergeant Murchison where she could find a Detective Steve Carella. Murchison picked up a phone, pushed a button on it, said a few words into the receiver, and then told her to go up the steps there to the second floor and down the corridor.

Carella was waiting inside the slatted wooden railing to greet her. He opened the gate, led her in, and offered her a chair at his desk.

Still wearing black – her husband had been dead only four days, after all – she looked somehow taller than she had in jeans and a turtleneck, perhaps because she was wearing high-heeled pumps with the black skirt and jacket. She sat, crossed her legs, and said, 'Is this an inconvenient time? I sense a changing of the guard.'

'Not at all,' Carella said. 'I had some papers to file, anyway.'

Pamela looked at him and nodded.

He sensed that she didn't quite trust him.

He said, 'Really, I'm in no hurry. How can I help you?'

Still, she hesitated.

'Really,' he said again.

She sighed heavily. Nodded again.

'I found some letters,' she said.

He glanced, he hoped surreptitiously, at the clock on the wall, and he thought, What this case doesn't need at a quarter to four in the afternoon, ten to four already, after a long hard day when I'm ready to pack it in and go home to my wife and family, what this case definitely does not need is more complications, this case already has enough complications.

Ollie had called him earlier to tell him the gun was found on the wrong side of the hall. Now here was the murdered man's wife telling him she'd found some letters, which he somehow suspected were not letters from her mother.

'Letters from whom?' he asked.

'Someone named Carrie.'

'As in Grant?'

'No, as in Stephen King.'

'A woman.'

'Yes. A woman.'

Landing on the word heavily. A woman. Yes.

'To whom were these letters addressed, Mrs Henderson?'

'To my husband,' she said.

Carella pulled on the white cotton gloves.

THERE WERE THREE letters in all.

All of them written in a delicate hand, in purple ink on pale lavender writing paper. The stationery was obviously expensive, embossed with the monogrammed initials JSH. If there had been matching envelopes to go with the single sheet of paper in each envelope, they had not been used for these mailings. Instead, Carrie – for such was how she'd signed her name – had used plain white envelopes she could have bought in any variety store for ten cents apiece. In her same delicate handwriting, she had addressed the letters to Councilman Lester Henderson at his office downtown. Hand-lettered across the face of each envelope were the councilman's name and address and the words PERSONAL AND PRIVATE. The envelopes had been postmarked at a post office in an area called Laughton's Market, one of the city's better neighborhoods.

The first letter read:

My darling Lester:
 I can't believe this is really happening! Will we

really be alone together for two full nights? Will you really not have to watch a clock or catch a taxi? Will I be able to sleep in your arms all night long, wake up in your arms the next morning, linger in your arms, make love to you as often as I like, spoil you to within an inch of your life? Will this really happen this coming weekend? I can't believe it. I'm afraid if I pinch myself, I'll wake up. Hurry to me, my darling, hurry, hurry, hurry.
    Carrie

The second letter read:

My darling Lester:
    When you receive this, it will be Tuesday. On Saturday morning I'll be boarding an airplane that will fly me to the Raleigh Hotel in a city I've never visited, there to await the arrival of the man I love so very much. I cannot wait, I simply cannot wait. I love you to death, I adore you.
    Carrie

Carella slipped the letters back into their envelopes.
'You know,' he said, 'maybe it would be better if I . . .'
'I've read them all,' Pamela said. 'Don't worry about me. I'm beyond shock.'
He nodded, and opened the third envelope.

My darling Lester:
    It will be Friday when you receive this. Tomorrow morning, I will take a taxi to the airport, and fly into your waiting arms. I love you, my darling, I adore you, I am completely and hopelessly madly in

love with you, am I gushing? So allow me to gush.
I'm nineteen, I'm entitled.
   Carrie

'So, uh, where'd you find these?' Carella asked, folding the last letter, sliding it back into its envelope, busying himself with the task, not looking at Lester Henderson's widow, who sat beside the desk in monumental silence.

'In his study. At the back of a drawer in his desk.'

'When was this?'

'This morning.'

He didn't ask what she was doing in his desk. A man dies, you go through his things. Death robs everyone of privacy. Death has no respect for secrets. If you're fucking a nineteen-year-old girl, don't leave her letters around. Death will uncover them.

'Does the name mean anything to you?' he asked.

'Nothing.'

'You don't know anyone named Carrie?'

'No one.'

'How about the monogram. JSH. Do those initials ring a bell?'

'No.'

'They don't seem to match the name "Carrie."'

'No, they don't.'

'Did you suspect any of this?'

'No.'

'Any idea your husband was . . . uh . . .?'

'No. This came as a total surprise.'

'Any . . . uh . . . past history of . . . uh . . .'

'Never. As far as I knew, he was completely faithful to me.'

'May I keep these letters?'

136

'Of course. That's why I brought them here. Won't there be fingerprints on them or something?'

'Well, yours certainly, and your husband's. And, yes, maybe the girl's, too.'

Nineteen. He guessed that was a girl. He guessed that was still a girl.

'If you'll let us take your prints before you go,' he said. 'For comparison.'

'Yes, of course.'

'We have your husband's,' he said. He did not mention that cadavers were routinely printed at the morgue. He did not mention that even if they recovered some good prints for the girl, chances of finding anything on her in the system were exceedingly slim. Nineteen years old? Had she ever been in the armed services? Had she ever held a government job? What was the likelihood that a nineteen-year-old girl who wrote letters on expensive monogrammed stationery had ever been arrested for anything? Still, you went through the paces, and sometimes you got lucky.

'Will you let me know if you learn anything?'

'I'll call you right away,' he said.

'I hate him for this,' she said out of the blue.

THE BAR TWO BLOCKS from the Eighty-seventh Precinct station house was called Shanahan's. At four-thirty that afternoon, forty-five minutes after the day watch was relieved, Eileen Burke and Andy Parker met there with Francisco Palacios, who was not too terribly tickled to be seen in a place where so many cops went for drinks after work. The Gaucho liked to keep a low profile.

On the other hand, if he was involved in the business of supplying information to the police, would he be doing it so blatantly out in the open? Mindful of the fact that another person in his profession – an informer named Danny Gimp – had been killed in a public place while sharing coffee and chocolate eclairs with yet another detective from the Eight-Seven, Palacios kept a roving eye on the people coming in and out of Shanahan's, lest he, too, be cold-cocked for no reason whatsoever.

He was here this evening to tell Parker and Eileen what he had learned about the drug deal that would go down this Tuesday at midnight. The date and the time hadn't changed. Neither had the names of the principal players. But he was now able to give them with some degree of certainty the exact location of the impending transaction.

'The thing is she's being very careful, this woman,' he said. 'I think she got burned once before, really bad, by some sharpies up from Miami, so she wants to make sure nobody does it to her again. Five times already, she changed the location. It's always a basement, she likes to do business in basements cause nobody can get in and out too fast if they have to run up and down steps. When the Miami guys took her, it was on a rooftop. She figured a rooftop would be safe, *verdad*? Instead, she handed over the crack and next thing you know she's looking at half a dozen Glocks and the Miami guys are jumping over to the next roof, and it's so long, see you on the beach, honey. Ever since then, it's basements. Does anybody want another beer?'

'I'm fine,' Eileen said.

'I could use one,' Parker said.

Palacios signaled to the waiter, who slouched over to the table and took their order for two fresh brews. A pair of heavy-looking guys came through the front door, and Palacios gave them the once-over, but they turned out to be two off-duty cops who went over to join some buddies at another table. Eileen was still trying to find out a little bit more about this mysterious deal that was about to happen in some mysterious basement.

'Who are the players here?' she asked. 'You say they haven't changed, so who are they?'

'I think you had traffic before with the lady selling the crack,' Palacios said. 'You remember a black woman named Rosita Washington, she's half Spanish?'

Eileen shook her head. 'Who are the buyers?'

'Three guys who are total amateurs,' Palacios said. 'They're the ones who are dangerous. Ah, *gracias, señor*,' he said to the waiter, and immediately picked up his beer mug. Tilting it in Eileen's direction, he said, 'To the beautiful lady,' and drank. Eileen acknowledged the toast dead-panned. 'The three of them think all black people are stupid,' Palacios said, 'but if they try to rip off Rosie Washington, there's gonna be real trouble, I can tell you.'

'All black people *are* stupid,' Parker said, not for nothing was he a close friend of Ollie Weeks.

'Not as stupid as these three jerks, believe me,' Palacios said. 'You heard of The Three Stooges? Shake hands with these guys. I don't know how they raised the three hundred thou they need for the deal, *if* they raised it. But I can tell you, if they go in empty-handed they're dead on the platter. Rosie ain't gonna get stiffed a second time.'

'Who are they?' Eileen asked.

'Three jackasses named Harry Curtis, Constantine Skevopoulos, and Lonnie Doyle. You know them?'

'No,' Parker said.

'No,' Eileen said.

'Grifters from the year one. Which is why I think they might try to rip off Rosie, in which case run for cover, *niños*, run for cover. Thing you should do, you want my advice, is go down the basement, yell "Cops, freeze!" and bust all of them before any shooting starts. You nail Rosie for possession of the coke, and you nail the three dopes for tryin'a buy it, is my advice.'

'Thanks,' Parker said drily.

'Where is this basement?' Eileen asked.

'3211 Culver. Between Tenth and Eleventh.'

'I gotta pee,' Parker said, and rose, and headed for the men's room. One of the heavy-looking guys who'd come in earlier walked over to the juke box, put some coins in it, and pushed some buttons. Sinatra came out singing 'It Was a Very Good Year.' You didn't hear Sinatra too often these days. Eileen missed him. She sat listening, swaying in time with the music. He was singing now about city girls who lived up the stairs.

'Do you like to dance?' Palacios asked.

'Yes, I like to dance,' she said.

'You want to come dancing with me sometime?'

She looked at him.

'No, I don't think so,' she said.

'Why not? I'm a very good dancer.'

'I don't doubt it, Cowboy.'

'So?'

'You also have four wives.'

'*Had*,' Palacios said. 'Past tense. Had. I'm divorced now. Four times.'

'Terrific recommendation,' Eileen said.

'Come on, we go dancing one night.'

'Cowboy, we've got enough on you to send you away for twenty years.'

'So? Meanwhile, we go dancing.'

'I'm a cop,' Eileen said.

'So? Cops don't dance?'

'Let it go, Cowboy.'

'I'll ask you again.'

She looked at him another time. She was thinking he was handsome as hell, and she hadn't been to bed with anyone for the past six months now, and she'd heard Hispanic lovers were the cat's ass, so why not go dancing one night? She was also thinking you don't get involved with guys on the other side of the law, this man would be doing time at Castleview if we hadn't let him walk in exchange for his services. So thanks, Cowboy, she thought.

'Thanks, Cowboy,' she said, 'but no.'

Parker was back.

'Lay it out for me one more time,' he told Palacios.

OH SHIT, Suzie thought, it's about to get complicated again.

Just when I dared hope things would stay clear and simple forever, Harry brings his dumb-ass friends home with him again, and they're sitting there in the living room playing cards at eight o'clock at night, and talking about their next brilliant scheme to make a million dollars without having to work for it.

The last time they had a great idea was four weeks ago, when they decided to stick up a floating crap game in Diamondback. Twelve humongous black guys in the game, any one of them could've broken these three wimps in half without lifting a finger, they decide to go stick it up. What happened was it was raining that night, and the game got called off, which was lucky for her husband and his pals, or there would've been three broken heads around here. So now they were planning another one of their grand capers, but maybe – if they got lucky again – it would rain again and save them a lot of heartache and grief.

She sometimes wondered why she stayed married to Harry Curtis. Sometimes wondered, in fact, why she'd married him in the first place. Well, she always did go for big men. Suzie Q, they used to call her when she was in her teens – well, some of her friends still called her that. Short for Suzie Quinn. Now she was Susan Q. Curtis, twenty-three years old and married to a man who was twice her age and big all over, including his ideas.

The thing of it was that Harry Curtis thought all black people were stupid, and all you had to do was trick them out of their money, usually by sticking a gun in their face. It really was a good thing him and his bright cronies hadn't held up that crap game because from what Luella told her down at the beauty parlor where she worked, the people in that game were truly Diamondback 'gangstas,' Luella's word, a bit of information her brilliant husband shrugged off when she later told him about it.

It was Suzie herself who had casually mentioned the time and location of the crap game to Harry, who in turn had mentioned it to his two brainy buddies, who had decided that here was a score worthy of their combined talents. Never mind she also later mentioned the guys in the game were gangstas, that didn't scare them off, oh no, they were three big macho men with three big pistolas, and they weren't afraid of no niggers up there in Diamondback. Lucky thing it rained that night. Though now Suzie wondered what kind of gangstas these guys could've been if they'd got scared off of their game by a little rain. Well, a lot of rain.

She could hear their voices coming from the other room.

'Cocaine,' one of them was saying. Lonnie. Her husband's oldest friend. Went to high school together, went to jail together, but that was another story. And besides, it was only for a year and a half after all was said and done. And they'd met some nice people there.

'See your five and raise you five,' her husband said.

'High grade snow,' Lonnie said.

'What does that make it?'

This from Constantine, the one with the dopey grin and the fidgety shoulders. Constantine in motion was a wondrous thing to behold.

'It makes it a ten-dollar raise,' Harry said.

'Too steep for me,' Constantine said.

'Asking price, three hundred thou,' Lonnie said. 'Call.'

'So it's just you and me, Lon,' Harry said, and chuckled. She guessed maybe that was one of the reasons she married him. That deep low chuckle of his. And also his size, of course.

'Where we gonna get three hundred thou?' Constantine asked. She could visualize his shoulders twitching. As if he was trying to shake off bugs.

'We don't hafta get it,' Lonnie said.

'Beat kings full,' her husband said.

'Four deuces, sport,' Lonnie said.

'Then how we gonna buy the coke?' Constantine asked.

'We *ain't* gonna buy it,' Lonnie said. 'We gonna *steal* it.'

Of course, Suzie thought.

Otherwise it would be too damn simple, am I right?

10.

ON FRIDAY MORNING, AFIS — the Automated Fingerprint Identification Section — identified the larger of the
prints, the man's prints, as belonging to Lester Lyle
Henderson, who had served a stint with the US Air Force
during the Gulf War. Some of the smaller prints matched
the ones Pamela Henderson had allowed them to take.
For the other small prints, presumably left by the Carrie
who'd written the letters, there was nothing.

The lab downtown identified the plain white envelopes
as a product of the Haley Paper Company, available in
any variety store, any office supply store, any supermarket
across the entire nation. Carella suddenly felt like the FBI
trying to track down the envelopes used by whoever'd
been mailing anthrax hither and yon.

The monogrammed stationery was another matter.

The lab identified it as a quality paper made by
Generation Paper Mills in Portland, Maine, a supplier to
Carter Paper Products in Philadelphia, Pennsylvania, the
manufacturer of an exclusive line of stationery called
Letter Perfect, which was carried by only two department
stores and seven specialty shops in the city. Both depart-
ment stores were located in the midtown area. Carella and
Kling went to visit them first.

Except for charge customers, neither of the stores kept
sales records going back earlier than a year ago. Within
the past year, there was no record of any customer — cash

or charge – having ordered Letter Perfect stationery with the monogram JSH. One of the stores did not keep charge records for more than two years. The other did not keep them for more than eighteen months. In any case, it would take some time to peruse the earlier files; they would have to get back to Carella.

The prospect was even dimmer at the seven specialty shops. None of them remembered a customer with the initials JSH, and none of them had time to go through their back records just now. They promised to call the detectives if anything turned up.

Carella still felt like the FBI.

THE OFFICES OF Councilman Lester Lyle Henderson were close to City Hall, in a part of town still referred to as the Old City. Here stood the ocean-battered seawall the Dutch had built centuries ago, the massive cannons atop it seeming to control the approach from the Atlantic even now, though their barrels had long ago been filled with cement. Here at the very tip of the island, you could watch the Dix and the Harb churning with crosscurrents where the two rivers met. The streets down here had once accommodated only horse-drawn carriages, and were now too narrow to permit the passage of more than a single automobile. Where once there had been two-story wooden taverns, a precious few of which still survived, there were now concrete buildings soaring into the sky, infested redundantly with lawyers and financiers. And yet – perhaps because the Atlantic was right here to touch, rumbling majestically off toward the Old World that had given the city its life – there was still the feel here of what it must have been like when everyone was still very young and very innocent.

There was no sense of the Old World in Henderson's

offices. Neither was there the slightest whiff of innocence. Youth, however, was in rich abundance. The girl sitting behind the reception desk couldn't have been older than twenty-three. Pert and blond, wearing a very short green mini and a white-buttoned navy-blue blouse, she sensed immediately that Kling was the single guy in this dynamic duo, and turned her full attention to him.

'How can I help you?' she asked, smiling radiantly.

She sounded Southern. North Carolina? Georgia? Kling wondered what she was doing in a politician's office up north.

'We're here for Alan Pierce,' Kling said.

'Is he expecting you?'

'He is.'

'And you are?' she asked.

Kling felt as if he'd just asked her to dance at the senior prom, and she wanted to know which home room he was in.

'Detective Kling,' he said, and opened the leather fob to which his shield was pinned. 'This is my partner, Detective Carella.'

'Is he in?' Carella asked.

'Let me see, sir,' she said.

Sir. Made Carella feel like forty. Which he was.

The blonde lifted a phone receiver, tapped a button on the phone base, smiled up at Kling, listened, and then said, 'Alan, there are two detectives here to see you.' She listened again, said, 'Right,' and then put the phone back on the receiver. Smiling at Kling again, she said, 'Through the door there, and into the main office. Then through that to Mr Pierce's office at the far end. If you need me, just whistle.'

The line sounded familiar to Kling.

They walked past a wall hung with framed campaign

posters of bygone years to an unmarked door with a brass knob. Beyond that door was a huge open room banked on one side with windows now open to breezes that blew in off the water where the rivers clashed. There were perhaps twenty desks in this room, all of them the same color as the computers sitting on top of them, an array of greens and purples and grays that seemed as cheerful as spring-time. Behind each desk sat the so-called T-Generation, kids who had come of age when the terrorists bombed America, none of them older than twenty-five, all of them staring at their computers as if transfixed, fingers flying, performing God only knew what political tasks for their now deceased leader. None of them looked up as Carella and Kling worked their way to the rear of the room where three identical doors sat like props in a stage farce. One of them bore a plaque that read: A. PIERCE.

'Lauren Bacall,' Carella said. '*To Have and Have Not.*'

Kling looked at him.

'The next line is, "You know how to whistle, don't you, Steve? You just put your lips together and blow."'

'Oh,' Kling said. 'Yeah,' and knocked on the door.

'Bogart's name was Steve,' Carella explained. 'In the picture.'

'Come in,' a voice called.

Alan Pierce was a man in his late thirties, Carella guessed, old by comparison to the cadre of kids manning the computers outside. He came from behind his desk with his hand extended, a tall, slender man exhibiting the obvious end results of hours in the gym, a flat tummy, a narrow waist, and wide shoulders clearly his own since he was in shirtsleeves. 'Gentlemen,' he said. 'Nice to see you. Sit down. Please.'

Carella wondered if Pierce was doing an imitation of President Bush, who couldn't seem to get through a

147

sentence longer than five words without parsing it. 'We are. Going to. Find and destroy. The Evil One.' Pierce here seemed to go him one better. Or perhaps this was just a memorized way of greeting people. He shook hands vigorously now, as if he were soliciting votes.

'How can I help you?' he asked.

Same words the blond receptionist had used. Carella wondered if this was office protocol. He suddenly realized he did not trust politicians. And he wondered if this attitude had been reinforced by the letters Henderson had received from someone named Carrie – which, after all, was why they were here today.

'Mr Pierce,' he said, 'I under . . .'

'Alan,' he said. 'Please.'

'Alan,' Carella said, and cleared his throat, 'I understand that you and Mr Henderson flew up to the state capital together last . . .'

'Yes, we did.'

'That would have been last Saturday, is that right?'

'Yes. Saturday morning.'

'April twentieth, right?'

'Yes.'

'Just the two of you?' Carella asked.

'Just the two of us, yes.'

'And you came back the next morning, is that correct?'

'Correct. Sunday the twenty-first.'

'Alone.'

'I came back alone, yes.'

'You left Mr Henderson up there and flew back alone.'

'Yes. I had some personal matters to attend to here in the city. And he no longer needed me.'

'What'd you guys do up there, anyway?' Kling asked.

'Attended meetings. As you probably know, the Governor had approached Lester about running for mayor.

148

We met with his people on Saturday. And Lester had a lunch meeting with the Governor himself scheduled for Sunday. That's why he stayed over. It was a summit thing, just the two of them.'

The telephone rang.

Pierce picked up the receiver.

'Yes?' he said. 'Who? Oh, yes, certainly, put him through. Sorry,' he said to the detectives, and then, into the phone again, 'Hello, Roger,' he said, 'how can I help you?'

There it is again, Carella thought. How can I help you?

'Well, I have to tell you frankly,' Pierce said, 'I find it not only premature but also somewhat ghoulish for you people to be asking that question so soon after we put the councilman in the ground.' He listened and then said, 'I don't care *what* the Governor's office is putting out. No one has talked to me about it, and I just told you I don't wish to entertain any questions about it.' He listened and then said, 'Then can you please extend me that courtesy?' He looked at the detectives, rolled his eyes, listened again, and then said, 'When I'm *ready* to discuss it. When a decent interval has passed. *If* then. Goodbye, Rog,' he said, 'thanks for calling.'

He put the receiver back on the cradle rest, said, 'I'm sorry, gentlemen. They keep asking me if I plan to run for mayor now that Lester . . .' He shook his head. 'No fucking decency left in this world, is there? Forgive me, but they're like animals.' He sighed heavily, sat in the big leather chair behind his desk again, and said, 'We were discussing?'

'Your coming back home early,' Kling said.

'No, I'm sorry if I gave you that impression. I never expected to stay any longer.'

'I thought . . .'

'No.'

'When you said you had some personal matters . . .'

'Yes, but I knew before I went upstate that Lester would be lunching with the Governor. This wasn't something that came as a surprise.'

'Sorry I misinterpreted it,' Kling said.

'Sorry if I misled you.'

'What sort of meetings did you have up there?' Carella asked.

'Well, first with some members of the Governor's exploratory committee, it's called, and then with the Governor's campaign people, and then with people from the national party itself. Mayor of this city is a big deal, you know. Both parties would like their own man in there.'

'This was all day long?' Carella asked. 'The meetings.'

'Well, the first one was at ten Saturday morning. We broke for lunch, and then met with the campaign people at two. Our last meeting was at four.'

'What time did that end?' Carella asked.

'Oh, around six, six-thirty.'

'What then?'

'We had dinner and went to sleep. I had an early flight the next morning.'

'You had dinner together?' Kling asked.

'Well, no, actually. I called room service. I don't know where Lester ate. I imagine he did the same thing. We'd had a long day.'

'Did he say he was going to call room service?'

'Well, no. I'm just assuming . . . I really don't know.'

'Was there a restaurant in the hotel?'

'Oh, sure.'

'So he might've had dinner there.'

'He might've. Or anywhere else in town, for that matter. There are lots of good restaurants up there. Italian ones, especially. There's a large Italian constituency up there. Population, I should say.'

'Did you talk to him on Sunday morning?'

'No. I was catching a seven A.M. flight.'

'Didn't want to wake him, was that it?' Carella asked.

'Exactly. Besides, there was really nothing more to say. We'd said it all the night before.'

'Had a talk the night before?'

'Yes. After our last meeting.'

'At around six, six-thirty?'

'Around then, yes. We had a drink in the lobby . . .'

'Just the two of you?'

'Yes. To rehash the day. Then I went to my room, had dinner, and went to bed. I don't know where Lester went.'

'He didn't say where he *might* be going, did he?'

'No.'

'But you think he might have called room service.'

'That was just a guess. He seemed tired . . . that was just an educated guess.'

'Were there any women at these meetings?' Kling asked.

'Oh yes. This isn't Afghanistan, you know,' Pierce said, and smiled.

'Did any of these women come up from the city?' Carella asked.

'No. They were all based up there.'

'Any of them named Carrie?'

'Carrie?'

'C-A . . .'

'No, not that I recall. Carrie? Where'd that come from?' Pierce asked.

'Does that name mean anything to you?'

'No. Who is she?'

'You don't know anyone named Carrie?'

'No one at all.'

'Did Mr Henderson know anyone named Carrie?'

'Not to my knowledge.'

'This wouldn't have to be professionally,' Carella said.

'I'm not sure I . . .'

'Personally. This would have been someone he knew personally.'

'You'd have to ask Pamela about that. She'd be more familiar with their personal acquaintances.'

'She doesn't know anyone named Carrie,' Carella said.

'I don't, either. I'm sorry.'

'You were Mr Henderson's aide . . .'

'Yes.'

'His assistant.'

'Yes.'

'His right-hand man.'

'Yes.'

'He would have told you if he knew someone named Carrie, wouldn't he?'

'I suppose so. Gentlemen, I'm still not sure I under . . .'

'How do you suppose a letter without a return address on it got through to Mr Henderson?'

'I have no idea. Everything coming into the office is screened. No one in public life takes any chances nowadays.'

'Would anyone besides Mr Henderson have had access to an envelope marked "Personal and Private"?'

'An envelope with no return address on it?' Carella said.

'Well . . . Josh maybe.'

'Coogan?'

'Yes.'

'We'd like to talk to him. Is he here?'

'No, I'm sorry, he's not.'

'When will he be back?'

'He won't. He's gone for the day. You have no idea how many calls we've had following Lester's murder. Both of us have been running around like crazy.'

'I'm sure,' Carella said. 'Can we reach him at home?'

'I'll give you his address, sure,' Pierce said. 'But you'd have a better shot at the school.'

'The school?'

'Ramsey U. He takes film courses there at night. He wants to be a director.'

'What time is he usually there?'

'Mondays, Wednesdays, and Thursdays. Seven to eleven.'

'Today's Friday,' Kling said.

'So it is,' Pierce said, and both cops suddenly disliked him intensely.

'Just one other question,' Carella said. 'When you were upstare with Mr Henderson, did you at any time see him in the company of a nineteen-year-old girl?'

'Not that I can recall. Do you mean at any of our meetings? Most of the women were older than . . .'

'No, I mean alone. Alone with a nineteen-year-old girl.'

'No. Never. Lester? Never.'

'Thank you,' Carella said.

In the corridor outside, Kling said, 'He's lying about the girl.'

'I know,' Carella said.

AINE DUGGAN pronounced her name Anya Doogan. This was surprising to Emilio, but then again he wasn't Irish. She told him one time, while they were both stoned on crack when it was still fashionable, that Aine was an old Celtic name. He believed her. She certainly looked Irish. Or even Celtic, what with her bright-green eyes, when she wasn't stoned, and hair that had a burnt October look, somewhat like what he imagined Livvie's hair to be. He had known Aine for it had to've been seven, eight years now, when crack was all the rage and you could get high for a few bucks, man, those were the days. That was before either of them started hooking.

Back then, Aine was still bartending and Emilio was working as a dishwasher at the same little Italian restaurant down near the Quarter. But even after they both began using, there always seemed to be enough money for their daily needs plus a movie every now and then or a rock concert out on The Bight, crack was so friggin *cheap* then. It was one of the busboys first turned them on to crack. Emilio hardly ever saw Aine socially anymore. No time for music or flicks anymore, too busy out there rushing the buck.

She looked tired these days.

Twenty-five years old, she looked tired.

He wondered if he looked the same way.

'What I'm searching for is a bar named O'Malley's,' he said.

'Must be ten thousand bars named O'Malley's in this city,' Aine said.

She still talked with a Calm's Point accent, the Irish variety, not the Italian or black style. On the telephone, Emilio always could tell if he was talking to a Spanish person like himself or somebody Irish or Italian or black or Jewish. Some people said you couldn't tell a book by its cover, but that was all democracy bullshit. On the telephone, the minute anybody opened his mouth, Emilio nailed him. When Aine opened her mouth, it was like you pulled a cork from a bottle and shamrocks fell all over the table. She was wearing this afternoon a flared skirt and a white blouse, white ankle socks and brown loafers. She looked like an Irish teenager instead of a junkie, except that she also looked so friggin tired.

'No, that's what I thought, too,' he said, 'but I looked in the phone books, and there ain't no O'Malley's.'

'You look in all the phone books?'

At eleven that Friday morning, they were sitting in the park counting the time to their next fixes. When they first started using, they would try all kinds of shit. It was like a big supermarket of drugs out there. The hubba, of course, so cheap, so convenient, somebody shoulda put that on the TV as a commercial, So Cheap, So Convenient, Come Get Your Crack Cocaine Right Here, Kiddies. Or Just Say No, if that's your choice, tee-hee. But they also smoked gremmies, which were coke and weed rolled in a cigarette, or sherms, which were these cigarettes laced with PCP. If Emilio remembered correctly, they even did some fry before they started slamming their drug of choice, good old hop, directly in the vein, honey.

It was Aine went on the street first.

Good-looking Irish girl, shapely white legs, red hair hither and yon, she looked like a virgin Catholic school-girl in a pleated skirt and jacket with a gold-thread crest on it, Saint Cecilia of Our Infinite Sorrows, all she needed was books under her arm, some virgin. By that time, she'd been had fore and aft, upside down and backwards.

Emilio started a little later, and wasn't doing too well peddling ass till he discovered he looked better in a skirt than he did in jeans. Shaved his legs, bought first a red wig, thinking him and Aine could go on the street together like Miss Dolly Ho and her sister Polly. But the fake red wig didn't go with his dark complexion or her real red hair, in fact made him look like a male wearing a very bad rug instead of a juicy female tart who just happened to have a cock under his or her skirt. He tried on a lot of other wigs, even some pink and purple ones before he settled on the blond. Business picked up almost at once, though he wasn't necessarily having more fun.

'I tried every book I had,' he said. 'No O'Malley's.'

'Which books do you have?'

Addicts tended to be somewhat precise, Emilio noticed. They would often argue a point like monks in a seminary or judges on some high tribunal. Emilio didn't particularly like this about addicts, even though he recognized it as one of his own faults.

'I have the Riverhead book, and the one here for the city.'

'That leaves out three very big parts of this town,' Aine said.

'I know, but I have a feeling this bar is right here someplace.'

'What gives you that feeling, man?'

'First thing, I ripped off this bag outside the King. Next thing . . .'

'What bag?'

'Had confidential information in it. Next thing, there's this lady detective in it talking about diamonds, and she's locked in a basement . . .'

'Whoa now.'

'Where'd I lose you, Ahn?'

'There's this lady detective in a *bag*?'

'No, in her report. And her precinct is a few blocks away from this bar she called O'Malley's. Also, did you ever hear of a precinct called the Oh-One?'

'No. The Oh-One? No. What's the Oh-One?'

'I'm thinking the First Precinct.'

'No. The First Precinct is the First Precinct. I never heard it called the Oh-One. Never. That makes it sound like there's a decimal point in front of it, the Oh-One.'

'Also, if there's an Oh-One, there's also an Oh-Two, and an Oh-Three, and so on. Which as you know, there ain't,' Emilio said. 'So I figure Livvie made up this fake what you might call terminology to throw any evil-doer off the track.'

'Any evil-doer, huh?'

'Somebody tryin'a get those diamonds.'

'Diamonds, huh?'

'You help me find them, Ahn, we'll both go down to Rio together.'

'Why Rio?'

'It's nice down there, I hear. Also, they have carnival.'

'I have carnival right here every time I shoot up.'

'You used to be a bartender, am I right?'

'You know I used to be a bartender.'

'So where's there a bar two blocks from a police station?'

'Everywhere,' Aine said.

AT FIVE O'CLOCK that Friday evening, Josh Coogan seemed surprised to find two men who identified themselves as police detectives waiting for him on the steps outside his building.

'I thought this was the fat guy's case,' he said.

'We're working it together,' Carella told him.

'How'd you know where to find me?'

'Alan Pierce gave us your address.'

'So what's up?'

'We want to ask you some more questions.'

'What about? I already spoke to the fat guy, you know.'

'Briefly, yes,' Kling said.

'Well, I thought I answered all his questions.'

'We're sorry to be bothering you again, but we thought . . .'

'I mean, am I a suspect in this thing?'

The question they all asked sooner or later.

But Coogan had about him the air of confidence most college kids exude – especially those pursuing arts programs. They didn't yet realize they would never become a Hemingway or a Picasso or a Hitchcock or a Frank Lloyd Wright. The world was still their oyster. Kling, who'd never been to college, and Carella, who'd never finished college, envied the attitude. But they had both read Fat Ollie's report, and they remembered him describing Coogan as 'flustered and unsure of himself.' He did not appear that way tonight.

'Do you know anyone named Carrie?' Carella asked.

'No. Is that a man or a woman?'

'It's a nineteen-year-old girl,' Carella said.

'No, I don't know her. Am I supposed to know her?'

'Lester Henderson was supposed to know her.'

'Does that mean what I take it to mean?'

'What do you take it to mean?'

'Was he messing around with a nineteen-year-old girl?'

'You tell us.'

'Let me say I wouldn't be surprised. He definitely had an eye for the women.'

'Did you ever *see* him with a nineteen-year-old girl?'

'Our office is full of nineteen-year-old girls. But if you mean . . .'

'Any of them named Carrie?'

'No.'

'Did any letters addressed to the councilman and marked "Personal and Private" ever cross your desk?'

'No. His mail went to him directly.'

'All of it?'

'All of it.'

'In spite of the anthrax scare?'

'Was it anthrax that killed him?' Coogan said, and raised his eyebrows, and nodded sagely.

11.

IT TOOK THREE HOURS by train to the state capital. It would have taken them a half-hour to get to the airport and – with security what it was these days – another two hours to get to the gate, all for an hour-long flight. If Carella had opted to drive up, the trip would have taken almost four hours. He figured it was six of one, half a dozen of the other. Besides, on the train, he and Teddy could talk.

Communicating with a person who could neither hear nor speak required, first, that you be able to see each other's hands (because that's what signing was all about, Gertie) and next that the impaired (what a word!) partner be able to see the other person's lips so that she could read them.

Car rides were difficult. Without risking an accident, Carella could not turn his head away from the road to look at Teddy. And without leaning over at an impossible angle and virtually flashing her fingers in his face, Teddy simply could not communicate. They had tried. They knew. The only way it worked was to translate through the kids, Carella speaking, the kids in the back seat signing, and then Teddy signing back to the kids, and the kids speaking the words out loud to their father. But alone in a car? Forget about talking.

The train was a good solution.

Besides, this was Saturday, and Carella's day off, and he was entitled.

The morning train they caught was virtually empty. He bought coffee and donuts in the café car and carried them back to where they'd spread out like pashas on two reclining seats. Leisurely, they watched the countryside flashing by outside, and talked about things there hadn't been time to discuss in their busy workaday schedules.

Carella was most concerned about having to give away both his mother *and* his sister at their joint weddings this coming June. How was he supposed to do that? Come down the aisle with one of them on each arm? Or lead his mother down first, a nod to seniority, and then go back up for his sister. While Luigi . . .

'I really wish his name wasn't Luigi,' he said, signing simultaneously. 'It really makes him sound like a wop.'

He's Italian, Teddy signed. *That's a very common name in Italy.*

'Yeah, well, this is America,' he said, and then something occurred to him. 'You don't think she'll be *moving* to Milan, do you?'

Well, of course, she will, Teddy signed. *That's where he lives.*

'How come I didn't think of that till now?'

Maybe that's what's troubling you about taking them down the aisle.

'Maybe *everything* is troubling me about taking them down the aisle.'

Get over it, Teddy signed.

He nodded, and then fell silent for a while, thinking again that his mother shouldn't be remarrying so soon after his father's death, and his sister shouldn't be marrying the man who'd unsuccessfully prosecuted his father's slayer. Well, get over it, he thought. You should have got over it last Christmas already, put it to rest, okay?

They're getting married, you're giving them away, put on a happy face.

Come June sixteenth, his mother would be Mrs Luigi – Jesus, I hate that name! – Fontero, and his sister would be Mrs Henry Lowell, whom he suspected he'd have to start calling 'Hank,' the way his sister did, 'Could you please pass the gravy, Hank?'

Luigi and Hank.

Jesus.

Teddy was talking again. He turned to watch her hands. He loved the way she signed, her fingers moving almost liquidly, her eyes and her face adding expression to what she was saying, her lips mouthing the words her hands signaled. She was telling him she had to find a job. She was telling him she was tired of addressing envelopes at home, she wanted to get out into the real workplace. She'd been checking the want ads, but these were difficult times, and being so limited . . .

'You're not limited,' he told her.

Well, if I can't hear, I won't exactly be hired as conductor of the Philharmonic, she said, and burst out laughing

Carella laughed with her.

'How about moderator on a talk show?' he suggested.

Good idea, she said. *Or a translator at the UN.*

The countryside flashed by.

Spring was alive out there.

It was a very short ride.

THEY TOOK A TAXI to the Raleigh Hotel, and Carella settled her in the coffee shop while he went to find the manager.

The manager's name was Floyd Morgan. He told Carella at once that he hated the job up here because the winters were so damn cold. 'Well, look at it,' he said.

'It's already the end of April, and there's still snow on the ground up here, can you believe it?' He told Carella that the last managerial position he'd held was in the Bahamas, at the Club Med there on Columbus Isle. 'Now *that* was a job,' he said. 'Great people to work with, wonderful food, and an atmosphere of . . . *joy*, do you know? Happiness. Not like here. Here it's doom and gloom all winter long and by the time May rolls around, you're ready to jump out the window. Have a seat,' he said, 'let me get some coffee for us. You've had a long journey, you must have a lot of questions to ask.'

Carella did indeed have a lot of questions to ask.

In police work, it was always a matter of how best to utilize one's time and assets, especially now that travel had become so difficult. It would have seemed simpler and cheaper all around to have done this by telephone; he'd had to call, anyway, to set up this Saturday appointment. But there were too many people he needed to talk to here, and he couldn't have done that on the phone. Moreover, there were no nuances in a phone call. You could not see a person's face, his eyes, you could not detect the tremor of a lip, or a slight hesitation. A catch in the voice, a change of tone, any of which might indicate a lie or merely a bit of information being withheld. Face to face, you saw and heard it all.

He let Morgan have it flat out.

'I'm trying to find out if Lester Henderson had a woman with him last weekend,' he said.

Morgan hesitated, and then said, 'You understand, of course . . .'

Carella was about to hear the speech he'd already heard from 10,012 hotel managers, the one about the privacy of guests and the hotel's responsibility to protect a guest's rights and privileges, the same speech he'd heard from priests and lawyers and even accountants, on occasion, so he cut immediately to the chase by saying the magic words, 'Yes, but this is a homicide.'

Smiling understandingly as he said the words.

Yes, I know the difficulties of weighing civic duty against corporate obligation. But a grievous breach has taken place here, and I am but a mere public servant attempting to address this wrong and correct it, so I truly would appreciate candor and honesty because this is a homicide, you see, and that is the worst possible crime, sir, so please help me solve it because this is a homicide.

'I would have to check our records, sir,' Morgan said.

He led Carella into the Business Office and asked someone there to pull up the registration records for the past weekend. As Carella suspected, Lester Henderson had occupied a single room, albeit with a king-sized bed, and had registered as he himself alone, Lester Lyle Henderson.

'The rate would have been higher for a double,' Morgan said.

Carella was tempted to ask why hotels charged more for double occupancy than single. A room was a room, wasn't it? No matter how many people were in it? Well, maybe they provided more towels and little bottles of shampoo if they rented it as a double. He was sure there had to be a reason. Maybe this went back to the so-called blue laws, when women weren't allowed to drink at the bar, or – for all he knew – occupy hotel rooms with men who weren't their husbands.

'Could you check your records for a woman with the first name Carrie?' he asked. 'Who also might have been here last weekend.'

'That . . . might be difficult,' Morgan said.

'This is a homicide,' Carella said.

'Let me see if the computer can do a find.'

The computer did, in fact, 'do a find' – but it found nothing for anyone named Carrie.

'How about the initials JSH?' Carella said.

'Really, I don't see how . . .'

'Do a find for last names beginning with the letter "H,"' Carella said. 'Then narrow it to first names beginning with "J," and if you get lucky, close in on the "S." This would've been a woman, too.'

'JSH,' Morgan said.

'Please.'

Three women whose last names began with the letter 'H' had checked in last Saturday. All three worked for IBM. Only one of them had a first name beginning with the letter 'J.' She had signed in as Miss Jacqueline Held, no middle initial, and had given an address in Charlotte, North Carolina.

'How old was she, would you know?' Carella asked.

'Our records would not show that,' Morgan said.

'How about the room clerk who checked her in? Would he remember?'

'She,' Morgan corrected. 'Everyone behind the registration desk is a woman.'

'Would the same room clerk be working today?'

'Usually we have the same people on weekends, yes.'

'Can we find out which one of them checked in Miss Held?'

'Nothing is impossible,' Morgan said, and then added – somewhat sarcastically, Carella thought – 'This is a homicide, you know.' But he was smiling.

The clerk who'd checked in Miss Jacqueline Held recalled her as a dark-haired woman in her forties with a distinct Southern accent.

'What room was Henderson in?' Carella asked.

'We'll have to go back to the Business Office,' Morgan said, and briskly led the way down the corridor. Carella got the impression that he was beginning to enjoy himself. Well, it had been a long hard winter.

The computer showed that Henderson had stayed in room 1215, which was occupied at the moment.

'How about the maid who cleaned that room?' Carella asked. 'Is she working today?'

'Well, let's see if we can find her, shall we?' Morgan said, sounding positively ebullient now.

Two maids had worked the twelfth floor that weekend. Both of them were from Brazil. One of them was short, the other very tall. The short one spoke only Portuguese. The tall one's English was halting at best. She told Carella that she vaguely remembered the people who had occupied –

'People?' he said.

'Man and girl,' she said, and nodded.

'Can you describe them for me?'

'Man short, eyeglasses, maybe forty-five. Girl blond, maybe eighteen, nineteen. Maybe was daughter, no?'

The short maid suddenly began shaking her head and speaking in rapid Portuguese.

'What is it?' Carella asked.

'She says wasn't daughter. The girl.'

'She saw her, too?'

'*Você também a viu?*'

'*Claro que vi ela. Eles estavam esperando o elevador.*'

'She says, Yes, she saw her. They were waiting for the elevator.'

'What makes her think this wasn't his daughter?'

'*Por que você acha que ela não era filha dele?*' the tall one asked.

'*Porque eles estavam se beijando,*' the short one said.

166

The tall one turned back to them and shrugged.

'Because they were kissing,' she said.

The Business Office showed no room service charges for Henderson on Saturday night. Neither had he charged anything to the hotel restaurant that night. The records did reveal, however, that he had charged his stay to an American Express card. Carella copied down the number and expiration date of his card, and then asked if he could use a telephone.

He stopped in the coffee shop first, found Teddy sitting alone at a table near the window, sneaked up behind her, kissed her on top of the head, and then came around to sit opposite her at the table.

'You okay?' he asked.

Her hands flying, she told him it was very nice sitting here in the window, watching all the comings and goings outside, somewhat like seeing a foreign movie with actors she didn't recognize. She kept making up stories about them in her head. Which of them were married, which of them were having affairs. which of them were business-men or spies . . .

I think I saw one who was positively a detective, she said.

He watched her hands, watched her lips mouthing the words.

'How do you know he was a detective?' he asked.

First off, he was very handsome . . .

'I don't know any detectives who are handsome,' he said.

I know one, she said.

He took her hands, kissed first one, and then the other.

'I have to make one phone call,' he said. 'Then we can have some lunch and start home. Will you be okay here?'

If I have any more coffee, I won't be able to eat lunch, she said.

'This'll take maybe ten, fifteen minutes,' he said.

Morgan found him a phone in a private little office, and provided him with an 800 number to call for American Express. The woman at the other end wanted to know how she could tell for sure he was a police detective. He gave her his shield number, gave her the number at the precinct, gave her his lieutenant's name, even gave her the name of the Chief of Detectives and the number to call at Headquarters to verify that he was for real. She asked him to hold while she talked to her supervisor.

Carella waited.

The woman came back some five minutes later.

'Sorry, Detective Carella,' she said, 'we have to check. What can I do for you?'

He explained what she could do for him.

AT LUNCH, he told Teddy what he had learned today.

'He was definitely here with the girl. One of the maids saw him kissing her while they were waiting for an elevator.'

Romantic, Teddy signed.

'Very. Unless you're married to someone else.'

You'd better never, she said.

'My guess is she checked into a separate room, snuck down the hall each night to sleep with him.'

Like the English do, Teddy said. *At country houses on weekends down from London.*

'Yes, exactly like the English do,' he said. 'How do you know what the English do in country houses on weekends?'

Movies, she said, and shrugged.

'His Sunday morning room service charge was for *two* breakfasts. Bit careless, huh?'

Not if you don't think anyone'll come around checking.

'American Express gave me two restaurant charges for him. One for dinner on Saturday night, the other for dinner on Sunday. Nothing for lunch Saturday, that's when he was with the Governor. The Saturday night dinner cost two hundred bucks . . .'

Teddy rolled her eyes.

'You said it. Dinner on Sunday was a hundred and eighty. These were the best restaurants in town, but he couldn't have been alone unless he had an enormous appetite.'

Teddy nodded agreement.

'I'd like to check both restaurants, if you still have the patience. What it looks like, he sent his aide home, dallied with the blonde on Saturday and Sunday nights, and then . . .'

You didn't mention she was a blonde.

'A blonde, yes.'

Do you like blondes?

'Everyone likes blondes.'

How about you? *We're talking about you here. Do you like blondes?*

'I like brunettes with big brown eyes and enormous appetites.'

Am I eating too much?

'Not if you're hungry.'

I'm very hungry. How about one of these women who sign to the deaf on television shows? The ones you see on the side of the screen in a little box?

'Hey,' he said. 'Now *that's* a good idea.'

You think so?

'I really do.'

Wouldn't I have to hear what the anchors are saying?

'They work from scripts. You'll have a script.'

Is that what they do?

'Absolutely.'

The problem is . . .

Her hands stopped.

'What?' he said.

I'm not pretty enough, she said, and shrugged.

'You're beautiful,' he said.

Her eyes were suddenly brimming with tears.

But worthless, she signed.

He reached across the table and took her hands.

'Beautiful and valuable,' he said.

To you.

'To anyone with any sense at all,' he said, and got up in the crowded restaurant and walked around the table and tilted her face to his, and kissed her on the lips.

Someone across the room applauded.

THE MAITRE D' AT Amboise, the restaurant Henderson and his little blond friend had dined at on Saturday night, remembered the couple well.

'Yes indeed,' he said. 'He was a man in his late forties, I'd say, short, slim, with one of those haircuts you see on all those television politicians. They ought to get new barbers, don't you think?'

'And the woman with him?'

'Oh, very pretty. Very. A young blond girl, I thought at first she was his daughter.'

'What changed your mind?'

'Well, to begin with, he asked for a quiet table. And the girl said, 'A *romantic* table, please,' and squeezed his arm, you know the way they do. He ordered a bottle of champagne before dinner, and when they toasted, they looped their arms through each other, you know, hooked their arms together, and brought their heads close over the table, whispering to each other, you know the way they do. And they were holding hands all through dinner, and ... well, to put it plainly, they were behaving like sweethearts. I've never seen a father and daughter behave that way, and I've been in this business thirty-one years now.'

'How old would you say she was?'

'Eighteen? Nineteen? No older than that.'

'You didn't happen to hear her name, did you?'

'No, I didn't.'

'Wouldn't have heard him calling her "Carrie," would you?'

'I'm sorry, no.'

'What time did they leave here?'

'Well, the reservation was for eight, I think they left at around nine-thirty, it must have been. He had his arm around her. They were definitely not father and daughter. He told me the food had been delicious, and the girl said, 'Oh, yesss,' gushing, you know the way they do. Well, I'm *sure* she enjoyed the meal, she came back for lunch the next day.'

'What do you mean? He brought her here again on Sun . . .?'

'No, no. She was here alone. The girl. She came back alone. Walked in at about twelve-thirty, asked for the same table they'd had the night before. I was happy to oblige. We don't get much of a lunch crowd.'

'How did she pay?' Carella asked.

'Credit card,' the maitre d' said.

'I don't suppose . . .'

'Let me check.'

THE NAME ON the credit card was Carolyn Harris.

This did not jibe with the JSH monogram on the

stationery, but then again it never had, and now at least they had a last name.

And a first one, too, for that matter.

Carella called Kling from the train station and told him what he had. Kling said he'd get on it right away. The time was four fifty-nine, and the clock was ticking: Carella's train left at five-oh-seven.

Kling could find no listing for a Carolyn Harris in any of the city's phone directories.

Her credit card company adamantly refused to reveal her address. Kling told a supervisor in Arizona or wherever the hell she was that he would have to petition for a court order. She told him she was sorry he felt that way, but she had to protect the confidentiality of their clients, and so on and so forth, but at least she was live, which was better than listening to a menu with four hundred choices. But she knew damn well he would not petition for a court order.

Instead, he went down the list of the stores carrying Letter Perfect stationery, dialing each one in order, this time asking each and every one of them to please check for any monogrammed stationery order with the last name 'Harris,' the first initial 'J,' and the middle initial 'S.'

Each of the stores promised to get back to him.

One of them phoned at six-thirty that Saturday night, just as Kling was about to leave the squadroom.

The woman on the phone told him they'd taken that particular stationery order six months ago, on the phone, from a charge customer named Joanna Susan Harris, who lived in Fort Lauderdale, Florida. Kling wrote down her address, dialed 411 for information, and phoned her not a moment later. He told her who he was, and then asked if she had a daughter named Carolyn.

'What is it?' Mrs Harris said at once. 'Has something happened to her?'

'No, ma'am,' Kling said, 'she's fine. But we're investigating a case here . . .'

'Has she done something wrong?'

'No, no, please, believe me, she's not in any sort of trouble. We'd like to ask her some questions about the victim, though, a man we think she may have known.'

There was a long silence on the line. When Mrs Harris spoke again, she sounded suddenly very distant.

'I see,' she said.

'Would you know where we can reach her, ma'am?'

'Why?'

'So we can . . .'

'Is she going to need a lawyer?' Mrs Harris asked.

'I don't think so. Why would she need a lawyer?'

'You said victim.'

'Yes, ma'am, this is a homicide we're investigating.'
Another long silence. Then:

'Is she a suspect?'

'No, ma'am.'

'Then why . . .?'

'We're tracking the victim's whereabouts, we think your daughter may have been with him on the day before the murder.'

'Then she *is* a suspect.'

'No, ma'am, I would not say she's a suspect.'

'I won't give you her address,' Mrs Harris said, and hung up.

He called her back at once.

'Mrs Harris,' he said, 'don't hang up on me again, okay? This is a homicide we're investigating, and we need to know your daughter's address. If I can't get it from you on the phone, then I'll go to the Grand Jury here for a subpoena compelling you to testify. Our DA will make a call to the prosecutor in Broward or Dade, or wherever you are, and he'll go to a local court for an order supporting the subpoena. Next thing you know, there'll be a sheriff on your doorstep, and you'll be flying up here to face the Grand Jury, who'll either get the address from you or charge you with contempt. Air travel is no picnic these days, ma'am, so why not save all of us a lot of trouble and give me the address right here and now?'

'You are a bully, young man,' Mrs Harris said.

But she gave him the address.

12.

The Needle got back to me on Wednesday morning, the day after Mercer Grant came to report his missing wife. By that time my associate Barry Lock had trailed Grant to several different apartments in the city and could not say with certainty that Grant lived in any of them. He had finally lost him when he went into the Barnes & Noble on Thirty-fifth Street, where Lock observed him reading several magazines he did not offer to buy, while sipping a cappuccino he had apparently purchased.

But that's where Lock lost him because, you should pardon this, Commish – and this is just between you and I, or maybe even you and me – he had to relieve himself. And while he was in the back of the store where the men's room was, Grant took it in his head to depart, whether by coincidence or design. In short, I still didn't know where he lived. So it was with considerably great expectations that I took the call from The Needle that morning. Hopefully, The Needle . . .

Or perhaps I hoped The Needle . . .

Or maybe I was even hopeful that The Needle . . .

Hopefully, The Needle would have some information on Grant or his missing wife Marie or his cousin Ambrose Fields. To which extent, I held my breath and prayed to the good Lord above.

'What have you got for me?' I asked.

'Well, the picture ain' bright, but neither be it dim. I can't find neither hide nor hair of him.'

'Then how do you figure the picture's bright, Morty?'

The Needle did not like being called Morty when his true and honorable name was Mortimer. He once told me that Mortimer is a name from the old Anglo-French, and that it means 'one who lives near the sea,' which might have been okay if he was still living in Jamaica, which was surrounded by water, but not if you lived in this city, which was surrounded by thieves of all kinds. Besides, I didn't like Jamaicans putting on airs, so every now and then I called him Morty to get a rise out of him. It did not get a rise out of him that morning. He went on with his report as if I hadn't even addressed him.

'I tink I know what dee RUF mean. But it ain no di'mons, it's a whole 'nother scene.'

'If it's not diamonds, what . . .?'

'These conflic' di'mons, they also called "blood." An' the folks dat trade 'em is nothin but crud.'

'What makes you think the RUF isn't involved here?'

'Blood di'mons is rare on dee street dese days. What we lookin' at here is a new kinda craze.'

'Like what, Morty?'

176

'What I got from a lady whose name is Grace, is dee RUF is a <u>underwears</u> place.'

'Underwear?'

'What you put on first . . .'

'I <u>know</u> what underwear . . .'

'. . . when you gettin dressed. So yo outer clothes dey don' get all messed.'

'What do you mean by an underwear place? A lingerie shop?'

'What I mean is a <u>fac'try</u> by dee River Dowd. Where dey makes underwears for dee upper-class crowd.'

'What kind of underwear?'

'Lacy bras, garter belts, frilly panties an' such. If you want to hear more, it won't coss you too much.'

'<u>How</u> much, Morty?'

'Fo' dee name, fo' dee address, pay me juss a fin . . .'

'No way!'

'Make it four an' a half, and I'll cave right in.'

'That's still too high.'

'Den how about four, do dat sound too dear? Shall I take a walk, or you want to hear?'

'Three hundred is all I can go, Morty.'

'Mother mercy of God, why dee girl so <u>cheap</u>? Kinda money like dat ain' wurt even a peep!'

'Morty, I'm not in the mood for a stickup in a dark alley!'

'Okay den, fine, make it t'ree twenty-five. Do we have a deal? Are we still alive?'

'Three twenty-five. Let me hear it. And it better be good.'

'On dee River Dowd, Queen Elizabeth side,' Mortimer said, his voice lowering to a whisper. 'Tink I'll come along wid you, juss for dee ride.'

'What's the name and address?'

'I tell you doze when I gets dee pay. Otherwise I see you some udder day.'

'Trust me, Morty.'

'Run hide dee silver, cause dee lady wants trust . . .'

'Morty . . .'

'Never see her again once she makes dee bust.'

'You can trust me, you know that. What's the name and address?'

Mortimer sighed deeply.

'Juss between you an' I, or perhaps you an' me, it's the Rêve du Jour Underwears Factory.'

'Rêve du Jour Underwear,' I said. 'Never heard of it. Where is it?'

'Accordin to dee lady whose name is Grace, it's twenty-one, forty-four Riverview Place.'

'Thank you, Mortimer.'

'You owe me t'ree an' a quarter,' he said.

The trouble with Livvie's city was that it was imaginary. The people, the places in her pages were all fictitious. For all Emilio knew, even the police routine was phony and not based on established investigatory technique. He realized that this was what she'd had to do in order to throw the bad guys off her track, but man it certainly made things difficult for a person trying to rescue her.

He thought of himself as her rescuer.

Her savior.

Her knight in shining armor.

The person who would kick in the door to that basement, wherever the hell it was, clutching her brave report in his hands and crying, 'I'm here, Olivia, what ho!'

Was what they cried in novels and movies.

But, still, he wished she hadn't made it so damn complicated. Things were complicated enough these days without imaginary cities with imaginary places in them. For example . . .

Where was this bar two blocks from Livvie's station house?

And where was this factory across the river?

He had just learned from reading her report yet another time that there was a ladies underwear factory across the river, which was exciting in itself, all garter belts and panties and such. He supposed 'dee River Dowd' was the River Dix in real life, and he further guessed that the 'Queen Elizabeth side' of the river was Majesta, directly over the bridge. But none of this brought him any closer to finding the basement Livvie was trapped in.

He wondered if he should read her report yet another time from top to bottom because, to tell the truth, it was very lively reading and it gave him some very keen insights into the workings of a woman's mind, which he could use in his business, as it were, or even was. On the other hand, wouldn't it be more profitable to take a stroll over the bridge, scope the neighborhood there, see if there was anything that even *sounded* like Rêve du Jour Underwear Factory at 2144 Riverview Place, which of course was a phony street name in Livvie's imaginary city.

He wondered if Aine would like to come with him.

Sometimes, if you offered a dealer a two-fer, he gave you a break on the price.

Emilio let her phone ring a dozen times.

Either she was out looking for a bar two blocks from a police precinct, or else she was laying on the floor stoned out of her mind.

So he headed for the bridge all by his lonesome.

THE STREETS ON either side of the Majesta Bridge were perhaps among the noisiest in the entire city. Teeming with vehicular traffic, the approaches to the bridge seemed miles long, although in actuality they measured only several blocks. The din was relentless. Taxis, trucks, passenger cars honked their horns incessantly.

The building Carolyn Harris lived in was in the shadow of the bridge. If Emilio Herrera had looked down as he started across the bridge that morning at ten, he would have seen two detectives talking to the doorman outside. He wouldn't have recognized them, and in any case he wouldn't have known they were detectives. Emilio had met many detectives in his checkered career, but not these two. Besides, the only detective on his mind right now was Olivia Wesley Watts.

The doorman was telling Carella and Kling that he'd seen Miss Harris leaving the building for church at a quarter to nine this morning. He expected she'd be back by eleven. What she usually did was go to nine o'clock mass, take holy communion, and then have breakfast afterward at a deli on Bradley.

'Did she do that last week, too?' Kling asked.

'No, sir,' the doorman said. 'She was out of town last week.'

'Bradley and where?' Carella asked.

They recognized her at once because she was the only blonde eating in the place, sitting in a booth, her back to the entrance doors. They debated just going in and sitting opposite her in the booth, and then decided to wait outside until she'd finished her breakfast. They let her walk a respectable distance from the deli, and then caught up with her on the street corner. Even on a Sunday, the noise was horrific.

'Miss Harris?' Carella said.

She turned, surprised.

She was sporting a shiner the color of Burgundy wine.

'Yes?' she said.

'Detective Carella,' he said, and flashed the tin. 'My partner, Detective Kling.'

She knew at once.

'This is about Lester, isn't it?' she said.

'Yes, miss, it's about Lester. What happened to your eye?'

'Nothing. A bee stung me.'

Which was perhaps more inventive than 'I walked into a door,' or 'I got hit with a tennis ball,' or 'I fell off the toilet bowl,' or any one of the dozen or more reasons abused women found to alibi the men who were abusing them.

Carella let it pass. For now.

'Few questions we'd like to ask you,' he said. 'If you've got a minute.'

They walked several blocks downtown and then south to the river where a pocket park nestled at the water's edge. The noise was less frightful here; it merely sounded like distant thunder. Across the river, they could see Majesta with its factories and smoke stacks. They did not know, nor would it have meant anything to them, that at about that time, Emilio Herrera was just leaving the bridge's footpath and coming down the steps to the street below.

'How did you find me?' Carrie asked.

'The stationery,' Carella said.

181

'My mother's,' she said, and nodded. 'I shouldn't have used her stationery. She let me take some home with me when I went down to see her last winter. She lives in Florida, you know . . . well, I guess you *do* know if that's how you got to me, her stationery.'

'Miss Harris,' Carella said, 'where were you last week at around this time?'

'I was with Lester Henderson.'

'Where?'

'The Raleigh Hotel. Upstate. The capital.'

'You had a room at the Raleigh, did you?'

'Yes. But we spent most of the time in his room.'

'Did you have dinner with him last Saturday night, at a restaurant called Amboise?'

'Yes, I did.'

'Did you go back there for lunch alone the next day? Sunday?'

'Yes.'

'And did you have dinner with him that Sunday night at a restaurant called The Unicorn?'

'Yes, I did. We did.'

'Did you spend Sunday night with him as well?'

'Yes.'

'Did you accompany him home on Monday morning?'

'Yes, we took the same plane back to the city, yes.'

'The same early plane.'

'Seven-ten, it was, I believe.'

'Then what, Miss Harris?'

'I don't know what you mean.'

'Where did you go from the airport?'

'Home.'

She looked surprised. Where do you think I went? Where would you go from the airport? You'd go home, wouldn't you? Well, that's where I went. Home.

'You didn't go to King Memorial, did you?'

'No, of course not. Lester went his way, I went mine. He's married, you know.'

Carella refrained from saying, Yes, *I* know. Did *you* know?

'What happened to your eye?' he asked again.

'I told you. I got stung by a bee.'

'When?'

'When?'

Again the surprised look. What difference does it make *when* I got stung? Did you ever get stung by a bee? Then don't ask me *when* I got stung!

'Yes,' Carella said. 'When?'

'Last night, okay?'

'Looks older than that,' Kling said. 'Did you see a doctor about it?'

'No. I put an ice pack on it.'

'Last night?'

'*Yes*, last night,' she said, her voice rising in indignation, a host of unspoken words once again flaring in her eyes and curling on her lip: Why are you asking me the same question over and over again, don't you *believe* me? Why would I lie about a goddamn bee sting? How dare you not *believe* me? My mother has a condo in Fort Lauderdale, my mother orders monogrammed stationery that costs a fortune!

All of this in her eyes and on her face.

'Who hit you?' Carella asked.

'*Not* Lester, if that's what you're thinking.'

'Then who?'

'Nobody.'

'Nobody, but not Lester, huh?'

'What is this? You don't think *I* killed him, do you?' she said, and tried a laugh. 'Is *that* what you think?' The

183

laugh died, the indignation flared again in her green eyes. My mother has *attorneys*, her eyes said. How dare you?

But somebody had smacked her in one of those lovely green eyes, and the flesh surrounding it was still discolored red and purple and blue.

'Who hit you?' Carella asked again. 'And *when?*'

'My *boyfriend*, okay?' she shouted.

THE WAY SHE tells it, she was going steady with this boy from school . . .

'I go to Ramsey U,' she said, 'I'm a sophomore there, an English major.'

. . . when she met Lester Henderson while he was giving a talk for the Political Science Department. She went up to chat with him afterward, and to get him to sign this book he'd written titled *Why the Law?*, and to ask the questions she hadn't had a chance to ask from the floor even though she kept waving her hand at the guy with the microphone. Mr Henderson . . .

'I was still calling him Mr Henderson then.'

. . . told her if she'd like to continue the discussion over a cup of coffee, he'd be happy to, and she said sure because he was so very cute and all in a dynamic, forceful, vibrant, vigorous sort of way, not like Lucas at all.

'Lucas is my boyfriend,' she said. '*Was* my boyfriend.'

'Lucas what?'

'Riley,' she said.

'Is he the one who hung the shiner on you?'

'Yes.'

'Last night?'

'No.'

'When?'

'Monday morning. After I got back to the city.'

'Why?'

'He found out about Lester.'

The way she explains it, she kept seeing Lucas because, after all, he'd pinned her and everything. But at the same time she was seeing Lester once or twice a week, sometimes three or four times, depending on how often he could get away from his wife, and how often she could tell Lucas she had to study for a Chaucer test or something. This had been going on since last November, you know, when Lester spoke at the school, just after Thanksgiving, between Thanksgiving and Christmas was when it started. But Lucas never suspected anything at all, well, you know Lucas, he's so laid back about everything. Until Monday morning.

'On Monday, he came to my apartment . . .'

'What time was this?'

'Around eleven-thirty.'

'Came to your apartment, yes.'

'And told me he knew where I'd been that weekend . . . and . . . and started to hit me.'

'Did he know you'd been with Henderson?'

'Yes.'

'He told you that?'

'Not in those words.'

'What words?'

'He called him "That fucking cheap politician."'

'But he knew it was Henderson.'

'Yes, he knew.'

'Where does your boyfriend live?'

'He's not my boyfriend anymore.'

'Where does he live?'

'831 Granger. Near the school.'

FATS DONNER didn't call Ollie until twelve noon that Sunday. He announced himself to the desk sergeant as

'William Donner,' which didn't ring a bell until Donner said, somewhat impatiently and heatedly, 'Fats Donner, tell him it's *Fats* Donner,' at which time the sergeant recognized a snitch if ever there was one. He put Donner through at once.

'You should tell your people to be more alert,' Donner said.

'Why, what happened?' Ollie asked.

'I'm calling with valuable information, and the man doesn't recognize my name.'

'Gee, I'm sorry about that,' Ollie said. 'What have you got for me?'

'I've got Emmy,' Donner said.

ROSIE WASHINGTON was not an easy person to keep in sight. A not uncommon mix of Hispanic and African blood, she was a good-looking, light-skinned woman in a community that boasted of many such racial blendings. If she were Chinese, it would be a different story. But the only Chinks up here ran laundries or places that gave women manicures, though Parker supposed the girls who worked in the nail parlors were all Koreans, same fuckin difference.

What Parker was trying to do was ascertain that the buy this coming Tuesday night would indeed take place in the basement of the building at 3211 Culver Av. Toward that end, he thought it might prove providential to put a discreet tail on the lady. His reasoning was that if three hundred large was about to change hands on Tuesday at midnight, the lady would at least case the joint first to make sure she wasn't stepping into another setup like the one on the rooftop with the Miami spics. The Gaucho hadn't actually *said* they were spics, but what else could dope buyers from Miami be? Anyway,

Palacios was a spic himself, so what did you expect him to say? My *compadres* ripped off a nice Spanish lady?

All things considered, Rosie Washington was in fact rumored to be a nice lady. That is to say, in a racket where sudden extermination was always a distinct possibility, she hadn't killed anyone yet – or at least she hadn't committed any murders the police *knew* about yet. This was not to say there weren't a multitude of bodies at the bottom of the river or in the trunks of cars at the airport, or even buried in somebody's basement, maybe even the basement in which the lady would be selling cocaine worth three hundred thousand dollars this Tuesday night. It merely meant that for someone who'd been in the business as long as Rosie had, she'd managed to stay remarkably beyond the reach of the law. Except for a minor possessions charge when she was nineteen years old and presumably still learning her trade, there was nothing on her in the files.

Parker hoped to change all that this Tuesday night.

Actually, following Rosie was not such a terrible chore. In fact, it was almost enjoyable. For a woman who was now forty-seven – according to her date of birth at the time of the single possessions bust – she had a very sweet little ass that was a definite pleasure to observe. Swinging up the avenue in a tight black skirt, she looked like any one of the hookers patrolling this turf. Then again, to Parker *all* Puerto Rican girls looked like hookers.

But where was she going in such a hurry?

ROSITA WASHINGTON knew she was being followed.

This troubled her.

The buy was supposed to go down this coming Tuesday at midnight, and this was now already past twelve o'clock on Sunday afternoon and some clumsy cop who

187

looked like a homeless person was on her tail. It was one thing to have to worry about the people supposed to be buying the product from you. It was another to have to worry that maybe the cops had found out. But how?

Two brothers coming toward her from the opposite direction smacked their lips and rolled their eyes and craned their necks at her as she went by. She wanted to tell them Yo, mind your fuckin manners, okay? but you never knew who was carrying a box cutter these days, or even a gun, so it was just better to keep your mouth shut and let them come in their pants.

She stopped to look in the window of a shop selling running shoes and barbells and all kinds of fitness shit, when all she wanted to do was take a quick peek up the street to see if Mr Law was still on her ass. There he was, stopping to light a cigarette as if he was paying her no mind, oh my what a smart detective you are, mister. Made you the minute you picked me up outside my building, now the problem is how to *shake* you.

She went in the A & P up the street, and then hurried to the ladies' room at the back of the store, figuring to stay in there awhile, let him believe he'd lost her. She'd have gone out the back way, but there wasn't no back way cause there were too many thefts in the hood, you had only one way in and out most stores so you could keep an eye on a woman suddenly got pregnant with a sack of potatoes under her coat. He was waiting outside when she finally hit the street again, pretending to be studying the Mother's Day display of flowering plants on a cart outside the store – was Mother's Day already here? Man, the way these holidays snuck up on you! She marched right past him without skipping a beat, just as if he wasn't there, and kept on walking till she got to a place she *knew* had a back door.

The lettering on the plate glass window of the shop read:

EL CASTILLO DE PALACIOS

She opened the door and went in.

A little bell tinkled over the door. She closed the door behind her, glanced quickly through the window to make sure the cop was still with her, and then smiled as The Gaucho came out from the back to greet her.

13.

WELL NOW, Parker thought, isn't this interesting?

The Gaucho is giving us information on a Rosie Washington deal going down this Tuesday night, and here's Rosie herself marching into his shop big as daylight on Sunday afternoon, will wonders never?

Of course, they were both spics, so who knew *what* evil the two of them had cooked up together?

Half-spic, anyway, in her case.

He took up a position across the street, thinking maybe he should try to get a court order to plant a bug in The Cowboy's shop.

THE FIRST THING Palacios thought as he came through the beaded curtains from the back of his shop was that Rosie knew he'd ratted her out.

'Hey, hello, Rosie,' he said, smiling. 'What brings you here?'

'I need a dreams book,' she said. 'For my cousin.'

Not everyone knew what kind of a shop Palacios ran *behind* his shop. Most people truly did come in for religious, paranormal, or supernatural items. So it was entirely possible that Rosie had a cousin who needed a book that would explain the significance of a recent dream so that she'd know whether she was going to win the lottery or fall under a spell instead. No one but the police knew that Palacios was an informer. Well, of course not.

If everyone knew how he picked up a few extra pennies, how could he ever garner any information at all? It was terrifying to think that Rosie had somehow discovered he'd be getting a tidy little sum after they busted her this Tuesday night. Rosie was not in the business of selling violets to opera goers. Rosie was in a business where people broke other people's heads and shot them in the balls.

'What kind of dreams has your cousin been having?' Palacios asked.

'She's been dreaming that a cop is following her,' Rosie said, and Palacios went pale. 'Gaucho,' she said in a rush, 'I think the law is on my tail. Can I go out your back door?'

Palacios almost wet his pants in relief.

AT FIRST, Ollie thought the girl sitting on the park bench with Donner was the Emmy he was looking for. The girl was a blonde, wearing a short blue skirt and knee-high blue socks, flat brown shoes, and an abundant white blouse. As he came closer to the bench, however, he realized that the girl couldn't be older than thirteen.

'Go play, Heather,' Donner told her. 'But don't get lost.'

'Okay, Bill,' the girl said, and smiled at Ollie, and then walked off toward the playground equipment on the hill.

'Little old for you, ain't she?' Ollie said.

'Yeah, well, times are difficult,' Donner said. 'You want to lecture me, or you want to hear about Emmy?'

'I'm listening.'

'She's a boy.'

Ollie looked at him.

'That's not what Stein told me.'

'Stein told you right. Emmy can pass for a girl any day of the week. But she ain't Emmy, she's Emilio. And Emilio's a boy.'

'Emilio what?'

'Ah-ha,' Donner said. 'That's where the cash comes in.'

'Do you have a last name for him?'

'I do.'

'Do you know where he lives?'

'I do not.'

'So how much do you want for this *valuable* information?'

'I told you. A deuce.'

'For just a name? No address?'

'The valuable information is that you're looking for a crossdresser. The minute I give you his name, you're on him like a bag of fleas.'

Ollie sighed.

'Lollipops cost,' Donner said philosophically.

Ollie opened his wallet. He took two hundreds from it, and handed them to Donner. Up on the hill behind them, Heather was on one of the swings, blue skirt flying, white panties showing. Donner fingered the bills.

'Herrera,' he said. 'Emilio Herrera.'

Of which there were probably ten thousand in this city alone.

LUCAS RILEY was perhaps twenty years old, they guessed, a skinny, blue-eyed kid some five feet, nine inches tall, freckles spattered all over his cheeks and the bridge of his nose, the map of County Donegal all over his face. He was wearing jeans, a Ramsey U sweatshirt, high-topped workmen's shoes, and a baseball cap turned backwards, the peak at the back of his head, the band on his forehead. They found him at last in the library at Ramsey U, and they asked him to come outside with them, please, and then walked him over to the school's football field, empty on Sunday except for some kids in jogging clothes running around the perimeter.

They sat in the stands under a clear blue sky.

The breeze was mild, the sun was shining.

But Lucas Riley had swatted a nineteen-year-old girl last Monday morning at eleven-thirty after he discovered she'd spent the weekend with Lester Henderson. And Henderson had been killed an hour or so before that.

'So tell us about it,' Carella said.

'I lost my temper.'

'Twice?'

'I don't know what that means.'

'Did you lose your temper with the councilman, too?'

'I never met the slimy bastard.'

'How'd you find out about them?'

'Her girlfriend.'

'Carrie's girlfriend?'

Lucas nodded. 'I called her Saturday night, I thought maybe Carrie was there studying with her, she told me she had a lot of studying to do that weekend. So Maria said No, she wasn't there, and she sounded sort of hesitant, you know, the way people do when they're hiding something, holding something back? So I said What is it, Maria? and she opened up, told me Carrie'd been seeing this older man since just after Thanksgiving, told me she was tired of making alibis for her, told me Carrie was upstate right that minute with the son of a bitch! I wanted to *kill* him!'

The detectives looked at him.

He seemed to realize what he'd just said, and immediately added, 'But I didn't.'

'You beat her up instead,' Kling said.

'I only hit her once.'

'Where were you before then?'

'Like say between ten and ten-thirty that morning?'

'I had an early class.'

'How early?'

'Nine o'clock. It let out at eleven. I went straight to Carrie's afterward. She was still unpacking from her big trip.'

'Where'd this class meet?'

'Morten Parker Hall. Room 713.'

'What's the instructor's name?'

'Dr Nagel.'

'What's his first name?'

'She's a woman. Phyllis, I think. Or Felice, I'm not sure.'

'Does she keep attendance?'

'I'm sure she does.'

'What sort of class is it?' Carella asked.

'Romantic Poetry,' Lucas said.

ROSITA THOUGHT these three people were total dummies, and she could not imagine how they'd managed to come up with three hundred thousand dollars, but they assured her they already had the money, and it was now merely a matter of ascertaining that she could deliver the product.

'How do we know you even *have* the jelly beans?' their apparent leader said.

His name was Lonnie Doyle, or so he'd said, she never believed any names that were exchanged in drug transactions. She herself had told them her name was Rosalie Wadsworth, which was close to Rosita Washington, but no cigar, thank you. She did not think Lonnie Doyle could possibly be this man's real name, but then again maybe he was stupid enough to have given her a square handle, who could tell when you were dealing with dummies?

One sure sign that these people were not playing with a full deck was the way they kept referring to the cocaine as 'jelly beans.' They were sitting at a back table in a little cuchi frito joint on Culver, maybe two or three other people in the place, plus the guy behind the counter. There was not the remotest possibility that anyone had planted a bug here, but they were using *code*, anyway, could you believe it! Jelly beans!

'I will have the jelly beans,' Rosita said. 'And they will be very high-grade jelly beans.'

Jesus, she thought.

Another one of the dummies, a guy who'd introduced himself as Constantine Skevopoulos, a phony name if ever there was one, asked if these 'jelly beans' would be in the quantity specified? He was a twitchy little man with a silly grin. 'Quantity specified' were the exact words he used. Dopey little grin on his face. Quantity specified.

'The *jelly beans* will . . .' Rosita started, and rolled her eyes, and because she knew there couldn't in a million years be a bug in this place, and since she knew Juanito behind the counter there was a little deaf in the bargain, she said flat out, 'The coke will come in ten-kilo lots at twenty thousand a lot, for a total of three hundred thousand dollars.'

The one named Harry Curtis looked suddenly alarmed, either by her having used the word 'coke' or else by the enormity of the purchase price, which Rosita had to admit was a thousand more per lot than the going price, but hey these were dummies. Harry Curtis – if that was his real name, which she felt sure it wasn't – was a huge man. He sat hunkered over the table like a grizzly bear, his eyes popping wide open when he heard Rosita talking about cocaine so openly. The other two looked startled as well, glancing around the room as if expecting an immediate raid, the dummies.

'So if we understand the purchase price,' Rosita said, 'and if we know how many *jelly beans* you'll be buying,' stressing the words, rolling her eyes again, 'all we need to settle, once and for all, is where the transaction will take place.'

'Don't say the address out loud,' Constantine said, twitching and grinning.

'Write it down,' Lonnie said.

'On a piece of paper,' Harry said.

Where else? Rosita thought. On the wall?

She opened her handbag, tore a sheet of paper from her address book . . .

'Letter it,' Harry said.

'So we can read it,' Lonnie said.

Constantine nodded and grinned.

In a large bold hand, Rosita lettered the address onto the sheet of paper:

3211 CULVER AVENUE

And then, just to show these dummies they were truly stupid to be worrying about a bug in a cuchi frito joint, she read the address out loud, anyway.

'Thirty-two eleven Culver Avenue,' she said. 'The basement. Be there. And bring the money.'

The three men hurried out of there as if their pants were on fire. Rosita lingered over her Coke – the soft drink, not the jelly bean – and then left the shop, passing a girl sitting at a table nearby. The girl was wearing a flared skirt and a white blouse, white ankle socks and brown loafers. She could have been your average Irish teenager were it not for the apathetic look that betrayed her for a drug addict. Rosita recognized the look at once; dope was her business. She nodded understandingly, perhaps even sympathetically, and walked past the girl and out of the shop.

The girl did not nod back.

The girl was Aine Duggan.

IT WAS NOT until ten past one that Parker realized Rosita had shaken the tail. He debated going into the shop and confronting Palacios with the accusation that he'd aided and abetted the very person Parker was following, but then that would alert the son of a bitch if he and Miss Washington with the swiveling little ass were trying to pull something funny here.

So he went back to the squadroom and told Eileen he thought the Washington woman had made him, and he suggested that Eileen pick up the surveillance. Otherwise they'd go down that friggin basement on Tuesday night —

He actually used the word 'friggin' in deference to Eileen's delicacy. Eileen found this amusing; in her many years as a cop, she had certainly heard the word 'fuck' in all its derivations. But even if she weren't a cop, which she most certainly was, all she had to do was go to the movies on any given Sunday, and she'd get an education she'd never received in church, believe me, Father Mulahy.

'Go down the friggin basement this Tuesday night,' Parker said, 'and find nothing there but cockroaches and rats. I think Palacios may be tryin'a pull something funny here.'

'Why?' Eileen asked. 'No bust, no money.'

Which was a thought.

'Maybe she's paying him more than we are,' Parker suggested.

'Why?' Eileen asked.

Another good thought.

'To steer us in the wrong direction.'

'You think Palacios would risk that?'

'I don't know what he'd do. I just don't want to look foolish on this thing.'

'So what do you want me to do?'

'Go down that basement tomorrow. Thirty-two eleven Culver. Check it out. Make sure we won't be walkin into some kinda booby trap there.'

'Why don't you go there yourself?' Eileen asked.

'Tomorrow's my day off,' Parker said.

'Then let's go there together. Right now.'

'It's almost quitting time,' Parker said.

'It's only two-thirty,' Eileen said.

'Yeah, but the clock is ticking,' Parker said. 'Time we got there, it'd be time we went home. Let it wait till tomorrow.'

'Okay,' Eileen said, and shrugged.

'What's that, that shrug?'

'I'll let it wait till tomorrow,' Eileen said, and shrugged again.

'You know, there's some things you ought to learn if you plan to stay here awhile,' Parker said.

'Oh, and what are these things?'

'These things are you don't try to second-guess your partner, and everything can always wait till tomorrow.'

'I didn't know I was second-guessing you.'

'And you don't sass him, either.'

'I see,' Eileen said.

'Just so we understand each other.'

198

'Oh, yes, perfectly. But tell me, Andy. Would you think I was second-guessing you if I checked out that basement right now? Because I have to tell you, the friggin clock *is* indeed ticking, and I don't want to walk into a mess of shit Tuesday night.'

'Be my guest,' Parker said, thinking he'd won the argument. 'You have the address.'

'I have the address,' she said, and turned and walked off with a hooker's strut, the bitch.

AINE DUGGAN was sitting in the hallway outside Emilio's apartment when he got back from Majesta at three that afternoon.

'Where you been?' she asked, rising and dusting off the back of her skirt.

'All over Majesta,' he said. 'There's no Rêve du Jour Underwear.'

'Gee, that's too bad,' Aine said.

She didn't know what the hell he was talking about.

'I walked all over the area. There's no such thing as Riverview Place, either.' He was unlocking the door. 'Not that I'm surprised,' he said, and retrieved his key. He swung the door open, and walked in ahead of her.

There was a mattress on the floor near the windows, an unpainted dresser he'd bought in a junk shop off Leighton, a floor lamp with a soiled and split linen shade, and that was it. Your everyday, garden variety junkie's pad. His toilet hadn't been cleaned since the day Julius Caesar got assassinated. Even Aine, who you could bet had seen some fine toilets in her life, was reluctant to pee in there.

'You running out of underwear?' she asked.

'No, I got plenty underwear.'

'So why were you looking for underwear?'

'I wasn't. I was looking for the diamonds.'

'What diamonds?' she asked, and flopped down on the mattress.

'In Livvie's report.'

'Livvie, right. *I* haven't worn underwear since I was seventeen,' she said. 'No bra, no panties, either.'

'That's evident,' he said, and glanced over at her where she lay somewhat carelessly on the mattress. Aine smiled like a blushing maiden, and pulled her skirt down over her knees.

'You still looking for that bar near a police station?' she asked.

'I am.'

'I think I found it.'

'Really? Where is it?'

'It's not called O'Malley's, though. It's called Shana-han's. And it ain't two blocks from the Oh-One, which as I suspected don't exist. It's two blocks from the Eight-Seven.'

'The Eight-Seven,' Emilio said, trying to place it. 'On Grover Avenue?'

'Facing the park, yeah. But the bar ain't on Grover. It's on St John's Road, two blocks over.'

'Too many streets in this damn city,' Emilio said.

'It's easy to find,' Aine said. 'I'll take you there, if you like. You ever feel like fucking anymore?'

'Not very often, no.'

'Neither do I. Smack's the best fuck I ever had.'

'Me, too.'

'Yeah,' she said.

They both fell silent, thinking about this basic truth, almost cherishing the knowledge that they were each and separately married to heroin.

'I think there's a big drug buy going down soon,' Aine said out of the blue.

'Good,' Emilio said. 'How do you know?'

'I heard these people talking in a cuchi frito joint on Culver. This Spanish broad, she looks Spanish, is selling ten-kilo lots at twenty large a lot.'

'That's a lot of lots,' Emilio said, making a joke, but Aine didn't catch it because she was doing arithmetic.

'Selling it for three hundred thou, that comes to fifteen lots.'

'That's a lot of lots,' Emilio said again, but she still didn't catch it. 'When's this gonna happen?'

'That's the only thing I don't know,' she said. 'A basement at 3211 Culver is where the buy's going down. A hundred and fifty keys of cocaine.'

Emilio looked at her.

'You don't think all that stuff's already down there in that basement, do you?' he asked.

THE BASEMENT was clean.

A table, four chairs around it, a wash sink in the corner.

Door at the back leading to the alley outside.

Steps coming down from the ground floor of the building above.

Eileen figured it'd be best to come in through the back door. Bust it open with a battering ram, surprise them at the table testing the dope and handing over the money. Rosita Washington wouldn't be coming here alone, that was for sure, not if the story about the Miami boys ripping her off was true. Her people would be armed. And so might the three grifters buying the stuff. She planned to ask Byrnes for a full-force raiding party, Kevlar vests and assault rifles, never mind any heroics Parker might have in mind.

She walked over to the back door, confirmed that a

Mickey Mouse lock was on it, looked around the room one last time, and then pulled the chain on the hanging overhead light bulb. In the scant daylight spilling from the narrow street-level windows, she found her way to the steps, and climbed them to the ground floor. She listened at the door there before letting herself into the building. A woman carrying two bags of groceries and climbing the steps to the first floor gave her only a backward glance. Eileen walked to the entrance foyer and let herself out into the street.

A young Hispanic male and an Irish-looking female were just approaching the building. The male stopped dead in his tracks. His mouth fell open. He looked directly into Eileen's face and said, 'Livvie?'

'Sorry,' Eileen said, smiling, and walked on past him.

Emilio turned to Aine and said, 'It was her, wasn't it?'

Or even she.

THE GIRLS usually started their stroll at nine, nine-thirty, sometimes even later. They'd learned from experience that nobody wanted to get laid too soon after dinnertime. These men were different from the ones who frequented the massage parlors. Those guys went upstairs at any time of day, whenever the urge hit them, some of them for quickies on their way to the train station before going home to their sweet little wives in the burbs. The johns here in Ho Alley were different.

You rarely saw a man on foot here. First off, it was too dangerous, and secondly you had to accommodate somebody like that with a room, and a room cost money, not to mention all the bother of finding one, it just didn't pay. The men looking for tail here usually cruised by in automobiles, casing the merchandise, and then drove up to the curb and parked, and waited for a girl to come over, and lean into the window, and talk business. The price of a handjob was fifty bucks. A blowjob cost a hundred. Nowadays, you couldn't get laid for less than three, and most girls didn't want to bother with intercourse at all. Most girls found intercourse too complicated, what with having to take off their panties and lift their skirts and place themselves in a vulnerable position on the back seat of a car in case the law showed. A handjob or a blowjob, you could perform on the front seat, sitting like a lady, fully clothed. Besides, most girls found intercourse too intimate. It wasn't any different on the street than in high school. Nowadays, in high school, a blowjob was the equivalent of a goodnight kiss.

Except for cops they knew, who were on the take and who would look the other way in return for any quick sex they could get, the girls were ever on the alert for the law. You got some jackass uniformed cop who didn't know how the system worked, he'd come around like some dumb preacher spouting hellfire and damnation, and next thing you knew you were in a holding cell waiting for night court. Or sometimes even a detective, although most of them knew better, they'd been around a long while, they knew how it worked, they couldn't care less if you blew the Mayor in broad daylight on the steps of City Hall. It was the young cops you had to watch out for. The ones who still believed.

The girls on stroll that night spotted Ollie for a cop the moment he entered the street. Maybe it was the arrogant stride, or the know-it-all look on his face. Or maybe it was because, first of all, he was on foot, and next he didn't seem to be seriously looking for a piece of ass. The hungry, desperate, guilty appearance of a bona fide john just wasn't there. In ten seconds flat, half the girls on the street disappeared into doorways, or walked around the corner, or simply went home for the night, they didn't need trouble from a fat flatfoot. The other half were otherwise engaged in parked automobiles all up and down the street. Ollie floated up Ho Alley like an aircraft carrier steaming into the Persian Gulf. He was looking for a blond Puerto Rican cross-dressing hooker named Emilio Herrera.

The first girl he talked to was just coming out of a parked Caddy near the closed Korean nail place up the block. She swung her legs out of the car, adjusted her short skirt, waggled her fingers goodbye to the white man behind the wheel, and turned to find a person who weighed perhaps a ton and a half standing there in her path, oh shit, she thought, a cop. The Caddy pulled away from the curb in a wink.

'Hi,' she said cheerily. 'You lost?'

'I'm looking for a friend of mine,' Ollie said.

'Oh?' the girl said, and looked him up and down. 'Maybe I can help instead.'

Maybe he wasn't a cop after all. Though a quick glance up the street revealed an amazing lack of pulchritude on display, a sure sign that the other girls on stroll had made him for what he was and had split the scene toot sweet.

'I'm really looking for this one particular person,' Ollie said.

Still hadn't flashed the tin, though, so who could tell? And if he was merely here looking for sex, why hand him over to anyone else?

'What's her name?' she asked. 'Though, you know, maybe I can help you.'

'She's a he,' Ollie said, and grinned like a hyena. 'Emilio Herrera, you know her? Him?'

'No, I'm sorry, I don't,' the girl said at once, and

then, 'In fact, I was on my way home, so if you'll excuse me . . .'

'Hold it just a second,' Ollie said. He was still smiling. The girl was thinking he was either a fat pig of a john who dug boys, in which case she didn't want to have anything to do with him, or else he was a fat pig of a cop looking to bust Emilio for narcotics use or breaking and entry, both of which pursuits Emilio was pretty good at. In which case she *still* didn't want to have anything to do with him.

'Emmy?' he said. 'He goes by the name Emmy?'

'Never heard of him *or* her,' the girl said.

'And what's your name?'

'Why is that important to you?'

'Because we like to know who's impeding the progress of a police investigation,' he said, and out came the tin, all blue and gold, Detective/First Grade it said on it. Oh shit, she thought again.

'I'm Talu,' she said.

'Talu indeed,' he said, 'ah yes.'

She wondered who he was imitating.

He sounded like Al Pacino in some movie she saw ages ago, before she got in the life.

She was wondering, too, how she could get him off her back about Emilio, whom she knew only as a transvestite junkie who catered to faggots who didn't know they were faggots. She didn't want trouble here tonight. A minute ago, she'd told him she was on her way home. Right now, that's all she wanted to do, go home, fast.

'And what may your last name be, m'little chickadee?'

'Diaz,' she said.

'In which case, you might be familiar with this Herrera girl or boy, as the case may be, who is yet another person of the Hispanic persuasion, not to mention the profession you both share.'

'I don't know what profession that is you're talking about,' Talu said.

'Ah me, a poor innocent adrift on the night,' Ollie said.

'If you don't mind, Detective, I'd really like to go home now.'

'Ah, but I thought I detected a faint glimmer in your eye when I mentioned the name Herrera,' Ollie said.

'No, I don't know the man.'

'Then I must have been mistaken, Talu.'

'Yes, you surely were.'

'In which case, do go home. And may God bless you,' he said.

She couldn't believe her own ears.

She turned and was out of there in a Taliban minute.

Ollie was thinking he'd hit the files when he got back to the office, see if they had anything that might connect little Miss Talu Diaz here, with her twitchy little ass and mile-high heels, to Mr Emilio Herrera, with his blond wig and big tits, who had not showed up on the computer, and who so far was –

A redheaded girl wearing a short black skirt and a pink halter top was coming around the corner. She spotted Ollie, smiled, came swiveling over on her spike heels, and said, 'I'm Anya,' it sounded like. 'Looking for a date, sweetheart?'

'IT'S DEFINITELY YOU he's looking for,' Aine said. 'He gave me your name. Emilio Herrera. He gave me your street name, too. Emmy. He said you're a blonde with big tits.'

'Well, I *am*,' Emilio said, and laughed.

He was high on marijuana. This was unusual for a heroin addict. She almost resented him being high. In fact, she *did* resent it. She was trying to give him important information here, and he was acting like a giggly little girl.

'Now that is very funny,' he said, and laughed. 'A big fat cop looking to fuck a little Puerto Rican boy with fake *tetas*. That is truly comical.'

'He wasn't looking for *sex*,' Aine said. 'He was looking for *you*. Do you understand me? He thinks you're involved in some kind of crime.'

'Well, I *am*,' Emilio said, and laughed again. 'Did he say which crime? Did he say possession, did he say burglary, did he say grand theft, auto, did he say prostitution? I am involved in a great *many* crimes, Aine. The man should have been more specific.'

'Well, he wasn't. He was on a fishing expedition, is what it was.'

'But you got the feeling he thought I was involved in some crime or another.'

'Yes, that's the impression I got.'

'He told you he was looking for me . . .'

'Yes.'

'. . . because I was involved in some crime or . . .'

'No.'

'He did *not* say I was involved in some . . .?'

'No, he didn't come out and say that. But it's what I discerned.'

He loved it when she used big words. He found it very amusing when she used big words. He wondered what crime he was supposed to be involved in. What did this fat cop want from him? Did he even *know* any fat cops?

'A *fat* cop, did you say?'

'Oh *man*, fat,' Aine said, and rolled her eyes.

'Did he tell you his name?'

'Detective Weeks.'

'From what precinct?'

'The Eight-Eight.'

'I'll bet he thinks I'm involved in that diamond deal.'

'What diamond deal?'

'In Livvie's report.'

'Who the fuck is Livvie?'

'The report she wrote.'

'Oh, *that* again,' Aine said.

'I'll bet he's after all those blood diamonds Livvie is locked up with in that basement,' Emilio said, and suddenly looked very sober, though he wasn't. 'Do you think it was her?' he asked. 'Do you think she got out of that basement somehow? Do you think she might be somehow involved in the big dope deal going down? Though I have to say I didn't see no dope down there, did you see any dope down there?'

'You know I didn't.'

'Are you sure you heard the address right? 3211 Culver?'

'I'm sure I heard what I heard,' Aine said.

'Maybe we should check out that bar you located,' Emilio said. 'What do you think, Aine?'

'You got any more of that grass?' Aine said.

14.

THE MINUTE OLLIE walked through the door of his apartment, the phone started ringing. He ran across the room, and was breathless when he picked up the receiver. Fats Donner was on the other end.

'I found your opera singer,' he said. 'Where can we meet?'

Ollie named a pizzeria on Culver and Sixth; what the hell, he thought, kill two birds with one stone.

'And don't bring your kindergarten class,' he said.

'I'll pretend I don't understand that,' Donner said, and hung up.

Ollie grabbed a bite from the fridge before heading out.

IF DONNER WAS remembering correctly, this was the same pizzeria where two hitters shot and killed Danny Gimp not too very long ago. This made him uneasy. He dimly recalled that the killing had had nothing at all to do with the profession he and Danny shared, but it still made him nervous to be sitting here in a public place with a cop as conspicuously large as Ollie, especially since he himself was not all that invisible. Such a pair could easily attract attention, he figured, and wished he'd asked Ollie to meet him at The Samuel Baths again.

'So who is she?' Ollie asked.

'How'd you make out with Herrera?'

'So far, he ain't worth the deuce I paid you, and I ain't all over him like fleas, either.'

'Maybe you're not such a good detective, dad.'

'Maybe I am. Maybe it's your information that stinks.'

'Then maybe you don't want to know who this opera singer is.'

'Maybe you'd like to give me her name free of charge, considering the Emilio Herrera stuff wasn't worth shit.'

'He's out there, all you have to do is find him. Do you want this on the opera singer, or do I walk?'

'Let's have a pizza,' Ollie said.

They ordered two pizzas, not for nothing were they men of considerable girth. Ollie ordered another one, which they split. Donner was thinking Ollie would try again for a free ride here. He was right.

'So tell me her name,' Ollie said.

'I'll need a hundred.'

'I already gave you two.'

'This is fresh information.'

'Like the last information was fresh, huh? Who has no record in the files and who I still can't find on the street.'

'Maybe you're looking on the wrong street.'

'Tell me why I should trust this new stuff?'

'Sure, dad. Number one, she *is* an opera singer. Number two . . .'

'She *what*?'

'She's an opera singer. In fact, she's currently doing a recital at Clarendon Hall. Are you familiar with Clarendon Hall?'

'Where the terrorists hit around New Year's?'

'The very.'

'She's singing there?'

'Right now.'

'Thanks,' Ollie said. 'Then I won't need her name.'

'You aced me, you fat hump,' Donner said, and bit into his pizza.

VERONICA D'ALLESANDRO was still onstage when Ollie got to Clarendon Hall at ten-thirty that night. He showed the manager his police identification and told him it was urgent that he speak to Miss D'Allesandro as soon as she came off. The manager thought this was about another terrorist attack.

Ever since the Israeli violinist was killed by a suicide bomber here last December, everyone in the city was on edge. The World Trade Center attacks hadn't helped much, either. Nor had what happened at the Pentagon. This was a nation of people walking on eggs. You saw anybody who looked like an Arab, you wanted to call the FBI. Ollie hated Arabs as much as he hated Jews or anybody else in this world. Ollie was an equal opportunity bigot. He felt anyone who didn't look or sound the way he himself did deserved a swift kick in the ass. The manager's name was Horowitz, which Ollie would have considered a major coincidence if he'd been at all familiar with classical music, which he wasn't. All he heard was a money-lending Jewish name, and suspected Horowitz would charge admission to go backstage. He was surprised when the man took him at once to the singer's dressing room.

Veronica D'Allesandro looked like that lady in all the Marx Brothers films, Geraldine Dumont or whatever her name was. A pouter pigeon chest with pearls hanging down its front, her hair clipped close to her head in what used to be called a bob, a pretty face for a woman her age. Ollie told her how much he'd enjoyed her performance, which he hadn't even heard, and then asked her if perchance she had purchased from a Jewish

211

pawnbroker named Irving Stein a tan pigskin Gucci dispatch case . . .

'Why yes!' she said, her eyes opening wide in surprise.

Ollie figured he'd impressed her.

'I'm sorry to have to tell you this, Miss Doll-a-sandri,' he said, 'but that case was stolen and is . . .'

'No!' she said.

'Ah, but yes,' he said. 'It is evidence sought in an auto smash-and-grab that took place on April twenty-second, the day before you purchased it.'

'Oh dear,' she said.

'I'm afraid I must reclaim that case,' Ollie said. 'Would you happen to . . .?'

'But I paid for it!'

'Seven dollars, if I'm correct.'

He was already reaching for his wallet.

'Yes, seven dollars,' she said, shaking her head in wonder.

Ollie figured he was still impressing her.

'The Department is required to reimburse you for reclaimed evidence,' he said, which wasn't true. 'Would you happen to have the case here with you?'

'Yes. I bought it for my music. I was carrying my music in it.'

'An appropriate use, ah yes,' Ollie said, and counted out seven singles and handed them to her. 'I hope you haven't handled it too much, we'll be looking for fingerprints.'

'Oh dear,' she said again.

'Yes, dear,' Ollie said, and smiled cordially. 'The case, please.'

The Rêve du Jour Underwear Factory was a squat brick structure nestled among a line of

212

similar but taller buildings on Riverview Place, at the edge of the River Dowd. I know you are familiar with many languages, Commish, this being a rainbow coalition city of many desperate or even disparate tongues. But in case you do not know what 'Rêve du Jour' becomes when it is translated from the original Spanish, which runs rampant in this city, then let me give you a bit of assistance.

'Rêve du Jour' means 'River of Joy.'

It was my guess, as I approached the building, that perhaps the owner or owners had derived the name from the proximate closeness of the factory to the river, but that was mere speculation, and detectives are not paid to speculate. Besides, a person – even a Spanish person – would never in a million years consider the Dowd a 'river of joy,' since it was more polluted than an Irishman on St Patty's Day – no offense, Commish, just a little metaphor there, or perhaps a simile.

A girl with short black curly hair and dark brown eyes was sitting behind the reception desk. She was not wearing a bra, which was surprising to me since this was an underwear factory. I must tell you that it is very difficult for a girl to find a proper bra these days, which is perhaps why the young lady behind the desk wasn't wearing one. The trick is to find something that enhances and supports simultaneously, but that also makes it look like you're not wearing a bra. At the same time, it can't be too revealing. That is to say, it shouldn't show your nipples and all through your outer garments. That may sound like mere girl talk, but believe me, I spend half my off-duty time searching for the right bra to enclose and enfold my not inconsiderate breasts. What I'm saying is that either the girl behind the desk was not wearing a bra, or else she was wearing a very good bra that made it look as if she wasn't wearing one.

I introduced myself to her and asked if I might speak to the owner of the establishment, please.

'Mais oui, madame,' she said, in what I took to be French, which surprised me, when one considered the Spanish origins of the company name. 'Will you 'ave a seat, if you please?'

You have to understand that the reception room of RUF was decorated with mannequins of women wearing bras and panties and garter belts and slips and camisoles and merry widows in reds and blacks and whites and blues and pinks and even purples. I took a seat on a sofa behind which were life-sized photographs on the wall of young women modeling many of the items the mannequins around the room were actually wearing. In effect, then, I was surrounded by a sea of female pulchritude and vertiginous femininity, so to speak, partially though scantily dressed or undressed, that would have turned the heads of many of my colleagues up the squadroom. There are times I am grateful for my gender and not easily distracted, believe me.

I was here to learn why Mr Mercer Grant, not his real name, had brought up the little matter of the RUF, which I was supposed to believe represented an African group that called itself the Revolutionary United Front, but which – I had learned through the kind auspices of one Mortimer 'Needle' Loop – actually stood for a Spanish lingerie company called the Rêve du Jour Underwear Factory. I was here to learn whether or not the people who owned this place knew anything at all about the disappearance and possible murder of one Marie Grant, not her real name, or her relationship with her husband's cousin, whose real name was also not Ambrose Fields.

In short, I felt I was hot on the scent of getting to the bottom of all this – no pun intended, Commish, in that the lady in the photograph behind me was bending over from the waist in a thong bikini that exposed her buttocks in a way that might have seemed enticing to many males.

I could have sworn the receptionist said, 'Mercer will see you now, <u>madame</u>.'

But no, what she'd actually said was '<u>Monsieur</u> will see you now, <u>madame</u>.'

She indicated a red door set between a photograph of a very tall leggy blonde wearing a white camisole and white lace panties and a very tall leggy brunette wearing a black bra and black lace panties. I opened the door and entered a hallway hung with similar photographs of similar models wearing lingerie and scarce else, and walked to another red door at the end of the corridor. I knocked on the door.

A voice I thought sounded familiar said, 'Yes, come in, please.'

I opened the door and found myself face to face with Monsieur Mercer Grant.

He grinned, exposing the gold-and-diamond tooth at the front of his mouth.

'So, Detective Watts,' he exclaimed. 'We meet again.'

And that was when someone hit me on the back of the head with something very hard, and I swam downwards into oblivion on a sea of utter blackness.

And that was all she wrote.

Or so Emilio thought.

A HASTY RAIN broke over the city early Monday morning, followed by a rainbow that took the citizens by surprise, causing them to follow its arc by eye, hopeful they would catch a glitter that would signify a pot of gold at its end. Ollie considered the rainbow a good omen. Surely, there would be fingerprints all over the dispatch case. Surely some of those fingerprints would be Emilio Herrera's. And just as surely, a he-she hooker and petty thief would have run afoul of the law long before now; Herrera would have a record; Herrera would have a last known address.

Ollie immediately checked with AFIS to see if any of the prints triggered a hit. His own prints were on the case, and they came up in the system check. Well, of course; he was a law enforcement officer. There were prints on file for Veronica D'Allesandro as well; she was a resident alien, and the Immigration and Naturalization Service had taken her prints before issuing her a green card.

A match came up for someone named Thomas Kingsley, who had served in the US Army during the Gulf

War. A call to the Gucci store on Hall Avenue confirmed that he was the man who'd sold the case to Ollie's sister.

There was nothing for Isabelle Weeks, thank God. Nothing for Irving Stein, either. Worst of all, there was nothing for Emilio Herrera. The man – or woman, as he would have it – was clean.

Ollie liked to think of himself as The Lone Wolf. In fact, he visualized himself as a predator of the night, all sleek and svelte and lithe. He did not like working with other people, perhaps because he knew they did not like working with him. This was because most people in this world, especially law enforcement officers, could not accept the utter frankness Ollie considered his most admirable character trait. Well, that was too damn bad, really. If they couldn't cope with his special and praiseworthy brand of candor, a fart on them all, and to Tiny Tim a good night.

But there were times when he was obliged to deal with other people in the department, as for example when he'd needed the help of Hogan or Logan or whatever the fuck his name was, in bringing up those serial numbers on the murder weapon, never mind his two worthless spic assistants, Pancho and Pablo.

This was one of those times.

So he put in a call to Jimmy Walsh in Vice.

THAT SAME Monday morning, Carella and Kling went back to talk to Josh Coogan again. This time, they found him in the youth-oriented offices of Councilman Lester Henderson, who seemed to be somewhat youth-oriented himself. Coogan seemed harried. Everyone in the late councilman's offices seemed harried. Gee, that's too damn bad, Carella thought.

'It occurred to us that of all the people in the auditorium that morning, you had the best overview of what was happening,' he said.

'How do you mean?' Coogan said, looking puzzled. 'Overview?'

'You were up there in the balcony when the shooting started. You could see everything happening down there.'

'Well, so could the guy in the booth.'

'He had his mind on the follow spot. He had a job to do. You were simply observing.'

'No, I was listening to sound checks.'

'What did that entail?'

'Volume levels, clarity.'

'Required your *ears*, right?'

'Okay, I get what you mean.'

'So tell us what you saw that morning,' Carella said.

As Coogan remembers it, there was a buzz of excitement in the air because everyone was expecting Henderson to announce his run for mayor at the rally that night. He'd been upstate all weekend, and it was no secret that he'd met with the Governor's people and also with someone from the White House . . .

'We didn't know that,' Carella said.

'Well, that was the skinny, anyway. The whole team was on his side, was the impression I got. So naturally . . .'

. . . if the man was going to announce he'd be making a run for the mayor's office, everyone wanted everything to be just right. They'd worked with Chuck Mastroiani before, and they trusted him to make sure the place looked suitably patriotic and partisan, but he was nonetheless bustling around down there on the stage, ordering his crew to put an extra tuck in a draped bunting or supervising the placement of a fan so that an American flag would ripple with just the right amount of vigor.

Coogan himself was in the balcony listening to what was coming from speakers around the hall while Mastroiani's audio guy kept repeating the same sentences over and over again at the mike behind the podium. This must have been ten-fifteen, ten-twenty, they'd all been working since nine o'clock or a little after . . .

'What time did Henderson get to the hall?' Carella asked.

'Around nine-thirty.'

'Was he alone?'

'What do you mean?'

'Was there anyone with him?'

'No. He was alone.'

'Okay, so it's now ten-fifteen or so . . . what happened?'

'Well, Mr Henderson was rehearsing his entrance . . .'

. . . striding on from stage left toward the podium, the follow spot on him all the way, raising his arm in greeting the way he would do it tonight, stopping when he reached the podium, starting to turn to face out front when the shots came. Six shots in a row, bam, bam, bam, and Henderson was falling, it almost looked like slow motion, the follow spot on him as he went down to the stage. Mastroiani yelled, 'Kill the spot!' and when the guy in the booth was too slow to do that, he yelled again, 'Kill that fuckin' spot!' and the light went off. Alan yelled, 'Stop him! Get him!,' something like that, and went running off the stage to the right . . .

'He didn't tell us that.'

'Yes, he went running off with Mastroiani and some of his crew following him. I went downstairs the minute I realized what had happened. By the time I got on the stage, Alan and the others were already coming back. The shooter had got away clean.'

'Where'd they look for him?'

'In the building, I guess. Wherever. I really don't know. I didn't ask.'

'*You* never got a look at the shooter, did you?'

'I didn't even know from which side of the stage the shots had come from.'

'Well, it was stage right,' Carella said, 'we know that. You didn't see anyone standing there in the wings shooting, did you?'

'Not a soul. I was watching the audio guy behind the mike.'

'What happened then?'

'Pandemonium. Everyone yelling at once. Alan told me to call the cops, which I'd already done, by the way . . .'

'You're the one who placed the call to the Eight-Eight?'

'Well, no, I didn't know what precinct we were in. I just dialed nine-one-one.'

'When was that?'

'The minute I got downstairs and realized Mr Henderson was dead. I called from my cell phone.'

'Where were the others?'

'Still out in the hall, chasing whoever had shot him. In fact . . .'

Coogan hesitated, shook his head.

'Yes?' Carella said.

'Alan was pissed off that I'd placed the call without first consulting him. I mean, the guy is laying there dead, his sweater all covered with blood, I'm supposed to wait for *clearance* to call the police?'

'What'd he say?'

'He said this was a delicate matter, I shouldn't have taken the initiative on my own. I told him I didn't know what to do, there's a dead man here, I assumed we'd want the police notified at once. Anyway, it was academic. By the time he finished yelling at me, the police were already there.'

'He was yelling at you?' Kling asked.

'He was upset, let's put it that way. He'd just gone running all over the building trying to find whoever had done the shooting, and now an insubordinate little twerp had taken action on his own.'

'Is that what he called you?' Carella asked. 'An insubordinate little twerp?'

'No, those are my words. But that's probably what he was thinking.'

'Did you talk to the responding officers?'

'Just to tell them I was the one who'd made the call to nine-one-one. Most of the time, they were shmoozing with Alan. Till all the detectives got there, anyway.' He hesitated a moment and then said, 'I assume you never got anything more from that witness. Right?'

'What witness?' Carella asked at once.

'The old bum.'

'What old bum?'

'The one the blues were joking about.'

'Joking? About a *witness*?' Carella said.

'Well, they were telling Alan about this drunk they'd talked to outside the building.'

'Yeah, what about him?'

'The guy said he'd seen someone running out of the alley.'

'He *what*?'

'He saw some . . .'

'A *witness* saw someone running out of the alley?'

'That's what the blues were saying, anyway. But he couldn't have.'

'What do you mean he couldn't have? Why not?'

'Because the alley he saw the guy coming out of was on the wrong side of the building. Alan told them straight off this was impossible. He'd just finished chasing the killer all over the *other* side of the building.'

Carella was thinking that the gun had been found on the wrong side of the building, too. He was thinking that maybe the killer was a magician. Or maybe stage right and stage left were meaningless when it came to murder.

'Thank you,' he said, 'we appreciate your time.'

15.

OFFICER PATRICIA GOMEZ kept wondering how somebody who'd shot somebody from the stage-right wings of the auditorium could have dropped the murder weapon in a sewer in the alley outside stage left. Wouldn't this person have had to cross the stage in order to do that? And wouldn't someone in the auditorium have *seen* him crossing the stage?

Patricia stood now in the alley outside stage right, where the killer *should* have come out of the auditorium if reason had followed logic. The trouble with police work, however, was that very often nothing seemed logical or reasonable. She had been a cop for only four months so far, and in that amount of time she had seen and heard so many totally illogical and unreasonable things that sometimes she wished she'd become a fire fighter instead, which had been one of the options open to a Puerto Rican girl growing up in the Riverhead section of the city.

Patricia's first day on the job, walking her beat in her spanking new tailor-made blues, an eleven-year-old girl eating a jelly apple had stepped out of a bodega and onto the sidewalk just as two gangs disputing the same dope-dealing corner opened fire on each other. The girl had been caught in the crossfire. When Patricia came onto the scene, the girl's blood was staining the freshly fallen snow under her, and her grandmother was holding her in her arms and screaming, 'Adelia, no! Adelia! Adelia!' But the girl was already dead.

Patricia found this unreasonable and illogical.

Her sergeant told her, 'You get used to it.'

In the ensuing months, she'd seen a man with four big holes in his face where his wife had shot him when she found him in bed with the woman next door; she'd seen a baby whose face had been chewed to ribbons by rats after her mother left her alone in her crib while she went out to the movies with a girlfriend; she'd seen a woman trapped in a car that had crashed into a Mickey D's, and had watched while the ES guys scissored the car open and lifted the woman out all bleeding and broken and crushed, and she had thought this is unreasonable, this is illogical.

And only two weeks ago, she had thought the same thing when a man of seventy-five had had his throat slit by someone they still hadn't caught, who had also cleaned out the man's wallet and thrown it into the gutter where his blood was still running red when Patricia knelt beside him, and said, 'You'll be okay, hang on,' but he was dead, of course, and there was no hanging on, and it was all so totally fucking unreasonable and illogical.

She stood alone in the alleyway now, trying to understand what it might have been like to shoot somebody and then run from the scene of the crime. You shoot from stage right, you run away stage right. You don't cross a crowded auditorium, and exit stage left, and drop the weapon in a sewer on the opposite side of the building. You do not do that. I have seen too many illogical and unreasonable things in these past four months, but I have to tell you I would not do that if I had just shot and killed a man.

So what *would* I do? she asked herself.

I would come out through the doors there, and because I would have the murder weapon in my hand, I would immediately dump it in the most convenient place. Which would be the sewer right there under the drain pipe. But no. The killer had gone to the *other* side of the building and dumped the gun there. It didn't make sense. The gun should have been on *this* side of the building.

Unless.

Well, this was just supposing.

But suppose there'd been an accomplice? Suppose there'd been two of them in on it, *two* people who wanted the councilman dead for whatever reasons of their own . . . well, at the Academy they'd been taught there were only two reasons for murder, and those reasons were love or money. So *cherchez la femme*, honey, or follow the money, cause that's all there is to know, and all you need to know.

Suppose I shoot him from stage right . . .

. . . and I hand off the gun to an accomplice, who goes out the doors on the left side of the building and drops the gun there . . .

While meanwhile . . .

Now let's just hold this a minute, she thought.

No, that's right, *meanwhile* I'm on the right side of the building, no gun anymore, and I go strolling away from the building and up the avenue, nothing to attract attention anymore, no gun, no nothing, you solved the fucking crime, Patricia!

So how come nobody saw me? she asked herself.

I pop six caps from the wings there, nobody sees me?

How often do people get shot in this place?

I mean, okay, maybe nobody on the *stage* got a good look at me, I'm in the wings, after all, and there must've been a lot of confusion, somebody getting shot. But how about *off* the stage, *backstage*, whatever they call it? How about *there*? Nobody standing there with a broom or a mop? Nobody in the whole damn building who saw me leaving the place — whichever side I left it, right, left, who cares? — nobody saw me *leaving* the scene of the crime?

Didn't Ollie question anybody who *works* here?

I'll bet he questioned *everybody* who works here, he's a good cop, I *guess* he's a good cop, I'm only a rookie, what do I know? And besides, the patrol sarge is going to start wondering why I'm not out on the beat right this minute, where people might illogically and unreasonably be getting themselves killed.

She looked at her watch.

It was almost lunchtime.

She decided she would call in and say she was taking five.

Then, instead of grabbing a bite to eat, she would go into King Memorial for twenty minutes or so, and see if she could scare up a custodian or something.

ALTHOUGH OLLIE'S SISTER once told him there might have been a touch of the shamrock in their own heritage, he did not particularly like people of Irish descent. Ollie preferred thinking of himself as descending from British aristocracy. He knew for an absolute fact that his ancestry could be traced back to Norman times in England, when — according to the Domesday Book — a lord of the barony of Hastings held a knight's fief in Wikes, which Ollie supposed was a town, what else could it be? 'Wikes' was only one of the variants of the name 'Weeks,' just like Weackes or Weacks or Weakes or Weaks or for that matter Weekes. Of course, people whose name was Wykes — of whom there were many, and please don't write to me, Ollie thought – considered Weeks a variant of their name, same as people named Anne thought Ann was a variant and not vice versa, the world was full of fuckin nuts.

His sister – who always looked on the dim side because she herself was so dim, the jackass – told him he should stop putting on airs since there was absolute proof that there'd been a Robert Weeks living in Walberswick, Suffolk, in the year 1596, and he'd been a mere merchant. In fact, she had looked up his merchant's mark, and had needle-pointed it into a sampler for Ollie, which he kept in the bathroom, hanging over the toilet bowl.

'Please observe the way the letter 'W' is worked into the design,' she'd said, the jackass. She had given him the sampler, framed, for Christmas one year, a gift as worthless as the stolen dispatch case, which was why he was here to see an Irishman like Walsh in the first place.

He greeted Walsh with his favorite Irish joke.

'These two Irishmen walk out of a bar,' he said.

'Yeah?' Walsh said, grinning in anticipation.

'It could happen,' Ollie said, and shrugged.

The grin dropped from Walsh's face. Ollie guessed the man thought he was making some kind of remark about Irishmen being drunk all the time. Well, if he couldn't take a joke, a fart on him.

'I'm looking for a cross-dressing whore named Emilio Herrera,' he said, 'street name Emmy. Does it ring a bell?'

'I'm still thinking about that so-called joke of yours,' Walsh said.

He was perhaps six feet, two or three inches tall, a big redheaded mick going gray at the temples, wide shoulders, arms like oaks, the butt of a Glock sticking out of a shoulder holster on the left side of his body for an easy right-handed draw. He was in shirtsleeves on this bright April morning, the sleeves rolled up, the collar open, the tie pulled down. Ollie guessed Walsh thought he looked like a TV detective. TV detectives thought they looked like real-life detectives, which they didn't. Trouble was, real-life detectives watched TV and then started acting like TV detectives, who were acting the way they thought real-life detectives did. It was a vicious cycle. Ollie was glad he looked like himself.

'Don't worry about jokes,' he said. And then, because he was not only a real-life detective, but also a real-life writer, he added, 'Jokes are the folk lore of truth.'

'Does that mean it's true that two Irishmen can't *walk* out of a bar?' Walsh asked.

'It could happen,' Ollie said, and shrugged again.

'That's what's offensive about the joke,' Walsh said. 'Those words "It could happen." And the accompanying shrug, indicating that whereas it's a remote possibility that a pair of Irishmen *could* walk out of a bar, the teller of the joke has certainly never *seen* such a phenomenon in his entire life, though that doesn't mean to say it *couldn't* happen, two Irishmen *walking* out instead of *staggering* out or falling down dead *drunk* as they come out, is what that joke is saying,' Walsh concluded somewhat heatedly.

'Gee, is that so?' Ollie said, and shook his head in wonder. 'I never thought of it that way. Can you help me find this Herrera punk?'

*

THE MAN Patricia spoke to was a Serb named Branislav Something, she couldn't catch the last name. Something with no vowels in it. He had been working here at the Hall since last December, just about when she'd started on the beat.

'I tink I see you valking around,' he said, grinning. He had bad teeth and patchy hair. He was probably fifty years old, she guessed, and was surprised when he later told her he was only forty-one. He had nice blue eyes. He kept smiling all the while he talked to her. He had been in Kosovo when the Americans bombed, he said. 'I don't blame Americans,' he said, 'I blame Albanian bastards.'

'Were you here Monday morning?' she asked him. 'When the councilman got shot?'

'Whoo,' he said, and rolled his blue eyes. 'Vot a trouble!'

'Where were you?' she asked.

'In toilets,' he said. 'Cleaning toilets.'

'Are the toilets anywhere near the stage?'

'Some toilet near, some not,' he said. 'You tink I shot councilman?'

'No, no. I just wanted to know if you'd seen anybody running from the stage.'

'Nobody. Saw nobody.'

'Somebody with a gun?'

'Nobody. Saw nobody. Mop floors, wash windows, clean toilets, sinks, everything, make sparkle like new.'

'There are windows in these toilets?' Patricia asked.

'Two toilets got windows,' he said. 'Let fresh air come in.'

'Can I see these toilets?'

'Both for men's,' he said.

'That's okay,' she said, 'I'm a cop.'

When Patricia was eight years old and visiting her

grandparents in San Juan, her father took them to a show in one of the big hotels one night, and she had to go to the bathroom after the show, but there was a big line of women out in the hall, the way there always is. He came out of the men's room and saw her standing there, dancing from foot to foot, and he said, 'Come with me, it's empty in here,' and he took her into the men's room and stood outside the door to make sure nobody came in while she was peeing. That was the first time she saw urinals.

The next time she saw urinals was just last week at the Sony Theater on Farley and First, where somebody had mugged some kid in the men's room, smashing his face into a urinal that was running with blood and piss when she came in with her gun drawn and the perp long gone. *Harry Potter* was playing on the screen outside.

The first men's room Branislav showed her was just off the right side of the stage. The urinals here were sparkling clean, just as he'd promised. A pebbled glass window was on the wall opposite the urinals, at the far end of the room. The window was wide open. A hand dryer was on the adjoining wall. Patricia hated hand dryers. She did not know anyone who liked hand dryers. She figured hand dryers were designed not to dry a person's hands but to save money on paper towels. She went to the window, bent over, and looked out.

She was looking out onto what appeared to be an airshaft that ran from right to left across the back of the building.

So much for an accomplice theory, she thought.

PORTOLES AND DOYLE were just coming out of the Okeh Diner that Monday when Carella and Kling caught up with them. They seemed surprised to learn that the detectives were here about the murder at King Memorial; until now, they'd thought the Fat Boy was investigating that case.

'Was Weeks pulled off it?' Portoles asked. 'Is that it?'

'No, we're handling it together,' Kling said.

'You ain't shooflies, are you?' Doyle asked.

'No, we're just honest, decent law enforcement officers investigating a mere homicide,' Carella said.

Doyle looked at him, not sure whether he was kidding or not. Portoles wasn't sure, either. Sometimes Internal Affairs sent around guys pretending to be what they weren't.

'So what can we do for you?' he asked.

'We understand you talked to some bum in the alley outside the building,' Carella said. 'Is that right?'

'Yeah, a Vietnam vet, he said he was.'

'Did you get his name?'

'No, he was an old drunk.'

'How old could he be, Vietnam?' Kling asked.

'Well, he *looked* old, let's put it that way,' Doyle said.

'Did you get his name?'

'No. He was drunk, he didn't see a weapon, what's the uproar here?'

'You just didn't bother to take his name, is that it?' Kling said. 'An eye witness.'

'An old drunk,' Doyle insisted.

'Besides,' Portoles said, 'the TV lady got it.'

'Got what?' Carella said. 'What TV lady?'

'His name,' Portoles said.

'He had to sign some kind of release,' Doyle said.

'What was *her* name?' Kling asked. 'The TV lady. Did you get *her* name?'

'Oh *sure*,' Doyle said, beaming. 'Honey Blair, Channel Four News. *Everybody* knows Honey Blair.'

CARELLA CALLED HER as soon as they got back to the squadroom. He got her answering machine.

'Miss Blair,' he said, 'this is Detective Steve Carella, you probably won't remember me, we met around Christmastime at the Grover Park Zoo, the case with the lady and the lions, do you remember? I need to know the name of the Vietnam vet you talked to outside King Memorial on the day Lester Henderson got shot and killed. One of the responding officers told us the man signed a release for you. If we could have his name, we'd appreciate it. You can call me back at Frederick seven, eight, oh, two, four, thanks a lot.'

She called back ten minutes later.

'Well, well,' she said, 'Detective Carella.'

'Hi, Miss Blair, I'm glad you . . .'

'Honey,' she said.

'Thank you for returning my call, uh, Honey,' he said. 'I won't take much of your time. All I need . . .'

'You can take all the time you need with me,' Honey said.

'All I want is the name of the man you . . .'

'It's Clarence Weaver, 702 Huxley Boulevard, I don't have a phone number for him, what else is on your mind?'

'Nothing right now,' he said.

'When you think of something, give me another call,' Honey said.

There was a click on the line.

He looked at the receiver.

*

THE HAND-LETTERED wooden sign over the entrance door read DSS HUXLEY. The DSS stood for Department of Social Services. Huxley Boulevard had once been a tree-lined esplanade with elegant apartment buildings on either side of it. The trees were still there, but the apartment buildings were now run by the city and were used for welfare housing. 702 Huxley had once been a movie theater. The seats had been torn out seven years ago, when the building was turned into a shelter for the homeless. That was where they found Clarence Weaver on that Monday afternoon a week after Henderson's murder.

There were eight hundred and forty-seven cots in the shelter. Weaver was lying on cot number 312, his hands behind his head, his eyes closed. He was wearing khaki fatigues and a khaki-colored tank-top undershirt. He had taken off his shoes and socks. His feet were dirty, grime caked between the toes, the ankles smudged with filth from the streets.

Gently, Carella said, 'Mr Weaver?'

He sat upright, eyes snapping open. He truly looked too old and too frail ever to have served in Vietnam, a scrawny, unshaven, toothless black man with thin arms and a sunken chest, the stench of whiskey on his breath at two o'clock in the afternoon.

'Whut's it?' he said at once, and looked around wildly, as if he had just heard incoming mail.

'It's okay,' Carella said, and showed Weaver his shield. 'We just want to ask you some questions.'

Weaver studied the shield carefully.

'I'm Detective Carella, this is my partner, Detective Kling.'

He looked up at the detectives, swung his legs over

the side of the cot. 'That TV station never sent me a nickel,' he said, and shook his head. 'I axed was they a reward, the blond lady tole me to just please sign the release. I told them ever'thin I knowed, but nobody sent me nothin.'

'What is it you told them, Mr Weaver? What did you see that morning?'

As Weaver recalls it, he was planning to enter the alley on the side of King Memorial . . .

'They's two alleys,' he said, 'one to the right, one to the left. One of them usually has nothin but papers an' trash in the garbage cans, from the offices that side of the buildin. The other one sometimes has soda bottles in it, sometimes even food, from people usin the aud'torium for one reason or another. I was juss about to go in there to start mah search, when I seed this young feller come racin out the buildin . . .'

'When you say young . . .'

'Yessir.'

'How young?'

'Hard to say. You know how these young fellers look nowadays. Tall, kind of thin . . .'

'How tall?'

'Five-seven? Five-eight?'

Carella was thinking that wasn't tall. Kling was thinking the same thing.

'White or black?' he asked.

'White man. He was a white man.'

'Clean-shaven? Or did he have a beard? A mustache?'

'No, nothin like that. Clean-shaven, I'd say.'

'Any scars? Did you notice any scars?'

'No, he was comin too fast. An' the cap made it hard to see his face.'

'We understand he didn't have a gun.'

'That's right, he did not have a piece, suhs. I was in the Army, you know, I'm a Vietnam vet, I knows all about weapons. He did not have a weapon, this man. I was in Nam durin the Tet offensive, you know.'

'Yes, sir,' Kling said. 'Sir, can you tell us what this man was wearing?'

'I tole the other officers, he had on blue jeans and a ski parka . . .'

'What color parka?'

'Blue. Darker than the jeans. An' white sneakers, and this cap pulled down over his eyes.'

'What kind of cap?'

'A baseball cap.'

'What color was it?'

'Black.'

'Anything on it?'

'How do you mean?'

'Any letters for a team?'

'I still don't get you.'

'NY for New York, or LA for Los Angeles . . .'

'SD for San Diego? The Padres?'

'M for the Milwaukee Brewers?'

Weaver was thinking.

'The Phillies?' Kling said.

'The Royals?'

'Anything like that?'

'Yes, they was letters on it,' Weaver said at last.

'Which team?'

'I got no idea.'

'Well, what'd you see, sir?'

'SRA.'

'SRA?' Kling said.

'The letters SRA, yessir.'

'SRA,' Carella repeated.

'You sure it wasn't SF?' Kling asked. 'For San Francisco? The San Francisco Giants?'

'Or SL?' Carella asked. 'For the St Louis Cardinals?'

'No, it was SRA. I feel sure about that. I was a spotter, you know. In Nam.'

'What color were the letters?' Carella asked.

'White.'

'White letters on a black cap,' Kling said. 'What team do you suppose that can be?'

'Oh Jesus,' Carella said.

'What?'

'Smoke Rise. Smoke Rise Academy.'

16.

THE PLAYING FIELDS behind Smoke Rise Academy were empty as Carella and Kling drove past them at three-thirty that Monday afternoon. Girls and boys in their school uniforms – grey trousers and black blazers for the boys, grey skirts and similar black blazers for the girls – walked along country roads anomalous in a city as big as this one, wending their easy way homeward, chatting, teasing, skipping, laughing on an afternoon still bright with spring sunlight.

The same housekeeper who'd answered the door for Carella on his earlier visit opened the door for them now. She said she would inform Mrs Henderson they were here, and then politely left the door open a crack while she went to summon her. Pamela herself opened the door for them not three minutes later. She was still wearing black, a sweater and skirt this time, black pantyhose, black loafers.

'Has there been some news?' she asked at once.

'May we come in?' Carella asked.

'Please,' she said, and led them into the house and into the living room Carella remembered from the first time he was here. 'Would you care for some coffee?' she asked.

'No, thank you,' Carella said.

Kling shook his head.

The detectives sat on the sofa, their backs to the French windows and the Hamilton Bridge in the near distance. Pamela sat in a chair facing them.

'We're sorry to bother you again,' Carella said, 'but we'd like to ask a few more questions.'

'I was hoping . . .'

'Mrs Henderson,' Carella said, 'can you tell us where you were on the morning your husband was shot and killed?'

'I'm sorry?' she said.

'I asked . . .'

'Yes, I heard you. Will I need a lawyer here?'

'I don't think so, Mrs Henderson.'

'Why do you want to know where . . .?'

'You don't have to answer the question if you don't want to,' Kling said.

'Oh, I'll just bet,' she said, and then immediately, with a slight wave of her hand to indicate this was all nonsense, 'I was here at home.'

'This would've been around ten, ten-thirty . . .'

'Yes, I was here at home. Is that it? In which case . . .'

'Was anyone here with you?'

'No. I was alone.'

'No housekeeper, no . . .'

'Our housekeeper comes in later on Mondays.'

'Oh? Why is that?'

'She does the weekly marketing on Mondays. She doesn't get here till noon or thereabouts.'

'So she wasn't here at all that Monday morning, is that correct?'

'That's correct.'

'You were here alone.'

'Yes.'

'Children gone?'

'The children walk to school. They leave here at eight-thirty.' She looked at her watch. 'They should be home any minute, in fact. I would rather you were gone by then. If there are no further questions . . .'

'Do you drive a car, Mrs Henderson?'

'No. Well, do you mean do I have a *license* to drive? Yes, I do. But no, we do not keep a car in the city. My husband was a city councilman. We were provided with a car and driver whenever we needed one.'

'I believe you mentioned your son was on the school baseball team.'

'Yes, he plays second base.'

'Does he have a baseball uniform?'

'Yes?'

'With a baseball cap?'

'Yes?'

'A black cap with the initials SRA on it? For Smoke Rise Academy?'

'I'm sure he does.' She rose suddenly. 'I hear them now,' she said. 'If you don't mind, I must ask you to leave.'

They passed the children on the way to their car.

A boy of eleven, a girl of eight or nine.

'Hello there,' Carella said.

Neither of them answered.

THE UNIFORMED GUARD in the booth at the Smoke Rise gate wasn't sure he should talk to them.

'It's okay,' Kling assured him. 'We're just checking some stuff Mrs Henderson already told us.'

'Well,' the guard said, but then immediately relaxed into his five minutes of fame.

'Can you tell us what time the Henderson housekeeper got here last Monday?'

'Jessie? Around noon, I guess it was. She usually

comes in late on Mondays. Does the shopping for them, you know. Or used to. I don't know what it'll be like now.'

'How about Mrs Henderson? Did she leave the development anytime before then?'

'We don't call it a development,' the guard said.

'What do you call it?'

'People who live here call it a compound.'

'Did she leave the compound anytime that morning?' Carella asked.

'Saw her going out around nine,' the guard said.

'In a limousine or what?'

'No, in a taxi. Let him in a few minutes before that.'

'Around nine, you say.'

'Well, the cab got here at five to nine, it must've been. Drove out some ten minutes later? Quarter past, let's say. Around that time.'

'Yellow cab, was it?'

'Yellow cab, yes.'

'What was she wearing, did you notice?'

'Mrs Henderson? I just told you. She was in a taxi!'

'Yes, but did you happen to . . .?'

'How could I tell what she was *wearing*?'

'Thought you might have noticed.'

'No, I didn't.'

'You didn't glance in the cab or anything?'

'No, I didn't. I knew it was the same cab came in ten minutes before, I just opened the gate and waved him on through.'

'When did she get back, would you know?'

'Let me think a minute.'

'Take your time.'

The guard thought it over.

'I was having a cup of coffee.'

'Uh-huh.'

'Must've been around eleven, eleven-fifteen.'

'Yellow cab again?'

'Yeah, but a different one. The first guy was black. This guy was wearing a turban.'

'Sikh, huh?'

'No, he looked pretty healthy to me. Big guy with a turban. Probably a terrorist, don't you think?' the guard said, and grinned.

'Probably,' Kling said. 'Did you notice what she was wearing this time?'

'Well, yeah. Cause I looked in the cab to make sure it was somebody who lived here. When I saw it was Mrs Henderson, I waved her on in.'

'So what was she wearing?'

'She was dressed casual. Jeans, some kind of jacket, a baseball cap.'

'Any letters on the cap?'

'It looked like the school cap to me. The school here? The ones the kids wear? It looked like that. Hell of a thing, ain't it?' the guard said. 'I'll bet she went out to meet her husband. He'd been away, you know. She prob'ly went out to meet him, don't you think?'

'I think so, yes,' Carella said.

'I THOUGHT YOU MIGHT find this interesting,' Patricia was telling Ollie. He was eating, of course. She somewhat enjoyed watching him eat. Such gusto, she thought, and wondered if the word 'gusto' had Spanish roots. 'I got it from the manager at King Memorial. It's the architect's schematic sketch of the building. Shows what's what and where's where.' She spread it out on her side of the table. Without missing a beat, hands and mouth working, Ollie leaned over the table to study the drawing:

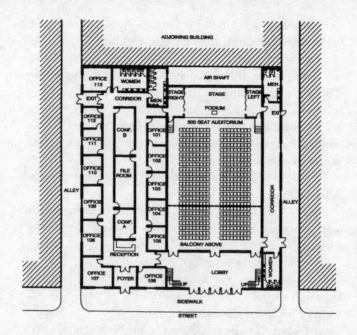

'Auditorium is here on the right of the building,' she said, 'offices on the left. You'll see that these two men's rooms, one left, one right, have windows opening on an airshaft. Little narrow passageway runs along the back of the building. The windows were wide open when I checked them out. I figured . . .'

'You checked them out?'

'Yeah. Earlier today.'

'That was very enterprising of you, Patricia.'

'Thank you,' she said. 'I figured it was funny, the windows wide open in rest rooms? What I did, you see, was walk the passageway from one side of the building to the other. I climbed out one window and in the other.'

He visualized her climbing out the rest room window on the left here, and walking across the back of the building and then climbing through the other rest room window on the right. And then . . .'

'I get it,' he said. 'You think that's what our killer did. He got into this rest room . . .'

'The men's room here on the left of the drawing, yes.'

'. . . went out the window, and ran across the back of the building to the other rest room . . .'

'The other men's room, yes.'

'And then out the exit doors here, and into the alleyway.'

'Where he ditched the gun down the sewer,' Patricia said, and shrugged. 'That's what I figure happened, anyway.'

'I think you're right,' Ollie said. 'Listen, is that all you're going to eat?'

'I'm not very hungry, really.'

'You're not?' Ollie said, surprised. 'I'm hungry all the time.'

'Maybe . . .' she started, and then shook her head.

'No, what?' Ollie asked.

'Maybe it gives you something to do,' she suggested, and shrugged.

'I got plenty to do,' Ollie said.

'I mean, something to . . . well . . . take your mind off whatever . . . problems you might have.'

'I don't have any problems.'

'Because eating is pleasurable, you know.'

'Oh, that I know,' he said.

'Instead of fighting City Hall,' she said.

'*Che si puoi fare?*' he said.

'I found out how to say that in Serbian, by the way.'

'You're kidding me.'

'No, the janitor at King Memorial taught me.'

'So how do you say it?'

'*Shta-MO-goo*,' she said.

'*Shta-MO-goo*,' he repeated.

'I also know how to say "Nothing." Ask me "What can you do?" in Serbian.'

'*Shta-MO-goo?*' he said.

'*Neeshta*,' she answered.

'What makes you think I got problems?'

'I don't.'

'You said I eat cause I got problems.'

'No, you eat cause it's pleasurable is what I said.'

'You said that, too, but you also said I got problems.'

'Well, I was wrong.'

He looked at her. His cell phone rang. He unclipped it from his belt, hit the SEND button.

'Weeks,' he said. 'Hey, Steve.' He listened. 'When? Okay. See you.' He pressed the END button, and hung the phone on his belt again. 'I gotta go up the Eight-Seven,' he said. 'Carella and Kling think they're onto something. Do you like to dance?'

'Yes, I love to dance,' Patricia said, surprised.

'You want to go dancing with me sometime?'

'Sure.'

'I'm a good dancer. I won a salsa contest one time.'

'I'll bet you are.'

'I really am.'

'I said so, didn't I?'

'So when would you like to go?'

'I don't know. You're the man. You say when.'

'How about this weekend?'

'Okay.'

'Saturday night?'

'Okay.'

'Put on a nice dress.'

'I will.'

'I'll wear my blue suit.'

'Sounds good to me,' she said.

'*Shta-MO-goo?*' he said.

'*Neeshta,*' she answered.

'**OKAY, SO TELL US** what you've got,' Byrnes said.

This was almost five o'clock already, and all of the detectives gathered in his office should have gone home an hour ago. But Carella and Kling thought they had real meat here.

'First,' Carella said, 'she knew her husband was having an affair.'

'*Everybody's* husband is having an affair,' Parker said. 'That don't mean you run out and shoot them.'

'Besides, why would she turn the bimbo's letters over to you?' Hawes asked.

'Throw us off the scent,' Kling said.

'Throw us off the scent?' Parker said. 'What is this, Sherlock Holmes? Throw us off the *scent?*'

'Let us think she was trying to help the investigation,' Kling explained. 'It's done all the time.'

'Okay, so we've got motive,' Willis said.

The men were sitting or standing or leaning everywhere in the lieutenant's corner office. Most of them were bone-weary after a long day. Ollie looked fresh and energetic. He was the only one eating the donuts and drinking the coffee the Loot had set out.

'We've also got opportunity,' Carella said. 'We have her leaving the compound at nine-fifteen . . .'

'Plenty of time to get there and do the job,' Brown said.

'Get back, too,' Kling said. 'We've got her coming home at eleven, eleven-fifteen.'

'How about means?' Meyer asked.

'Only smeared prints on the gun. We can't tie her to that.'

'So where's your probable cause?' Parker asked. 'Lady goes out to do some shopping . . .'

'No, her housekeeper was out doing that.'

'No alibi, huh?' Byrnes said.

'None.'

'You've still got no reason to arrest her,' Parker said.

'We've got a description from an eye witness. Same clothes the Smoke Rise guard saw her wearing.'

'We can get a search warrant for the hat,' Kling said.

'What hat?' Byrnes asked.

'The baseball cap she was wearing.'

'She's a baseball player?' Willis asked.

'Her son is.'

'Maybe *he's* the killer,' Meyer said.

'He's only eleven.'

'I've seen eleven-year-old killers,' Brown said philosophically.

'Not this kid. He comes up to my belly-button,' Carella said. 'Our witness saw somebody five-seven, five-eight. Which is about her height.'

'You still got nothing that warrants an arrest,' Parker said.

'I agree,' Byrnes said. 'Absent fingerprints on the gun . . .'

'How about we dust them window sills?' Ollie said, and bit into a chocolate-covered donut.

'What window sills?'

'In the toilets,' Ollie said. 'Where maybe the shooter went in and out after plugging Henderson.'

Byrnes didn't know what the hell he was talking about.

Neither did any of the others.

'My girlfriend went to the toilet,' Ollie explained.

NELLIE BRAND got to the precinct at seven P.M. that Monday night. She was wearing a tan linen suit that complemented her short blondish hair, a darker brown silk blouse, sheer pantyhose, and dark brown, French-heeled pumps. It was raining again, and she was carrying an umbrella which she deposited in a stand just inside the slatted wooden railing that divided the squadroom from the corridor outside. The day shift had been relieved three hours ago. A Chinese translator was sitting at Bob O'Brien's desk, talking to a man who'd been arrested two hours earlier. O'Brien sat looking bored as the two exchanged sing-song dialogue. The guy had killed both his wives; that was good enough for O'Brien, never mind the Mandarin or the Cantonese.

'Hello, Bob,' Nellie said, 'where are they?'

'The Loot's office,' O'Brien said, and the translator turned to him and said, 'What?' and he said, 'I'm talking to the DA,' and the translator said, 'Oh, solly,' was what O'Brien actually heard her say, 'solly.'

Nellie walked across the familiar squadroom to Lieutenant Byrnes's office, knocked on the frosted glass panel in the upper half of the door, heard Byrnes's voice yelling, 'Come!' and opened the door and went in. She recognized Carella, of course . . .

'Hey, Steve.'

'Nellie.'

. . . and Ollie Weeks from the Eight-Eight.

'Hello, Ollie.'

'Hi, Nellie.'

She had been briefed on the phone, and knew that the

two precincts were sharing the bust; Lieutenant Hirsch had already given permission for the Q and A to take place here at the Eight-Seven, since this was where Mrs Henderson had been apprehended. A police stenographer was seated at a small table across the room, near the windows that fronted the street, closed now against the rain and the noise of the traffic below.

Pamela Henderson was sitting in a straight-backed chair alongside her attorney, a man named Alex Wilkerson, with whom Nellie had crossed swords on many a previous occasion. Pamela was wearing a dark blue suit, a white blouse, blue pantyhose, and blue high-heeled pumps. Despite the expensive designer suit, she appeared somehow shabby, perhaps because the rain had dampened her hair and her clothes on her walk from the car to the front steps of the building. Nellie's first impression was one of shoulder-length hair that could only be described as mousy, matching eyes that were a trifle too large for the woman's narrow face, a thin-lipped mouth devoid of lipstick.

'Hello, Alex,' she said.

'Nice to see you, Nellie.'

A man in his late forties, Wilkerson affected the long, lanky, languorous style of a young Abraham Lincoln, favoring dark suits and bow ties, a shock of black hair hanging boyishly over his forehead. He was smoking a pipe now, even though a sign on Byrnes's desk read CANCER-FREE ZONE. Byrnes was frowning. He was thinking, Smoke your brains out, Counselor, we're gonna fry your client.

Nellie introduced herself, explained that she was here from the District Attorney's Office at the request of the arresting officers, and then asked if Mrs Henderson knew she'd been charged with second-degree murder . . .

'My client has been so informed,' Wilkerson said.

'Has she been informed of her rights?'

'She has.'

'Does she understand she can stop the questioning at any time . . .?'

'I've advised her not to answer any questions at all,' Wilkerson said.

'Then we've got nothing further to say here,' Nellie said. 'Let's get her printed, boys, and take her downtown for arraignment.'

'I'd like to add,' Wilkerson said, 'that you have no probable cause for arrest. Anything that's brought out from this moment on – including any fingerprints you take – will be fruit of the Poisoned Tree.'

'We'll take that risk, Counselor.'

'Be so advised.'

'Thank you.'

'I'd like to say something,' Pamela said.

'Mrs Henderson, I strongly suggest . . .'

'I'd like to know why I've been arrested.'

'Well,' Nellie said, 'the detectives here seem to think you shot and killed your husband, ma'am. If you'd like to convince us otherwise . . .'

'She's not going to answer any questions, Counselor, so please don't get fancy with us.'

'Well, fine, then let's get on with it. Boys? You want to . . .?'

'I have nothing to hide here,' Pamela said.

Nellie was happy to hear this. The ones who had nothing to hide already had one foot on the path to life imprisonment.

'They've placed you under arrest,' Wilkerson said. 'Answering their questions will only *help* . . .'

'My answers will be on the record, won't they?' Pamela asked.

'Yes, but you have the right to remain silent,' Wilkerson said. 'And if you *choose* to remain silent . . .'

'I don't *want* to remain silent!' Pamela said.

'I'm trying to say that your choice won't be held against you in court. They cannot compel . . .'

'I'll say it in court, too.'

'You may not wish to testify in . . .'

'I didn't kill him!'

The room went silent.

'So what'll it be?' Nellie asked. 'Questions, no questions? It's your call, Counselor.'

'I fear it's my client's call,' Wilkerson said.

'Mrs Henderson?'

'Ask your questions. I didn't kill him.'

'Counselor. That okay with you?'

Wilkerson spread his hands and sighed.

'Thank you,' Nellie said.

She took Pamela's oath, elicited her name, address, and occupation, reaffirmed once again that she had been informed of and understood her rights, and then began questioning her.

'Mrs Henderson, can you tell me where you were at ten-thirty on the morning of April twenty-second?'

'I was home.'

'Where was that?'

'26 Prospect Lane. In Smoke Rise. I gave you the address two minutes ago.'

The stenographer's fingers were flying over her machine.

Q: Can you tell me what you were wearing?
A: A simple skirt and sweater.
Q: Do you remember what color they were? The skirt? The sweater?

A: It was a matching set. An olive-green sweater and skirt. I have them at home. I can show them to you, if you like.

'Excuse me, Counselor, but where's this going?' Wilkerson asked, and looked to Byrnes for sympathy and encouragement. Byrnes sat dead-panned behind his desk. 'Why is my client's wardrobe on the morning of her husband's death of such importance to you?'

'Maybe because we have a witness who saw her wearing something entirely different that morning,' Nellie said.

'Oh, and who might . . .?'

'Alex, do you want me to swear *you* in? Or may I continue questioning your client instead?'

'Mrs Henderson?' he asked, turning to her.

'I have nothing to hide,' she said again.

Q: Mrs Henderson, do you own a pair of blue jeans?
A: I do.
Q: Do you own a blue ski parka?
A: I do.
Q: Do you own white sneakers?
A: No.
Q: White running shoes then?
A: Yes.
Q: How about a black baseball cap?
A: No. I don't own a black baseball cap.
Q: A cap with the letters SRA on it?
A: No.
Q: Weren't you wearing such a cap on the morning of April twenty-second?
A: No. I was wearing a green sweater and skirt set.
Q: No hat.
A: No hat.

Q: Any idea what those letters might stand for?

A: The detectives have already told me what they think those letters stand for.

Q: And what's that?

A: Smoke Rise Academy.

Q: Where your son goes to school, does he not?

A: That's where he goes to school.

Q: Does your son own such a cap?

A: You will have to ask my son.

'Excuse me, Counselor, but what does her son's *school* have to do with any of this? I must again ask where you're going. Mrs Henderson has already told you . . .'

Nellie sighed heavily.

'No theatrics, please,' Wilkerson said. 'We're not in court yet.'

'Counselor, your client said she wants to answer my questions. If she's changed her mind, fine. But if she still . . .'

'I just don't know where you're going,' Wilkerson said plaintively, and again turned to Byrnes for sympathy. Byrnes sat stonefaced.

'I don't know where you're going, either,' Pamela said.

'I'm going to King Memorial on the morning your husband was killed,' Nellie said. 'I'm going to an alleyway on the western end of the building, where the murder weapon was recovered from a sewer there. I'm going to a man named Clarence Weaver who almost got knocked over by someone running out of that alley. The person he saw was wearing what I questioned you about a moment ago. Blue jeans, a ski parka, white sneakers . . . or maybe running shoes, hm? . . . and a black baseball cap with the initials SRA on it. I'm suggesting that the initials on that cap stand for Smoke Rise Academy, where your son goes to school, and I'm further suggesting that you were wearing your son's hat on the morning of the murder when you ran out of that alley on St Sebastian's . . .'

'Well now,' Wilkerson said, 'that is one hell of a mouthful, Nell.'

'Don't call me Nell,' Nellie said. 'I wasn't raised in the woods with wolves.'

'Well, gee, excuse me, Mrs District Attorney. But now that you've told us where you plan to go, and now that you've made all your wonderful suggestions, do you think you might like to frame all that rhetoric in the form of a question? Because, I must tell you, my patience is wearing a bit thin and I'm on the edge of making a suggestion of my own, which is the one I made to my client in the first place, and that is to keep silent from this moment on.'

'Mrs Henderson,' Nellie said, 'were you the person our witness saw running out of the alley at King Memorial, yes or no?'

'No.'

'Mrs Henderson, did you almost knock a black man off his feet in your haste to get out of the Hall that morning, yes or no?'

'No.'

'Mrs Henderson, did you shoot your husband from the wings stage right . . .'

'No.'

'. . . and then make your escape by . . .'

'No.'

'Let me finish, please.'

'I don't want to answer any further questions,' Pamela said.

'Good,' Wilkerson said, and nodded in dismissal.

'You can stop answering questions, that's Miranda-Escobedo, and it still holds for some lucky citizens of these United States,' Nellie said. 'But you're still under arrest, and you can't stop me from asking you to put on a baseball cap like the one you were wearing when the witness saw you – who by the way is down the hall waiting to have a better look at you in a lineup – and you can't stop me from asking you to put your finger to your nose, or walk across a stage, or jump up and down for me three times, or sing "Eensy Weensy Spider" in the key of G! And please don't give me any bullshit about fingerprints and The Poisoned Tree, Alex. I've been informed by Detective Carella that we already have her prints on file, but I don't want to risk any technical nonsense later on about them not being hers, or whatever you might come up with, which from personal experience I know can be plenty. That's why I want her prints taken again, now, in my presence, which is exactly what we're *going* to do. And then we're going to compare them with the ones we lifted from two separate rest rooms at King Memorial. If we get a positive match, and I feel certain we will, your client can kiss . . .'

'*Can* they do all that?' Pamela asked suddenly.

'I'm afraid they can,' Wilkerson said.

'Then it's all over,' Pamela said.

17.

THIS WAS THE meat-packing section of the city.

During the daytime, trucks pulled in and out, and sides of beef were unloaded, and hung on platform hooks and then carried inside where they were weighed and refrigerated. Food stands and flower carts and stalls selling photographs suitable for framing lined the streets during the daytime, and African merchants in tribal robes hawked imitation Rolexes and Louis Vuitton luggage. During the daytime, there were restaurants and book shops and antiques emporiums and furniture stores, and couples wandered down to the river to watch the big steamers and the tug boats, and the ferries chugging over to Bethtown during the daytime.

At night, the streets were thronged with hookers.

'Vice don't bother with this petty shit anymore,' Walsh told Ollie. 'Ever since the terrorist business started, we got more important things on our mind. Hookers have it easy now. Terrorism made it easy for hookers.'

'How about you get some hooker commits a crime?' Ollie said.

'That's a different story. Every now and then, one of the girls'll stab a john gets out of line, that's an ADW no matter how you slice it, no pun intended.'

'I'm not talking about deadly assault, I'm talking about a minor crime like stealing somebody's dispatch case has something valuable in it. Does that attract your attention?'

'You know,' Walsh said, 'you sometimes have a snotty way of saying things.'

'Gee, really. What did I just say that was snotty?'

'You said, "Does that attract your attention?" with a little edge to it, you know? As if we're not doing our jobs or something. As if Vice has nothing to do all day long but worry about some fuckin dispatch case.'

'Well, you just told me you look the other way, you got more important things on your mind, you don't bother with this petty shit anymore . . .'

'That's just what I mean,' Walsh said. 'The way you just said that.'

'I was only repeating what you said.'

'It's the *way* you repeated it.'

'All I'm asking is whether a hooker who stole a dispatch case is worth your valuable time, is all I'm . . .'

'There you go again,' Walsh said. 'My valuable time. That little edge of sarcasm there. That snotty tone. I was trying to indicate to you that we've been on high alert for Arabs and other such types ever since 9/11. This is Vice here, we know every whore house in this city. These fucks pray to God five times a day, but then they go out drinking and lap-dancing before they crash an airplane into a building.'

Ollie suddenly liked the man.

'I tell you,' Walsh said, 'I wouldn't care to be some guy who looks even vaguely Middle Eastern when the only mischief on his mind is getting laid, though they ain't supposed to do that in their religion, anyway, go to a whore house. Unless they're Saudi Arabians in London,' Walsh said, and Ollie liked him even more. 'We got girls all over town waiting to call us the minute one of these creeps shows up. But that ain't *all* we do, Weeks.'

'Oh, I know that,' Ollie said.

'No, you *don't* know it, all your remarks about our looking the other way, or being sarcastic about my valuable time . . .'

'Don't be so fuckin sensitive,' Ollie said.

'Well, I *am* sensitive,' Walsh said. 'Vice ain't concerned only with prostitution. We're after the policy racket, bookmaking, loan sharking, ticket scalping, we're after the big boys, the ones running the show. We want to get 'em on RICO, send 'em up forever. That's why you tell me some hooker stole a fuckin *dispatch* case, I'm supposed to get all excited about it? Give me a break, willya?'

'I'm sorry, but that case had something in it very valuable to me.'

'You telling me it's *your* case?'

'Yes, it was my case this Herrera hump stole from my parked car and hocked.'

'So what was so valuable in this case of yours?'

'Well, now *you're* doing it.'

'Doing what?'

'Sounding sarcastic.'

'I didn't mean to sound sarcastic.'

'I mean, you tell me *you're* sensitive, well, *I'm* sensitive, too,' Ollie said.

'I'm sorry, okay? Tell me what was in the fuckin case, okay?'

'A novel I wrote.'

'You wrote a novel?'

'Yes.'

'So did I!' Walsh said.

Everybody wants to get in the act, Ollie thought.

'It's with my agent right this minute,' Walsh said.

He's got an agent, no less, Ollie thought.

'What's it about?' he asked.

'Police work, what do you think it's about?' Walsh said.

That's what we need, all right, Ollie thought. Another novel about police work. There used to be no novels about police work at all. Then, all of a sudden – God knows who or what the influence might have been – every shitty little town in America had a fictitious character working out of a detective squadroom. To look at all these police novels out there, you'd think every hamlet in America was overrun with crime. Dumb little village has a population of six hundred people, according to these novels there are murders being committed there every hour on the hour. Let's say you live in Dung Heap, Oklahoma, and your day job is you're a garage mechanic. You go to the local police chief and you tell him you're a writer and you want to set a series in his police station. The Chief says, 'Come in, sit down, I'll bare my soul to you.' Never mind being a *real* cop. Nobody's real anymore, Ollie thought, that's the trouble. Well, *Walsh* is real, but fuck him, the Irish hump! *He* wrote a police novel. That makes him competition.

'So let's find Herrera, okay?' Ollie said.

'One of these days, we have to have a beer together,' Walsh said. 'Talk shop.'

Yeah, one of these days next *year*, Ollie thought.

'Hey, fellas, wanna take a picture of my pussy?' a voice behind them said.

They both turned to see two girls standing there and grinning. The one with the camera seemed a trifle high. Not stoned high, just silly high. Marijuana, Ollie guessed.

'It's Polaroid,' she said, still grinning, extending the camera to them. 'You like what you see, we can talk about further exploration.'

Further exploration, Ollie thought. Everybody sounds literary these days.

'Thanks, no,' he said.

But to tell the truth, he was tempted.

The girl was wearing a short black skirt, a red silk blouse, and red patent shoes to match, no stockings. She looked like Dorothy in *The Wizard of Oz*. Well, the red shoes did. She had very lovely breasts, most of them showing in the low-cut peasant blouse. In fact, Ollie thought he detected the rosiest of nipples peeking out of the right side of the blouse. The girl had a beauty mark near the corner of her mouth, and black hair done in twisty little ringlets, and dark brown eyes. Ollie suddenly thought of Patricia Gomez.

'You want to look for Herrera or what?' Walsh asked.

'Be more fun taking my picture,' the girl said, and waggled her eyebrows.

'Some other time,' Ollie said, and winked at her as he turned to follow Walsh.

THE NAME The Cozy was lettered onto the plate glass windows out front.

'They may know something about him here,' Walsh said, and reached for the doorknob.

A little bell tinkled over the door as the detectives entered, making the place sound as cozy as it looked. The feeling was one of gingham and pine. Ten or twelve tables with blue, checked table cloths. Stools at the bar cushioned in the same blue check. A pine-framed mirror behind the bar. A blonde wearing a white T-shirt, red Larry King suspenders that exaggerated the thrust of her breasts, high-heeled pumps, and a short blue skirt was behind the bar. A second blonde, identically dressed, was working the tables. There were maybe six or seven people sitting here and there around the room. The detectives took stools at the bar. The blonde behind the bar came over. Ollie wondered if the other blonde was her twin sister.

'Are you drinking or working?' she asked Walsh.

'We're both off duty,' he said. 'What'll you have, Ollie?'

It'd been 'Weeks' before he discovered they were both literary people. Now it was 'Ollie.' Next thing you knew, he'd be asking how to utilize metaphor most effectively.

'A beer'd be fine,' Ollie said. 'You got Pabst?'

'Coming up,' the blonde said. 'How about you, Detective Walsh?'

'Just a shot of bourbon, Flo, little water on the side.'

The other blonde came to the bar, looked at her pad, read off, 'BLT down, hold the mayo, iced tea no sugar,' and then turned to Walsh and said, 'Hey, long time no see. How's your book coming along?'

'Finished it,' Walsh said. 'With my agent right this minute.'

'Oh, gee, good luck with it.'

'Thanks, Wanda. This is Detective Weeks here.'

'Hey,' Wanda said, and gave him the once-over.

Of the two blondes, Ollie guessed Wanda was the prettiest. Although to tell the truth, they were both quite attractive. Ollie had always liked the look of blondes, especially real blondes, which these two definitely did not seem to be, but then again you could never tell until the panties came off, could you? He thought it odd that he was now attracted to a woman like Patricia Gomez, all dark and exotic looking, not that he was attracted to her, per se, but certainly interested in her, to say the least. He wondered how she was, in fact. Wondered what she was doing right this very minute, eleven o'clock at night. He thought maybe he'd give her a call when he got home later on, ask her if she'd like to go for some pancakes or something. He sure liked the way she filled that uniform of hers.

As he was leaving the Eight-Seven tonight, he happened to mention to his good buddy Parker that he'd made a date to go dancing this Saturday night with a Puerto Rican girl.

'Is she a hooker?' Parker asked.

'Hell, no,' Ollie said. 'She's a cop.'

'I don't think you should date a fellow police officer,' Parker said, offended.

'I like the way she fills her uniform,' Ollie said, and winked.

'Never mind how she fills her uniform. Don't go dating a cop. Especially a Puerto Rican one.'

'Why's that?' Ollie asked.

''Cause she'll cut off your dick for a nickel and sell it to the nearest cuchi frito joint,' Parker said.

Ollie wondered about that now.

Wanda here, and her twin sister behind the bar, if that's what she was, certainly knew how to fill their own uniforms, these T-shirts with the red suspenders framing tits like melons, how do you like *that* for a fresh simile, Detective Walsh?

Wanda took the stool on his left.

'So, Detective, what brings you to this part of the city?' she asked.

One elbow on the bar. Leaning over it. Left breast pressing against the rounded edge. Short blue skirt sliding back very high over very white, very smooth-looking legs and thighs. Looking up at him. Blue eyes. Her sister had blue eyes, too. If Flo was indeed her sister.

'Oh, a little business down this way,' Ollie said.

'Are you Vice, too?' she asked.

'No, no. I'm with the Eight-Eight Squad. We just wrapped a murder,' he said.

'Oh my, a murder,' Wanda said, and rolled her delicious blue eyes. 'Who got killed? Or am I being presumptuous?'

Everybody so literary these days.

'No, not at all,' he said. 'You probably read about it in the papers. It's Councilman Lester Henderson.'

'Oh, wow, a big one,' Wanda said.

'But he's down here looking for a dispatch case,' Walsh said, leaning over to talk past Ollie.

'Actually, I recovered the dispatch case,' Ollie said.

'Oh. Then it's the book was *inside* the case,' Walsh said to Wanda. 'Ollie wrote a book, too.'

'Did you, Ollie?' Wanda said. 'May I call you Ollie?'

'Yes. But I used a pen name on it,' he said.

'What name did you use?'

'John Grisham,' Walsh said, getting even for the Irish joke.

'Actually, I used a girl's name,' Ollie said.

'Oh, really?' Wanda said, and leaned closer to him, her eyes widening.

'Ready when you are, hon,' Flo said.

'I'll be back,' Wanda said, and swung out sideways to get off the stool, the skirt sliding back even higher on her thighs, almost to Katmandu, in fact. She went to the other end of the bar, picked up her order, looked back over her shoulder at Ollie – who felt himself growing faintly tumescent in his pants – winked at him, and then swiveled over to a man sitting alone alongside the wall under a framed poster of Boy George.

'I wish I could write a book,' Flo said wistfully.

'Maybe I could give you lessons sometime,' Ollie said.

'Maybe you could give us *both* lessons,' she said.

'Maybe so. Let's ask Wanda when she comes back.'

Ollie was thinking he'd stepped in shit here. A three-way without any effort at all. How lucky could a person get? Walsh looked at him. There was a faint, smug, Irish look on his kisser. Probably congratulating himself on his wise-ass John Grisham remark, whoever the hell that was.

'Meanwhile,' Walsh said, 'we wanted to ask you girls about somebody who maybe you've seen in here.'

'What makes you think that?' Flo asked.

'Kind of place The Cozy is,' Walsh said.

'Hi, honey, you miss me?' Wanda said, and took the stool on Ollie's left again. Ollie put his left hand on her knee.

'How come you decided to put a girl's name on the book?' she asked.

'I thought it would sell more copies,' Ollie said, and slid his hand onto her thigh.

'That the only reason?' Wanda asked, and snuggled a little closer to him.

'Guy's a Puerto Rican switch-hitter,' Walsh told Flo. 'Goes by Emmy on the street. His square handle is Emilio Herrera. Ever see him in here?'

'Oh, sure,' Flo said. 'Emmy's a darling.'

'You know Emmy, too?' Ollie asked Wanda, just as he reached clear up under her skirt and got the shock of his life.

*

'**YOU SHOULD HAVE** told me she was a he,' he shouted at Walsh. The two men were striding up the street toward where Ollie had parked the car. One look at them, you'd know they were cops, that stride they had. Same way you took one look at a hooker, you knew she was a hooker, the strut on her.

'You were getting along so fine there,' Walsh said, grinning. 'I didn't want to . . .'

'And who the fuck is John Grisham?'

'. . . interrupt a beautiful . . .'

'Is the other one a man, too? Flo? Is she a man?'

'She is a man, yes, Ollie.' He grinned again, the fuckin Irish bastard. 'I guess that rules out both of them, huh?' he said.

Ollie walked on ahead of him. He was at the car, unlocking the door, checking the windows to make sure some other faggot junkie hooker hadn't smashed one of them, when Walsh caught up.

'You won't be needing me anymore, will you?' he asked. 'You got what you wanted, right?'

'I got a *location* is all I got.'

'They told you he lives in Kingston Station,' Walsh said. 'What more do you need?'

'Kingston Station is six blocks wide and a mile long,' Ollie said. 'That's a lot of territory to get lost in.'

'It's also Jamaican,' Walsh said.

'So?'

'Your man's Puerto Rican. He should stick out like a sore thumb.'

'I've been looking for the little fuck the past week,' Ollie said. 'So far he ain't sticking out so good.'

'What's your book called?' Walsh asked.

'Fuck you,' Ollie said.

'Nice title,' Walsh said, and threw a finger at him and walked away from the car.

THE TRUE AND PROPER NAME of the neighborhood now called Kingston Station was Westfield Station. Perhaps that was because when railroad tracks still ran along that side of the city, the station stop there was called Westfield. It was not until an overwhelmingly large number of Irish immigrants settled in Westfield Station that the neighborhood was familiarly dubbed Dublin Town. Russian Jews started pouring in at the turn of the century, and the place was popularly renamed Little Kiev. Upward mobility sent the Jews to the suburbs, ceding the area to Italians moving out of ghettos downtown. The area was still called Little Kiev, but the streets now resonated to cries of '*Buon giorno*' and '*Ba fahn gool!*'. But not for long.

Prosperity led to migration. The Italians, too, followed the trail to the suburbs. Nature abhors a vacuum. The Puerto Ricans came next, and finally the Jamaicans. So many Jamaicans, in fact, that first the rest of the white-bread city, and then the residents themselves, began calling the area Kingston Station. An enterprising mayor, gunning for the Jamaican vote, even suggested that the name be legally changed to what everyone was calling it, anyway. Nobody but the Jamaicans liked that idea. In everyday conversation, then, Westfield Station was Kingston Station. But the name on the maps remained what it had been back in 1878, when the railroad opened its route along the river.

Everybody in Kingston Station –

Well, everybody along James Street, anyway.

– had heard of the transvestite hooker who called himself Emmy, but nobody knew where the hell he was.

Ollie had been a detective for a very long time. He knew the word had gone out. Somehow, Emilio Herrera had learned that the law was looking for him.

So where the hell was he?

SHANAHAN'S BAR at midnight was full of policemen who'd just come off duty. This made Emilio and Aine somewhat uncomfortable. But they were here to learn if this was, in fact, the bar Olivia Wesley Watts had mentioned in her report to the Commissioner, and it certainly looked as if it might be.

Emilio was convinced that the woman they'd seen coming out of the basement on Culver Av was indeed Livvie, who had somehow escaped her captors. Aine thought this was a very far-fetched notion.

'She fits the description exactly,' Emilio said, and quoted from the report, which by now he knew by heart because he'd read and reread it so many times, searching for clues. ' "I am a female police detective, twenty-nine years old, five feet, eight inches tall, and weighing one hundred and twenty-three pounds, which is slender." '

'I weigh a hundred and six,' Aine said. '*That's* slender.'

'*That's* skinny,' Emilio said, and went on quoting from the report. ' "My hair is a sort of reddish brown, what my mother used to call auburn . . ." '

'My hair is red, too.'

'Your hair is not reddish brown.'

'But it's red.'

'It's carrot colored.'

'That's still red,' Aine insisted.

' "I wear it cut to just above the shoulders," ' Emilio quoted. ' "What my mother used to call a shag cut." '

'I wear my hair short, too,' Aine said.

'And shaggy,' he agreed. ' "My eyes are green . . ." '

'So are mine.'

' "I look very Irish . . ." '

'So do I.'

'Aine, what is your *point*?' Emilio asked, truly irritated now.

'My point is, do you think *I'm* Olivia Watts-her-name?'

'Of course not.'

'So why do you think some Irish babe you ran into on the street is her?'

'Because she was coming out of the very *building*!' Emilio said. 'Otherwise it would be too much of a coincidence!'

'The world is full of coincidence,' Aine said wisely.

'I don't believe in coincidence,' Emilio said. 'You believe in coincidence, then you don't believe in God. It's God makes things happen, not coincidence.'

'Oh okay. Then it was God made me a junkie and a whore, right?'

Emilio looked at her.

'What *are* you?' he asked. 'Some kind of atheist?'

'That's what I am, yes,' Aine said.

'Since when?'

'Since I was twelve years old and a priest felt me up in the rectory.'

'That never happened.'

'Oh no?'

'And anyway, you can't blame God for some horny priest.'

'What *do* I blame him for? All these fucking lunatics fighting wars in his name? Killing each other in his name? I don't know any atheists who kill people in God's name. Not a single one. I don't believe in a God who allows such things to happen. I believe in coincidence, is what makes things happen.'

Which was when Francisco Palacios walked in and took a stool beside them at the bar.

BECAUSE THE GAUCHO recognized Emilio as a fellow Puerto Rican, and because he had an eye for the women, especially if they seemed not to be wearing either panties or a bra, he struck up a conversation with the young couple, directing his conversation at first directly to Emilio, entirely in Spanish, because he didn't want the young Irish girl, was what she looked like, to think he was coming on to her, even though he was. This annoyed Aine, so she said, 'Are you guys gonna talk Spanish all night? Because if you are, I've got better things to do.'

The Gaucho leaned over the bar and began chatting with Aine about the latest movies she'd seen and her favorite color and did she like to walk hatless in spring rain, all the stuff he thought a woman liked to hear. Aine was in fact flattered by his attention. She was well aware of the adage that held if you wanted to succeed with a lady, you treated her like a whore, and vice versa. She knew he was treating her like a lady, which meant he suspected she was a whore, but that was okay with her. It was the thought that counted.

On the other hand, The Gaucho had no idea she was a working girl. In his eyes, she looked like a well-scrubbed Irish girl from one of the suburbs, albeit one of these anachronistic hippie types who ran around without under-wear. There was something sharp and snippy about her, qualities he liked in a woman. Qualities he had found in Eileen Burke, who did not, alas, seem too terribly interested in him. He looked at his watch. The detectives were now ten minutes late.

'Listen,' he said, 'I know you're here with your boy-friend and all . . .'

'He's not my boyfriend,' Aine said.

'Oh, well good,' The Gaucho said. 'I have an appointment here – in fact they're late – but it shouldn't take more than half an hour to discuss our business, and then I thought maybe you'd like to go for a drink someplace quieter than this, what do you think?'

Aine looked him dead in the eye.

Green eyes clashing with brown eyes, sparks flying.

'Sure,' she said, and smiled like an Irish shillelagh, whatever that was.

As coincidence would have it, Eileen Burke walked in just then.

EMILIO SHREWDLY CALCULATED that the other guy who came in some five minutes later was either a civilian like Palacios or a detective like Livvie. He was absolutely positive now that the girl with the reddish-brown hair was Olivia Wesley Watts.

All three of them had moved to a table over by the phone booths. From where he was still sitting at the bar with Aine, who had her legs crossed and who was nursing a very sugary non-alcoholic beverage, Emilio could not hear a word of their conversation. This was unfortunate because he was sure they were discussing the blood diamonds hidden in the basement from which Livvie had escaped earlier today.

They were instead discussing cocaine.

So were the three men in the living room of a tenement flat half a mile uptown.

*

SUZIE Q. CURTIS was never permitted to sit in on any of these brainstorming sessions between her mastermind husband and his two rocket-scientist associates. Her job was to keep them supplied with food, like the women in the *Godfather* movies. Although to see those movies, you sometimes got the feeling the gangsters in them were as interested in cooking spaghetti with clams, or sausage with peppers, as they were in killing people. Just nice homey fellows who if you looked at them cross-eyed, they would slit your throat.

Her husband and his cronies were talking about killing some people tomorrow night.

Listening from the kitchen, where Suzie was making tuna fish sandwiches with slices of tomato on them, she could hear their conversation clear as a bell.

'We go in shootin,' her husband was saying. 'Never give them a chance to frisk us.'

'Cause then we'd be at a disadvantage,' Constantine said. 'If we let them frisk us.'

She could just imagine him twitching and grinning.

'Exactly,' her husband said. 'We know she'll be there with the coke, she'd be stupid not to bring the coke when we went to all this trouble setting this up. We mow everybody down, grab the coke, and split.'

'She'll have goons with her,' Lonnie said.

'How many? Two, three? Even half a dozen? We got the element of surprise on our side.'

'That's right,' Constantine said. 'Nobody's gonna expect us to come in shootin.'

'Exactly!' Harry said, and laughed. 'Who'd think we could be that stupid?'

Me, Suzie thought, and sliced another tomato.

*

HE HAD TAKEN HER into the back room of his shop, where there were all sorts of sex toys. She had seen all of them before, of course – there was nothing she hadn't seen or done – but she looked at them all agog and amazed like an Irish virgin, and pretended to be shocked when he asked her to put on a leather merry widow and thigh-high leather boots, so where's the whip, honey? she was thinking. It turned out he wasn't into the dominatrix scene, after all; it was just the opposite. He merely wanted to see what a nice Catholic girl like Aine would look like all dressed up like a whore.

She figured she wouldn't break his heart just yet.

She'd go along with it, let him believe she was Cathleen the Colleen for a little while longer. Then she'd tell him she was a working girl, bro, and ask him for a deuce. Or whatever the traffic would bear.

Instead, he started talking about himself.

She kind of found this interesting about him.

The way he opened up to her.

He told her he was a spy named The Gaucho.

Shut *up*, she said, a *spy*?'

Verdad, he said. Or Cowboy, I'm sometimes called.

Boy, she said, a spy.

For the Police Department, he said.

So what it was, he was a snitch, was what it was.

She didn't say this to his face.

She let him talk.

And, of course, like all men, he wanted to show her how important he was.

So he told her he had been instrumental in uncovering valuable information that would lead the police to a big drug bust tomorrow night at midnight in the basement of an apartment building on Culver Avenue.

3211 Culver, she thought, but did not say.

Midnight, she thought.

That's when it's going down.

Midnight tomorrow.

A hun' fifty keys of coke will change hands, he told her.

Three hundred thousand dollars will change hands, he told her.

So she didn't ask him for any money, after all.

He had given her enough already.

And besides, it was kind of nice to make love instead of to be fucked all the time.

I FOUND THE LETTERS from her the night before.

I knew right then I had to kill him.

We kept a gun in the house. I don't know where Lester bought it. I think in a pawnshop someplace downtown, near his office. He bought it when the first of our children was born. Lyle. When he was born. We'd heard there'd been a kidnapping in Smoke Rise, many years ago, at the King estate, on the water. Douglas King. So we figured we needed a gun. I don't know whether Lester registered the gun or not. Frankly, I didn't care. Lester was a councilman, he often took liberties. I mean, he parked in clearly marked No Parking zones, he went through red lights when he'd had a little too much to drink, he was a great one for breaking the rules. He felt he was privileged, do you know? A city councilman. Only this time, he broke one rule too many.

I know I'm not a beautiful woman, but I've always been a good wife. To think of him with a nineteen-year-old girl – how could he? I had to kill him. That was all I knew. Never mind confrontation, never mind asking for explanations, never mind forgiving him, I wanted him dead, I wanted to kill him. I knew he'd be going directly to King Memorial after his trip upstate. I knew what time he'd be getting there. I knew all this, he'd told me all this on the phone. The only thing he hadn't told me was that a young girl was in bed with him.

The gun was in the safe in his study. Same place I found the letters. The desk in his study. I wasn't looking for the letters, I was looking for his appointment calendar. Because we were supposed to go to a dinner party that Sunday when he got home, and I had the time written in my calendar as six o'clock, which sounded early, so I wanted to check it against his calendar, to make sure. But I couldn't find it anywhere on his desk, his calendar, so I started looking through the drawers, and that was when I found the letters, at the back of the middle drawer to the right of the kneehole, buried under a stack of papers.

I wanted him dead.

I read the letters, and I went directly to the wall safe, and opened it, and took out the gun, and loaded it. We kept it unloaded, because of the children. The box of cartridges was in the safe, with the gun. I loaded the gun, and then I went upstairs to dress.

I dressed for expediency. Nothing else. I wasn't thinking of any kind of disguise, I had no thought of getting away with it, I just didn't give a damn. I merely wanted him dead. So I dressed for ease of movement. Baggy blue jeans I used when I was gardening, a T-shirt, white socks and Reeboks, my hair up under Lyle's baseball cap so it wouldn't fly all over my face, wouldn't get in my eyes when it came time to shoot him. I put on a ski parka when I left the house. We used to ski a lot before the children were born. The gun was in the right-hand pocket of the parka.

I took a taxi up to the Hall. I walked right in, nobody there to stop me, you'd think after all this terrorist stuff there'd be people frisking me or something. But no. I walked right in with the gun in my pocket. I opened the door at the back of the auditorium, opened it just enough so I could look in. He was onstage with a lot of other people, Alan Pierce, Josh Coogan, some other people I didn't know. I closed the door and came around the side of the auditorium, to where there were a lot of offices and a corridor running between them. I went down the corridor almost to the end of it, and then opened a door that led to the stage.

My heart was beating very fast.

I opened the door and found myself in this backstage area, the wings I guess you'd call them, looking out at the stage. It was very dark where I was standing. There was no one around. Everyone was onstage, calling directions and adjusting lights and what not. Alan told Lester to go off left and then walk toward the podium so they could make sure the follow spot was on him, something like that. I took the gun out of my pocket.

Alan said Okay, start your cross, and Lester stepped out of the wings on the other side of the stage and began moving toward the center of the stage, this bright light on him, it was as if they were illuminating him for me, so I could kill him, the son of a bitch.

My hand was shaking.

When he reached the podium, I shot him.

I fired six times. I don't think all of my shots got him. But I saw him falling, and I could see blood all over his pink sweater, so I figured I had got him good. Then everyone started screaming and yelling. I turned and ran.

That was the first time I had even a notion of survival.
Of getting away.

Before then, I'd only wanted him dead.

I could hear yelling behind me.

I kept running.

There was a corridor with an EXIT sign at the end of
it. I was heading for the door under it, when someone
came out of an office at the end of the hall, a woman, and
I turned and started running in the opposite direction
again, back toward the stage. But there were voices ahead
of me now, coming off the stage, so I opened the nearest
door and went in whatever it was, I didn't know what it
was, I was just trying to hide.

The room was dark except for faint daylight coming
through a narrow window at the far end. I could hear
people running by outside, shouting. In the dim light, I
saw urinals. I was in a men's room. I ducked into one of
the stalls just as someone cracked open the door. Anyone
in here? a man's voice yelled. I held my breath. The room
was dark, the light from the window filtered. Where's the
fuckin light switch? the man asked himself. Silence. I
heard him fumbling around on the wall. Then he asked
Anyone in here? again, and muttered something, and
closed the door, and was gone. I heard more running
outside, voices passing by, fading. I waited.

I didn't know where to go. I wanted to cry. I had
killed him, and now I wanted to cry. Not because he was
dead, the son of a bitch. But because they would catch
me and put me in prison forever. The children, I thought.
I kept still in the dark, terrified that the man would come
back and put on the light this time, and search the room,
and find me, and take me away.

I don't know how long I waited there in the dark, in

the stall. At last, I came out of the stall and stood still, listening in the dark, for several moments. Then I went to the window. It was open a crack, just some three or four inches. I opened it all the way. I was looking out onto what seemed to be an airshaft, the sky far above, a narrow paved passageway below. I climbed up and over the sill and dropped to my feet on the other side. The passageway ran behind the building for the entire width of it. I ran down it, enclosed by walls on either side of me, and saw another window on the far wall. This one was open just a little bit, too. I reached up, and opened it all the way. Then I hoisted myself up and climbed into what I realized was another men's room, a smaller one this time, just two stalls, and a single urinal, and some sinks.

The lights were on.

A man was in one of the stalls.

I heard him coughing, and then I heard the toilet flushing.

I ran for the door at the other end of the room, opposite the sinks.

I opened the door, and stepped out into a long corridor. I was on the stage-left side of the auditorium. A door painted red was immediately to my left. An illuminated EXIT sign was above it. I opened the door and went out into an alley. Sunlight struck my eyes. I dropped the gun down a drainage sewer near the wall, and began running.

An old bum in army fatigues was just stepping into the alley at the far end.

I almost knocked him off his feet.

He said, Hey!

That was all he said.

Hey.

After I'd just killed a man.

*

THEY ASKED HER if there was anything she wished to change or add to her confession. She said No. They asked her to sign it, and handed her a pen.

She signed it.

It was all over but the shooting.

18.

This is what they call The Denouement, I thought.

I am not a writer, Mr Commissioner, but that is what writers call the chapter in the novel where everything falls into place and makes sense. It is alternatively called The Epiphany, which has religious overtones, I know, but which means some kind of dramatic change, as for example when a woman looks at herself in the mirror and sees looking back at her someone all bleary-eyed from being knocked unconscious, and all tied up to a chair in a basement she doesn't even know where.

A black woman came in carrying a tray upon which was, or were, a donut and a cup of coffee, when a person was starving to death. There was also an Uzi on the tray, which the black woman was careful to remove before placing the tray in front of me.

'Here you go, sister,' she said.

I asked her how I was supposed to eat with my hands tied behind my back.

'You won't have to worry about eatin too much longer,' she said, and burst out laughing, which I considered ominous.

'You goan be dead by midnight,' she added, which I also took to be a bad sign.

The clock was ticking.

Along about eleven-thirty, the door opened and Mr Mercer Grant himself came marching down the steps. Behind him was the French receptionist from the Rêve du Jour Underwear Factory.

'This is my wife Marie,' he said. 'By the way, those are our real names.'

'Then why did you tell me they were not your real names?' I asked.

'To lure you to the factory,' he said. 'It's called entrapment. It's done all the time.'

'How about your cousin Ambrose Fields?'

'You rang, madam?' someone asked, and a black guy as big as the one in The Green Mile, who could draw snot out of your body and make you able to urinate again, came walking down the basement steps, ducking under the hanging light bulb as he approached me. 'Dat is my real name, too,' he said, and grinned.

Nothing could surprise me anymore.

All I knew was that the clock was ticking.

'So where are the diamonds?' I asked.

'What diamonds?' Grant asked, grinning to show the gold-and-diamond tooth in his mouth. His wife Marie stood by his side, all curly haired and brown eyed, and not wearing a bra. She was grinning, too.

'The conflict diamonds,' I said. 'Isn't this all about blood diamonds?'

'Have you forgotten about the other blood diamonds?' Grant asked.

'I'll bet she's forgotten about the other blood diamonds,' Ambrose said.

'Oh dear, she's forgotten all about the other blood diamonds,' Marie said.

'I thought <u>you</u> were supposed to be dead by Tuesday,' I said.

'That was to throw you off the scent,' she said. 'It's done all the time.'

'Besides,' Ambrose said, 'don't worry. You yourself will be dead by midnight.'

'But <u>why</u>?' I asked.

And a voice I had heard somewhere before said, 'Because.'

I looked toward the stairway leading from above.

Someone I knew was coming down the steps.

AT MIDNIGHT that Tuesday, they came into the basement simultaneously, the six detectives in Kevlar vests, and the three men wearing ski masks. It would have been a regular traffic jam if Emilio and Aine had also showed up at the stroke of midnight, but at that very moment they were just coming around the corner to 3211 Culver. When they heard the shooting start, they almost turned and ran in the opposite direction.

It was Rosita's goons who started shooting first.

They did not know in which direction to turn. It was as if the Northern Alliance were coming down the stairs from the ground floor, and the Pashtun were breaking in the door from the back yard. Everybody had guns. Somebody was bound to get hurt. The goons figured it wasn't going to be them. So they started shooting.

They took out the three men in the ski masks first.

They were easy marks, these three. They came down

the steps one after the other, in single file. You shot the first guy in the row, he fell over and gave you a clear shot at the second one, and so on till all three of them were lying on the steps bleeding from a dozen holes, one of them between the eyes of the first guy's ski mask.

The guys in the Kevlar vests were another matter.

To begin with, they came in following the business end of a battering ram that sent wood from the door flying all over the place. And they were all six of them carrying assault rifles.

Rosita's goons – Rosita herself, for that matter – recognized the weapons as AR-15s, heavy Colt carbines that could tear off a man's head. As the goons turned toward the door, one of the guys coming in yelled, 'Police! Hold it right there!'

The guy was a woman.

The goons had no qualms about shooting a woman, police detective or not. It was only the AR-15 assault rifles that gave them pause.

The pause was all the team needed.

They swarmed over the room like fire ants, yelling and swearing, and snapping on handcuffs, and telling anyone in sight that he, or she in Rosita's case, was under arrest. Parker picked up the suitcase with the hundred and fifty keys of coke in it.

'Better file a report on that,' Eileen reminded him.

He shot her a dirty look.

As if he would ever *not* file a report.

EMILIO AND AINE huddled in the shadows near the building.

There were police cars angled into the curb now, their dome lights blinking. There were unmarked cars as well. It looked like the whole police department was here. The guy they'd seen in Shanahan's last night came out carrying a suitcase. Livvie came out behind a woman in handcuffs. There were other detectives with assault rifles. This had to be a big bust.

As Emilio took a step forward, Aine put her hand on his arm, trying to stop him. He shook it off.

'Detective?' he said.

Eileen Burke turned.

'Yes?'

'Don't worry about your report,' he said, and winked.

'What?'

'I burned it,' he said. 'The bad guys won't ever see it.'

'What?' she said again.

'But you don't have to worry. I memorized it,' he said, not realizing that in that moment he became one of a long line of traditional storytellers.

Eileen still didn't know what he was talking about.

Just then, Rosita made a sudden move as if to run. Eileen grabbed her by the arm, and said, 'Don't get any ideas, sister,' and shoved her toward one of the cars at the curb.

Emilio's only regret was that he would never know how she'd got out of that damn basement.

19.

THE CALL FROM the Reverend Gabriel Foster came at eleven o'clock that Wednesday morning. He asked to speak to Detective Kling, and when Kling came on the line, he said, 'I asked for you because of Miss Cooke.'

Kling said nothing.

'Your relationship with Miss Cooke,' he said.

'Deputy Chief Cooke, you mean,' Kling said.

'Yes, Deputy Chief,' Foster said, and Kling could swear he heard a chuckle. 'You asked me to call if I heard anything. My having a finger on the community pulse and all. Is what your partner said.'

'Uh-huh,' Kling said.

'This has nothing to do with the councilman, may he rest in peace, poor soul. I understand you've already cleared that one.'

'Yes, we have,' Kling said. 'What *does* this have to do with?'

'A big drug deal is about to go down,' Foster said, lowering his voice. 'Three hundred grand changing hands. A hundred and fifty keys of cocaine. I don't like narcotics in my community. You want to hear more?'

'We already heard more,' Kling said. 'It went down at midnight last night.'

'It did?' Foster said, surprised.

'It did.'

'Oh. Well,' Foster said. There was a long silence on

the line. Then he said, 'Give my regards to your lady,' and hung up.

EILEEN WAS JUST leaving the building, coming down the corridor from the squadroom to the metal steps leading below, when Kling came out of the men's room. Startled, she stopped dead in her tracks.

'Hey, hi,' she said.

'Hi,' he said. 'I hear it went down good last night.'

'Oh yeah, terrific,' she said.

'How's everything otherwise? Did you like working with Andy?'

'Joy and a half,' she said.

'Did he tell you any of his jokes?'

'Oh yes . . .'

'Which one?'

'The nuns peeing in a gasoline can?'

'Lovely joke.'

'Lovely,' Eileen said, and they both fell silent.

'Well,' he said.

'Listen . . .' she said.

'Yes?'

'I hope this isn't going to be awkward for you.'

'No, no. Awkward? Hey, why? Awkward?'

'Cause Pete gave me a little welcoming lecture, you know . . .'

'He did?'

'Yeah. Did he talk to you, too?'

'About what?'

'About this being one big happy family . . .'

'No. What? A big happy family? Why?'

'He also told me I'm a good cop, but "There's this thing with Bert," quote, unquote.'

'Oh.'

'So I was wondering if he'd given you the same, well, *warning* was what it was.'

'No. I'd have told him to shove it.'

'Really?' Eileen said, genuinely surprised.

'My private life . . . *our* private lives . . . are none of Pete's business. What does he think this is, a soap opera? We're professionals here,' Kling said. 'This really pisses me off, Eileen. I have a good mind to go in there and tell him . . .'

'Hey, slow down, Bert. I wasn't trying to incite a riot.'

'What'd you tell him? When he said there was this *thing* with Bert, or whatever it was he said.'

'I told him I didn't think there'd be a problem.'

'Well, there won't.'

'I know there won't. You're with Sharyn now, and I'm . . .'

I'm what? she wondered. Still looking for Mr Right?

'*I'm* perfectly content to be here at the Eight-Seven,' she said. 'I just wanted to make sure it's cool with you.'

'It's cool,' he said. 'Don't worry about it.'

'So, I mean, we don't have to avoid each other, or anything stupid like that, tiptoe around each other . . .'

'Is that what we were doing?'

'No, I meant it's not something we even have to *think* about anymore, is what I meant. We're two professionals, like you said, and this isn't a soap opera.'

'It certainly isn't. Besides, why should people have to *forget* what happened between them?' he said, and she could have hugged him then and there. 'Why can't they just remember the past, and move on?' His voice lowered, but he wasn't trying to be sexy or anything, he wasn't coming on or anything. 'There's a lot to remember, Eileen. No one can shoot us for remembering.'

'No one,' she said, and smiled.

'You going back inside?' he asked.

'No, I was just leaving,' she said.

'In that case,' he said, and bowed her in the direction of the staircase.

She suddenly remembered why she had loved him so much.

THE GAUCHO CALLED Aine at three o'clock that afternoon, hoping he could see her again tonight. He had enjoyed being with her, and now they really had something to celebrate; the bust had gone down as predicted, and he was in possession of five hundred bucks the generous cops of the Eight-Seven had given him as a reward for his services.

He let the number she'd given him ring a dozen times.

Aine didn't hear it.

She had shot up half an hour ago, and was lying stoned on the mattress in Emilio's apartment, her eyes closed, a dreamy expression on her face. Emilio didn't hear the ringing phone, either. He was on the toilet bowl, a needle still in his arm, the same peaceful look on his face.

The Gaucho hung up and went out front to greet a woman who was looking for herbs that would cure her insomnia.

CARELLA CALLED HONEY BLAIR at three-thirty that afternoon.

She came on the phone all treacle and smiles.

'Well, *hello*,' she oozed, 'how's it goin? What can I do for you?'

'My wife's looking for a job,' he said.

'I'm sorry, *what*?'

'My wife's looking for a job,' he said again, and then he explained that she was this beautiful speech- and hearing-impaired woman who could sign at the speed of light, and whose face spoke volumes besides, and he thought if the station was looking for someone who could appear in that little box in the left-hand corner of the screen to sign for the deaf while a news report was going on, she'd be perfect for the job.

'She's really the most beautiful woman on earth,' he said. 'You won't be sorry, I promise you.'

There was a long silence on the line.

'Honey?' he said.

'I'm here,' she said.

There was another silence.

Then she said, 'You are really unique, you know that? You are positively unique.'

He imagined her shaking her head.

'Have her send me a résumé,' she said, 'I'll see what I can do.'

And hung up.

AT THE EIGHT-EIGHT later that afternoon, Ollie ran into Patricia Gomez just as the shift was changing.

'I want to thank you for that wonderful work you did on the Henderson case,' he said.

'Well, hey, thank *you*,' she said.

'I already mentioned it to the Boss, he knows what a role you played.'

'Well, gee,' she said, 'thanks.'

There was an awkward moment of silence.

'Did you ever find that guy who stole your book?' she asked.

'No, all I still got is the last chapter.'

'I'll bet it's good.'

'Oh, yes,' he said. 'But I'll get him, don't worry. There's always another day, am I right?'

'Always another day,' she said.

He looked at her.

Quite seriously, he asked, 'Are you gonna cut off my dick for a nickel?'

'What?' she said.

'And sell it to the nearest cuchi frito joint?'

'Why would I do that?' she asked, and smiled. 'I don't even *like* cuchi frito.'

He kept looking at her.

'You still wanna go dancin Saturday night?'

'I bought a new dress.'

'So okay then.'

'So okay.'

'*Que puede hacer?*' he asked, and shrugged.

'*Nada,*' she said.

I watched him as he came down the steps into the basement.

'So, Olivia,' he said. 'We meet again.'

'Apparently so, Commissioner,' I said, narrowing my eyes.

'Does she know?' he asked the black man.

'Nothing,' Ambrose said.

'Then kill her,' the Commissioner said.

There was on his face a look of ineffable sadness. I could tell he felt badly, or perhaps even bad.

'It isn't midnight yet,' I said.

'But who's counting?'

'I am. Can you please tell me what's going on here?'

288

'Well, since you'll never be able to tell anyone else,' the Commissioner said, 'I see no reason why you shouldn't share my little secret.'

This was a line I had heard many times before in detective work, and I was surprised to hear it coming from someone as erudite, you should pardon the expression, as the Commissioner, who surely knew that if you told someone he or she would never be able to tell anyone else, then in the next thirty seconds or so he or she was going to kick you in the balls and tell everyone in the entire world.

Strengthened by this knowledge, I began working on the ties that bound me, so to speak, laboring secretly behind my back with a little razor I normally use for shaving my legs and armpits while the Commissioner began telling me what his little secret was.

It turned out that spilling red wine on his white linen suit was only the first of a series of real or imagined affronts he had suffered at my hands over the many years I'd been on the job. Never mind that this was his favorite suit, which he had bought after hearing Tom Wolfe speak at a Barnes & Noble one time long ago. Never mind that I had once crashed my motorcycle into the rear fender of his personal car, which happened to be a Mercedes-Benz – and this is not product placement, believe me; I am a police officer and above such mercantile pursuits. Never mind, too, that I had once – inadvertently – called him an asshole in the presence of several reporters, but that was when he was still only Chief of Detectives and I hadn't known at the time that he would become the Commish. What really bothered him –

And, honestly, I don't know how people can be so petty, I mean it.

What <u>really</u> bothered him – it now turned out as strand by strand I worked with the razor on the ropes binding me to the chair – was that I had once turned over to the Property Clerk's Office a large pile of so-called conflict diamonds without reporting to the Commish that I was about to do so.

This rough ice had come from rebel groups in Sierra Leone or Angola and was virtually impossible to trace, as some enterprising detective had undoubtedly figured out before he committed what was now famous in police archives as the African Connection Theft, later immortalized as a movie starring a promising young actor named Peter Coe, now serving a five-and-dime upstate for possession – but I digress.

As I was saying, or perhaps even <u>like</u> I was saying, the Commissioner himself could have been the one who got his hands on that pile of blood diamonds sitting on a shelf in the Property Clerk's Office, instead of some dumb detective from a precinct in the sticks, if only I had told him I was about to turn in the recovered loot as evidence. If I had mentioned my intentions, the Commissioner would now be sipping delicious Veuve Cliquot champagne at a fine Club Med someplace – which, again, is not product placement, but exactly what he said.

'You should have filed a report to the Commissioner,' he said. 'I should have been informed. If it hadn't been for you I would right this minute be sipping delicious Veuve Cliquot champagne at a fine Club Med someplace instead of standing here about to put a bullet in your head,' which was when he pulled a nine-milli-meter Glock from a shoulder holster under his jacket.

'Police! Hold it right there!' someone shouted from the stairway, and my good friend and sometime partner Margie Gannon, who got divorced every six years and shot every three, came charging down the steps with a gun in her hand.

By coincidence, it so happened that Margie had been shot almost three years ago to the day. So naturally, the Commissioner shot her once again, and she came tumbling down the stairs, yelling obscenities I won't repeat. I was out of the chair by then, my hands free. I grabbed a convenient lug wrench sitting in a box near the furnace, and I hit the Commissioner on the head with it, God forgive me for he outranked me, and then I turned on Ambrose and Marie and said, 'Okay, who's next here?'

Nobody was next here.

It was truly all over.

All Orion/Phoenix titles are available at your local bookshop or from the following address:

Mail Order Department
Littlehampton Book Services
FREEPOST BR535
Worthing, West Sussex, BN13 3BR
telephone 01903 828503, *facsimile* 01903 828802
e-mail MailOrders@lbsltd.co.uk
(Please ensure that you include full postal address details)

Payment can be made either by credit/debit card (Visa, Mastercard, Access and Switch accepted) or by sending a £ Sterling cheque or postal order made payable to *Littlehampton Book Services*.
DO NOT SEND CASH OR CURRENCY.

Please add the following to cover postage and packing

UK and BFPO:
£1.50 for the first book, and 50p for each additional book to a maximum of £3.50

Overseas and Eire:
£2.50 for the first book plus £1.00 for the second book and 50p for each additional book ordered

---

BLOCK CAPITALS PLEASE

name of cardholder ....

address of cardholder ....

....

....

postcode ....

delivery address
(if different from cardholder)

....

....

....

postcode ....

☐ I enclose my remittance for £ ....

☐ please debit my Mastercard/Visa/Access/Switch (delete as appropriate)

card number ☐☐☐☐ · ☐☐☐☐ ☐☐☐☐ ☐☐☐☐

expiry date ☐☐☐☐   Switch issue no. ☐☐

signature ....

prices and availability are subject to change without notice